Praise for Kevin Brockmeier's

the
Illumination

"Moving. . . . Skillfully explores the relationship between love and memory."   —*The New Yorker*

"The depth of [Brockmeier's] scrutiny makes his fiction glow."   —*The Plain Dealer*

"Brockmeier's characters are wonderful, and his images are dazzling."   —*Detroit Free Press*

"*The Illumination* imagines a real universe of pain and pleasure, connection and disconnection, and quest for meaning that defines human experience delightfully anew."   —*The Miami Herald*

"Brockmeier's consistently arresting observations have the throb of lived—rather than merely imagined—experience. . . . In *The Illumination* it isn't our agonies and discomforts that define us, but the selves we build in response to them."   —*Salon*

"Brockmeier's work has always been characterized by his crystalline and surprising descriptions. . . . Brilliant. . . . Thorough and honest."

—*Southern Literary Review*

"Lyrical. . . . Draw[s] the characters—and us—into the complex and vivid consideration of some of the fundamental questions that come with being human."

—*The Times Literary Supplement* (London)

"[A] sunlit novel."

—*Time Out Chicago*

"Fresh and ingenious. . . . Brockmeier has one of those imaginations that churns out picture-perfect imagery."

—*Elle*

"Brockmeier's book positively sparkles. . . . We've never read anything like it."

—*Daily Candy San Francisco*

Kevin Brockmeier

the
Illumination

Kevin Brockmeier is the author of the novels *The Brief History of the Dead* and *The Truth About Celia*, the story collections *The View from the Seventh Layer* and *Things That Fall from the Sky*, and two children's novels. His stories have appeared in *The New Yorker*, *Tin House*, *McSweeney's*, *The Oxford American*, *The Best American Short Stories*, *O. Henry Prize Stories*, and Granta's *Best of Young American Novelists*, among other publications. He teaches frequently at the Iowa Writers' Workshop and lives in Little Rock, Arkansas.

the
Illumination

the
Illumination

Kevin Brockmeier

Vintage Contemporaries
Vintage Books
A Division of Random House, Inc.
New York

FIRST VINTAGE CONTEMPORARIES EDITION, FEBRUARY 2012

Portions of this work were previously published in the following: "Ryan Shifrin"
in *Tin House*, "Jason Williford" in *The Toad Suck Review*, and an excerpt from
"Nina Poggione" (as "A Fable for the Living") in *Electric Literature*.

Grateful acknowledgment is made to Hugh Blumenfeld for permission to
reprint an excerpt from "The Strong in Spirit," words and music by
Hugh Blumenfeld, copyright © 1983 by Hugh Blumenfeld. Copyright renewed.
All rights reserved. Recordings: *The CooP: Fast Folk Musical Magazine*
(SE 201, Feb. 1983); *The String In Spirit* (Grace Avenue Records 1987,
Prime-CD 1994). Reprinted by permission of Hugh Blumenfeld.

The Library of Congress has cataloged the Pantheon edition as follows:
Brockmeier, Kevin.
The illumination / Kevin Brockmeier.
p. cm.
I. Title.
PS3602.R63145 2010 813'.6—dc22 2010020732

Vintage ISBN: 978-0-307-38777-6

Book design by M. Kristen Bearse

www.vintagebooks.com

Manufactured in the United States of America
10 9 8 7 6 5 4 3 2 1

Carol Ann Page

The strong in spirit wear bright clothes of fire.
They dance and burn. The light is worth the pain.
The light is worth the pain.
The pain stops when the flame dies out.

—Hugh Blumenfeld

It was Friday evening, half an hour before the light struck, and she was attempting to open a package with a carving knife. The package was from her ex-husband, who had covered it in a thick layer of transparent tape, the kind fretted with hundreds of white threads, the latest step in his long campaign of bringing needless difficulty to her life. She was sawing along the lid when she came to a particularly stubborn cross-piece of tape and turned the box toward herself to improve her grip. Her hand slipped, and just that quickly the knife severed the tip of her thumb. The hospital was not busy, and when she walked in carrying a balled-up mass of wet paper towels, her blood wicking through the pink flowers, the clerk at the reception desk admitted her right away. The doctor who came to examine her said, "Let's take a look at what we've got here," then gingerly, with his narrow fingers, unwound the paper from around her thumb. "Okay, this is totally doable. I don't mind telling you you had me worried with all that blood of yours, but this doesn't look so bad. A few stitches, and we should have you fixed right up." She had not quite broken through the nail, though, and when he rotated her hand to take a closer look, a quarter-inch of her thumb came tilting away like the hinged cap of a lighter. The doctor gave an appreciative whistle, then took the pieces of her thumb and coupled them back together.

She watched, horrified, as he fastened them in place with a white tag of surgical tape. "Miss? Miss?" The room had begun to flutter. He took her face in his hands. "What's your name? Can you tell me your name, Miss? I'm Dr. Alstadt. Can you tell me your name?" His hands were warm and soft, like the hands of a fourteen-year-old boy deciding whether or not to kiss her, something she remembered feeling once, a long time ago, and she gave him her name, which was Carol Ann, Carol Ann Page. "Okay, Carol Ann, what we're going to do is bring in the replantation team. They see this kind of thing all the time, so I don't want you to worry. You hang in there, all right? Is there anyone we can call for you?"

"No."

"A husband? A parent?"

"No. Not in town."

"All right then. It shouldn't be longer than a few minutes. In the meantime, I'm going to give you something to ease the pain," but instead he jotted a few sentences onto a clipboard and left the room. She lay back and closed her eyes, and when she opened them again, the doctor had been replaced by a nurse in dark green scrubs, who said, "You must be the thumb," wiped the crook of her elbow with a cloth that smelled like chlorine bleach, and gave her a shot. The shot didn't extinguish the pain so much as disguise it, make it beautiful, ease it, she supposed, just as the doctor had said it would. The nurse hurried out, and Carol Ann was alone again. A moment later, when she saw the light shining out of her incision, she thought she was hallucinating. It was steady and uniform, a silvery-white disk that showed even through her thumbnail, as bright and finely edged as the light in a Hopper painting. Through the haze of drugs, it seemed to her that the light was not falling over her wound or even infusing it from the inside but radiating through it from another world. She thought that she could live there and be happy.

After the surgery, when she woke, her hand was encased in an odd little glove that immobilized her thumb but left her fingers free to open and close. Her neck was stiff, and her lips were dry, and in her mouth she detected the iron-and-butter taste of blood. At first she thought she was making a sort of mental clerical error, mistaking the aftereffects of thumb surgery for the aftereffects of dental surgery, but when she swept her tongue over her teeth, she brushed up against a pad of cotton batting. She pushed it out onto her palm. A pale glow flickered from somewhere and then went out. She remembered her dream of light and consolation, the sensation of peace and abundance that had come over her, and a voice saying, "This is really freaking me out. Isn't this freaking anyone else out?" and a second voice saying, "We have a job to do, Clayton. Nothing here changes that fact," and then the feeling of escape as she stared into the operating lamp and sleep pulled her under. She was thirsty now, but when she to tried to sit up in bed, a boy in mocha-colored scrubs appeared by her side and said, "Whoa, there. You're still zonked out from the operation. What do you need? Let me get it for you." She asked for something to drink, and he took a bottle of Evian from the tray beside her bed, twisted the cap off, and brought it to her lips, his hand performing a slow genuflection in the air as he tipped the water out. She drained nearly the whole bottle without once pausing for breath. When she was finished, he nodded, a short upward snap of the chin, impressed. "Is there anything else I can help you with? The doctor should be in to check on you soon."

"My mouth. I cut my thumb—just my thumb—but when I

woke up, I found all this . . . *stuff* in my mouth." She was still holding the square of spit-soaked gauze she had discovered. When she opened her fingers to show it to him, he made a nest of his two good hands beneath her broken one so that she could dump it out. An image of her father came suddenly to mind: the sun was bright and the sky was clear and he was kneeling beside a stream in a state park, making a nest of his own good hands to give her a sip of water, and she paused and frowned, staring into the tiny pool he had created, transfixed by the way the light sent gray blooms of shadows gusting over his palms, and when she pointed it out to him, he laughed and called her his little Impressionist.

The orderly had taken her chart from the foot of the bed. "Says here you bit down on your cheek during the operation. Normally that doesn't happen. Just sometimes if there's an anesthesia problem you might wake up for a second and feel a little pain, and you'll have what they call a bite response. A B.R.—that's what this stands for."

"Brrr."

"Are you cold? I can turn the heat up if you want."

"No. I'm fine."

"Okey." That was how he pronounced it. "I'll be back in to check on you in a little while."

She had spoken to him for only a few minutes, and she felt so weak, and he was no one who loved her, and when she propped herself up on her elbows to watch him go, her head swam with a thousand colors. She spent a while studying her room: the television pinned by a metal arm to the ceiling, the window looking out on a stand of pine trees, the empty bed, with its sheets in a dead calm. In the hallway, a man walked by wheeling an IV tower with a sack of clear fluid on one of its hooks, his stomach glimmering through his hospital gown. Then a woman stumbled past carrying a flashlight in her left hand. By the time Carol Ann thought to wonder why she was pointing her light down a corridor that was already so clearly illuminated, the woman had slipped out of view. Her arms were trembling from supporting herself, so she lay back down again. The bed's side rails rattled as the mattress took her weight. The pillow rose up around her ears like bread. More and more she had the feeling that she was missing something.

It must have been another hour before the doctor who had first inspected her thumb, Dr. All-That-Blood-of-Yours, Dr. Alstadt, arrived and pulled a stool up to her bed. He sat down and asked her how she was feeling, then leaned in with his stethoscope. He was so close that her gaze was drawn to the smooth spot on his neck, a shape like Kentucky just above his Adam's apple, where the stubble had failed to grow. He smelled like mouthwash, and he used her whole name when he spoke to her. "Well then, Carol Ann Page, let's take a look at that hand of yours, shall we?" He undid the Velcro on her glove so that the material fell away like the peel of a banana, then unwrapped the bandage from around her thumb. Later she would find herself unable to remember which she noticed first: the quarter-inch of her nail that was missing, a straight line exposing the featureless topside of her thumb, or the way the light she thought she had hallucinated was still leaking out from around the wound.

"Your color is good," Dr. Alstadt said. "Can you go like this for me?"

She flexed her thumb in imitation of his. A thrill of pain passed through her hand, and the light sharpened, flaring through the black *x*'s of her stitching.

"Range of motion good, too. It looks like we got to you before any major tissue damage set in. Let me wrap you back up, and you can get a little shut-eye."

"Doctor, wait. What's happening to me? Don't you see this?"

He didn't need to ask, *See what?* She noted it right away.

"I forget you've been sleeping all this time. Well, I don't know much more than you do, I'm afraid. It started at eight-seventeen last night. That's locally speaking, but this isn't exactly local news. In fact, I bet if we . . . here." He picked up the remote control and turned on the television. An episode of an old courtroom sitcom filled the screen, the one with the lecherous prosecutor and the hulking bailiff, but when he changed the station, Carol Ann saw footage of what looked like the floor of the New York Stock Exchange. Silver sparks appeared to swirl through the bodies of the traders like the static on a broken television. The doctor changed the station again, and she saw a child soldier with his arm in a sling and his shoulder ablaze with light. Then the president of the United States stepping into a helicopter, raising a hand glowing with arthritis at its joints. Then a pair of boxers opening up radiant cuts on each other's faces. The images came one after another, so quickly that she barely had time to identify them. A woman in a blue burka, long pencils of light shining through the net of her veil. A team of cyclists with their knees and feet drawing iridescent circles in the air. A girl with a luminous scrape on her arm, her face caught in an expression of inquisitive fear. When the news anchor addressed the camera, saying how *from all around the world today we are receiving continuing reports of this strange occurrence: light, pouring from the injuries of the sick and the wounded,* Carol Ann noticed his eyes narrowing and saw something like the flat pulse of heat lightning flashing from his temples. *A phenomenon so new and unforeseen—* the anchor winced almost imperceptibly as his forehead grew momentarily brighter—*that scientists have not yet devised a name for it.*

Dr. Alstadt had finished dressing her thumb. Gently, as though cradling a bird's egg, he fit the glove back onto her hand. His voice came out tired and ragged. "Funny how quickly a person can get used to a miracle. Or how quickly a miracle can come to seem commonplace. If that's what this is, a miracle." He stopped, gave himself a derisory sniff, and for the first time since he had entered the room looked her directly in the eye. "See what I mean? 'If that's what this is.' The problem is we're in a hospital. Not exactly an environment conducive to quiet reflection. Well, Carol Ann Page," he said, and he smacked his knees as he stood up. He told her he would be willing to discharge her that afternoon, but that the hospital would be more comfortable if she would consent to stay until Sunday morning so they could watch the area of the injury for any signs of tissue rejection.

Those were his exact words.

The hospital would be more comfortable.

The area of the injury.

Tissue rejection.

When she agreed to remain overnight, he returned her hand to her stomach and said, "That's my girl." He muttered so softly that she wondered if he realized he had spoken. As he left the room she caught the briefest glimpse of the nape of his neck, where a hundred threads of light were twisting like algae in an underwater current.

She filled the morning with daydreaming and television and eating amorphous sogs of peach and pear from the fruit cup on her breakfast tray, and around noon she swallowed some blue tablets a nurse gave her out of a Dixie cup, and shortly after, she came to understand that there was no such thing as pain or solemnity in the world, as remorse or exertion, an anxiety that would not be stilled or a mourning that would not be comforted. She was not sure how long she spent idly pinching her arm, watching the light on her skin bud open and fade like a pair of lips, nearly outside of time, but eventually a couple of orderlies wheeled another patient past her, a woman her own age, and lifted her onto the second bed. "One and two and—" *Three,* Carol Ann finished for them. They brought the woman's blanket up to her chest and tucked a pillow under her skull, allowing her long hair to catch beneath her shoulders. Her head was fishlined to one side, exposing her neck to the air, but the orderlies did not seem to care, and who could blame them, who could blame them, in a room that drifted so lightly through the universe, who could blame them? They left a stack of the woman's belongings on the cabinet by her bed—a journal, a pocketbook, a plastic bag with her clothes and shoes inside it. She had the flawless features of a fashion model, and a face as placid as a kitten's, but there was a wound inside her so bright that Carol Ann could see it burning all the way through the layers of sheets and blankets.

"Are you awake?"

The woman's eyes were open, blinking every so often in a way that seemed almost deliberate, but she did not answer right away. Eventually she said, "I hope not." It was a hope Carol Ann understood, though it was not her own. From the earliest days of her childhood she had harbored the opposite hope—that when she was sleeping, she was actually awake. Her dream life had always been filled with fantasy, whimsy, beautiful reminiscence— never a chase scene, never a nightmare. She would follow a lost ball into a forest where she could understand the conversations of the animals. *I hope that I'm awake,* she would think. She would take two steps into the air and begin breaststroking over the rooftops. *I hope that I'm awake.* She would lie down next to her husband in the years when their kindness to each other was easy. *I hope that I'm awake.* Every morning she rose from sleep with the same feeling of vague disappointment she experienced when she picked up a ringing phone and heard only a dial tone. Someone had hung up on her.

The pills must have been losing their effect because she no longer felt as if her hands had been cast off from her body, and a thorn of pain went through her thumb when she tried to bend it. She was lying on her side, looking directly at the woman in the second bed, whose blue eyes watched her as she winced and gritted her teeth. "I cut my thumb. What happened to you?"

The other woman struggled free of her reverie. When she spoke, it was like a small bird pausing to appraise the landscape as it hopped across the grass, carefully forming each sentence before moving on to the next: "The car flipped over on the interstate," and then, "We hit an ice slick when we were going over the river," and then, "There was the truck carrying the steel rods, which we missed, but after that there was the concrete pillar," and finally, "Jason was driving. Not me."

"Who's Jason?"

"My husband."

"Is he all right?"

"They won't tell me. They say I need my rest. But I don't see how he could have . . ." Her voice sank out of hearing. "I kept asking him if he was okay—'Are you okay? Answer me if you're okay'—but he wouldn't, wouldn't answer. He just hung there upside down in his seat belt." Already Carol Ann had seen several hours of footage about the strange illumination of the injured. She imagined an incandescent lightbulb flooding the car with light until it burned out with a pop. She watched the woman swallow and then bow her head, inadvertently pulling her hair taut. "Every morning he left a note for me on the refrigerator with a different reason he loved me. He never missed a day. I write them down in my book. Would you like to see?"

She indicated the journal lying on the cabinet between their beds. Carol Ann reached for it and let it fall open to a random page: *I love those three perfect moles on your shoulder—like a line of buttons. I love the sound of your voice over the phone when you're trying to hide the fact that you're doing a crossword puzzle from me. I love your lopsided smile. I love the way you leave a little space between each piece of bacon on your plate: "amber waves of bacon." I love the way you sway and close your eyes when you're listening to a song you like—a dance, but only from the waist up. I love that moment in bed when you first climb on top of me, and the uprooted smell we leave behind when we're finished. I love the feel of your hands on my cheeks, even when they're " 'cold as tea.' 'Hot tea?' 'No, iced tea.' " I love the fact that when you accidentally pick up a hitchhiker, what you're worried about is that he'll steal the DVDs you rented. I love your fear of heights and bridges. I love the way you can be singing a song, and all of a sudden it will turn into a different song, and you'll keep on singing and won't even realize it.*

Carol Ann shut the journal, letting the silk bookmark trail over her wrist. "That's beautiful."

The woman in the other bed nodded, and it might have been intuition, or commiseration, or just the last timed dosage of the blue pills Carol Ann had taken, but she could tell that what she meant to say was, *Yes, it was beautiful. It was. It was.*

"You keep it," the woman told her.

"You don't mean that."

"I do. I couldn't bear to read it again."

"You don't want to give something like this away. It's too intimate."

The silence that followed had a strange bend to it. It drew itself out while an old man pushed a walker with tennis balls on its feet to the nurses' station at the far end of the hallway, then pivoted around with a series of metallic clacks. Eventually the woman let her breath run out, turned her face away, and said to Carol Ann, "You don't understand at all."

Later that day, around four in the afternoon, Carol Ann was watching a hawk wheel over the pine trees outside the window when the woman in the other bed lit up like a signal mirror. The glare was so bright that it suffused the glass, extinguishing the hawk in midflight. A team of doctors and technicians rushed to the woman's side. Carol Ann shielded her eyes as they worked over her body with their equipment, saying things like, "She's in full arrest, cardiac and respiratory," and, "Sunglasses! I need some sunglasses here!" and, a few minutes later, "S.C.D. at four . . . thirteen. You can stop now, Miriam. I've called it." One by one the doctors left, and the room fell quiet. The outlines of the shadows began to soften again. The light arising from the woman's bed slowly dwindled until her skin held only a cool spectral glow, like phosphorescent moss in a cave. Carol Ann did not have enough faith in her powers of observation to tell exactly when the light winked out, only that there came a moment when it appeared the woman's pain was no longer radiating from her body. Her hair had been freed from beneath her back. She lay with her eyes closed, her lips parted as if to take a breath. Once again, it seemed, she was confined to the borders of her flesh.

When the same orderly who had helped Carol Ann drink from the Evian bottle that morning came to box up the woman's possessions, Carol Ann stopped him from taking the journal. She slid it to her own side of the cabinet and pinned it down with her bad hand.

"No, that's mine."

The orderly shrugged. "If you say so, ma'am."

He turned his back to her as he finished his work, avoiding her eyes as he emptied the woman's lunch tray, folded her blanket, and with the help of another orderly hoisted her onto a gurney. Carol Ann knew that she would probably never see him again, and also that it would not matter if she did, for in that instant she had become a thief to him.

Soon after she left the hospital, Carol Ann developed a preoccupation with her wound, testing it a dozen times a day for signs of light and pain. Dr. Alstadt had warned her to avoid the temptation, but she could not resist it. At work or at home, whenever the thought crossed her mind, she would remove the glove splint from around her thumb so that she could trace the cut with her index finger. Her nail had grown over the top line of the incision, but the front and the sides were still exposed, and a narrow welt had formed there, healing up around the stitches. The pain was not as pronounced as it had been before, and neither was the light, but if she bent her thumb just right, guiding it into the injury, it would begin to radiate from the inside, pink and warm, showing a tiny net of capillaries and a curved silhouette of bone. It reminded her of the sleepover parties she used to attend when she was in elementary school, how all the girls would take turns shining a flashlight through their hands, making their palms sway around in the dark like Japanese lanterns. When she was finished examining herself, she would put the glove back on and seal the straps, and she would think about the hospital and the stand of pine trees and the tranquillity the blue pills had brought her, and if she was at home she would let her eyes drift to the light from the window, and if she was at work, to the light from the computer. She was employed by a subscription news service, compiling accounts of the day's major stories for various players in the stock and banking industries. Every day she devoted a portion of her assortment to what people had begun to call the Illumination. There was the story of the presidential task force that had been formed to investigate the phenomenon. The story of the Midwestern teenagers cutting luminous tattoos into their skin. The story of the Korean scientist who had spliced a gene of fluorescent jellyfish protein into a feline embryo to create a kitten that glowed in the dark. The story of the Palestinian suicide bombers who interpreted the footage of their brothers' lives ending in an explosion of golden mist as a sign that their cause was blessed by the Lord. She knew that some of these incidents would have no foreseeable effect on the marketplace, but since neither her boss nor her clients seemed to object to them, she kept including them in her packets.

Frequently her mind returned to the woman she had met in the hospital. Maybe it had something to do with her office door, which swung closed with a hitch at the three-quarters mark, brushing against the carpet and then continuing on with a pair of clicks, a sound that suggested the way the woman's voice had broken. Or maybe it was the simple fact that Carol Ann had never seen another person die. She remembered the woman's clear blue eyes, and her deliberate style of blinking, and how long it took the incandescence to fade from her body after the doctors pronounced her gone. And why, Carol Ann wondered—why would it have lingered like that? Were we outlived by our pain? How long did it cling to the world? She had held on to the woman's journal, and every day, after she got home from work, she allowed herself to read a page as she relaxed on the sofa: *I love the ball you curl into when you wake up in the morning but don't want to get out from under the covers. I love the last question you ask me before bedtime. I love the way you alphabetize the CDs, but arrange the books by height. I love you in your blue winter coat that looks like upholstery fabric. I love the scent of your hair just after you've taken a shower. I love the way, when I take my wedding ring off to do the dishes, you'll put it on your finger and walk around the house saying, "I'm married to me, I'm married to me!" I love how nervous you get when I'm driving. I love the way you say all the things you dislike are "horrible"—and how, when you're really upset, you pronounce it "harrible." I love the little parentheses you get beside your lips when you're smiling—the way the left one is deeper than the right. I love the fact that I know I can keep telling you things I love about you for the rest of our lives and I'll never run out.*

Sometimes she liked to imagine that the journal had a voice and that it was speaking directly to her—a gentle baritone that developed a bit of gravel when it used her name.

I love to wake up in the middle of the night and listen to you sleeping (*Carol Ann,* she added): *the funny noises you make when you dream, the tiny pop of your lips separating.*

"You're too sweet. Stop it."

I love kissing your tattoos one by one—first the bracelet on your ankle, then the heart on your shoulder, then the Celtic knot on the small of your back.

"That's some imagination you have. There's not a single tattoo on my body."

The truth was that she could extract any line from the book, any line at all, and find more kindness in it than she had heard from her husband in their four years of marriage. In the beginning, when they first started seeing each other, she had been just young and naïve enough to mistake his parched inhumanity for an elaborate comic routine. She still remembered the feeling of uneasy awareness shading into panic when she realized he meant every word he said, that *Nothing smells worse than an Asian who's just discovered dairy* and *Fat is still fat, even if it's only your wrists* were not examples of insurrectionary humor, as he saw it, but precise statements of fact. The day she arrived home from the hospital, she had mopped the blood from the kitchen floor and cleaned the tacky brown deposits that dotted the wall and table. She had even washed the carving knife that she somehow found the presence of mind to put in the dish drainer before she left. But she ignored his package, the one that had caused so much trouble, allowing it to sit there on the counter in its jacket of threaded tape. Maybe it was no more than a trick of the subconscious, but every time she saw it, she felt a sudden glinting sensation in her thumb. A week passed before she finally built up the nerve to finish opening it. This time she used a pair of scissors, wincing as each white thread burst apart like a tendon. Inside, beneath a mound of excelsior, she found that month's alimony check. His idea of a joke.

She spent eight hours a day sifting through stories about the economy and the Illumination, the vaccine shortage in Africa and the latest defense postures in the Middle East, so much misery that it made her head ache, and the last thing she wanted to do when she got home was watch the news. Usually, after reading a page of the journal, she would make a simple meal of soup or pasta for herself, take it to the dining room, and flip through one of the catalogs that had arrived in the mail that afternoon. Sometimes, in the endless inventory of throw rugs, wool sweaters, and fireplace cribs, she would momentarily forget everything that had ever happened to her, closing the last page and returning to her own life like a moviegoer stepping out of a darkened theater, dazed by the angle of the light.

She found it relatively easy to cook while she was wearing the glove, and to eat and type and drive, but not everything came so effortlessly. Shoes were a problem. Washing the dishes. Shaving beneath her right arm. She liked to knit every night before she went to bed, but knitting was impossible now, so instead she took to lying on the sofa watching rebroadcasts of various daytime talk shows—the one with the straight-talking Texan who walked offset holding hands with his wife, the one with the people who threw chairs at one another. Whenever the talk shows' guests were blindsided by grief, a kind of nimbus would settle around them, a colorless shimmering cloud that seemed to be exhaled directly from their pores, fainter even than the light from a hangnail. Was she seeing their emotional pain, she wondered, or its physical counterpart, like the raw throat that followed a bout of crying, or the stomach cramps that accompanied a wave of anxiety, or the gripping sensation you felt in your chest when you realized the man you were married to despised you? Physical or emotional, it didn't matter—the aura was unmistakable. Even on her old eighteen-inch Curtis Mathes, she could always tell when the people on the talk shows were really suffering and when they were merely playacting for the cameras.

She began to notice the same aura when she was out in public. She saw it on crossing guards, panhandlers, neighbors, coworkers. It was a simple matter of training herself not to dismiss the sight as a mirage. One day, a couple of weeks into the Illumination, she was on her lunch break when her joints began to ache and her skin felt cold to the touch and she knew she was coming down with a fever. The bottle of Advil in her purse was empty, so she pulled up to a convenience store and ran inside for a packet of pain relievers. A man was blocking the pharmaceutical shelf. Even from behind, she could see that he was distraught about something. The air wavered over his body like the air around the edges of a flame. He took a bag of cough drops from a hook, then looked up at her and gave a weak smile. "Carol Ann Page," he said, and tapped his thumb with his index finger.

In an instant she recognized him. "Dr. Alstadt."

"How's that thumb of yours?"

It was stinging, she realized, stinging and cold. A frigid glow had spread down through her glove, radiating past the bones of her wrist. "Not so good today. Are you all right? Did something just happen to you?"

He touched his brow, a nervous tic, smoothing down a cowlick that must have stood far back in the thicket of his hair when he was younger but projected from the bare curve of his forehead now like a minnow leaping out of a still pond. "And here I thought I was hiding it so well. A bad day at work, that's all. But here—let me take a look at you." He undid the glove from her hand, a gesture that seemed strangely intimate in the buzzing luminosity of the soda cabinet. A noise of concern escaped him. "Oh, Carol Ann. My. How long has it been like this?"

"Like what?"

"Do you see how the color changes here at the scar line? That's a sign of severe vasoconstriction. Let me ask you, does it hurt—does it light up and sort of *tighten* when you expose it to the cold?"

"Yes. It does do that."

"And when did you first notice the symptom?"

" 'The symptom'? I didn't know it was a symptom. It's been

sensitive to the cold ever since I came home from the hospital. Is that what you're asking?"

"No, that's to be expected. What I'm asking is when did you notice the *color* change?"

Just now, she supposed. Just this moment. When she cut her eyes across the floor, she saw a starfield of spinning dots, and she had lived in this world for so long, and she wanted so desperately for someone to be in love with her, and for a moment she had to lock her knees to prevent them from buckling.

"Dr. Alstadt, I'm not feeling so well."

He took her by the elbow. "Are you good to drive? I think we need to get you to the hospital." She waited to see if the dots would leave her head, and when they did, she straightened her back and nodded. "All right. Just to be on the safe side, I'm going to ask you to follow me, okay?" he insisted. "Let me check out first, and then we'll go."

He took the cough drops to the counter. While he was paying for them, she called the office and explained that she would be late returning to work that afternoon: "A medical emergency. I'm not sure really. Hopefully by three o'clock." She hung up and put the phone in her purse, listened to the cashier clearing his lungs. Glancing at him, she saw two dim blossoms of what must have been cancer showing through his polyester shirt. Cancer or maybe emphysema.

A mid-afternoon gloom had settled over the city, making the trees darker than the sky. A light rain was falling. As she followed Dr. Alstadt to the hospital, she thought about all the times she had sat in the backseat of the car when she was small and her parents were young and they were driving her to church or to school, watching windblown fleets of raindrops chasing one another across the glass.

The hospital's main doors opened onto an atrium with a gently sloping ceiling of metal trimmers and polished glass. She kept looking up at the rain on the roof and then down at its reflection on the floor, hundreds of semitransparent shadows that flowed across the tiles like snakes. A bird had built its nest into one of the ceiling's upper struts, and she wondered what it did on days like this: Did it tuck its head beneath its wings or just stand there stolidly and wait for the weather to turn?

She followed Dr. Alstadt down a chain of hallways and through the emergency ward, where a nurse was sorting patients into admission groups, saying, "Green group, green group, yellow group, green." In the last few weeks, it seemed, the hospital had established a system of treating patients based on the strength of the light emanating from their bodies. The Illumination had ushered in a new age of critical care. Doctors no longer had to rely on their patients to tell them how badly they were suffering. "Head light and heart light take priority, of course," Dr. Alstadt told her, "along with any obvious major traumas. Then we take all the other lights and make a visual determination of their severity."

The walls were tilting toward Carol Ann suddenly. She became aware that he had paused between sentences, and she made the noise she seemed to recall normal people making when they wanted to show an interest in something. The doctor steadied her with his hand. "Good Lord. You're really not feeling well, are you? Let's get you a bed."

He showed her into an examination room.

"You rest here a minute, and I'll go find the vascular specialist."

The curtains ballooned outward as he left, then settled back against the window. She saw that the pain assessment chart, with its six faces transforming from glee to agony, had been taken down from the wall. It was no longer necessary, she supposed, now that the Illumination had taken hold. She felt a pulse of blood traveling through her thumb, too much of it for so small a space, and she closed her eyes and waited for the twinge to pass, and before long Dr. Alstadt had returned with a young Indian man he introduced as Dr. Kimberley, his neck starlit with a fresh shaving rash.

Dr. Kimberley said, "I understand your injury has been misbehaving on you, Miss Ann-Page. Let's see what we can do about that. May I?" He removed her glove and took the base of her thumb between his fingers, pressing against the two indentations the splint's metal stays had left there, compacted to a smooth pale sheen. He was like a carpenter using a wood clamp, and as he tightened his grip, she watched her thumb change colors, instantly reddening below the line of the cut and gradually pinkening above it.

Dr. Alstadt made a grimacing noise with the corners of his mouth. Dr. Kimberley shook his head. "You see," he said. "This is what happens when you skip your follow-up appointments."

"But I didn't skip my follow-up appointments. I had a follow-up appointment last week. I have another follow-up appointment on Thursday."

"Oh. Well. Then sometimes these things happen."

The rest of it seemed to transpire very quickly. Once again she was given a shot in the crook of her elbow, and once again her skin began to tingle, and once again she had the sensation that all her life until just that moment she had been falling toward the ground and suddenly, instead, she was floating above it, and

the world looked so handsome, and the light so sweet and wel-
coming, and she cried as she lay there waiting for the orderlies to
take her into the strange, blue, humming, capacious elevator.
When she woke up and tried to wipe the grit from her eyes, she
found that there was a boxing glove on her hand, and then her
mind cleared and she realized that the boxing glove was a bandage, wrapped so tightly that it had fixed her fingers together into
a sort of trowel. A machine beeped next to her left ear. A woman
in dark green nursing scrubs came in to check on her. When
Carol Ann asked her how the operation had gone—*where was her
glove? could she go home now?*—the nurse looked at her chart and
said, "Maybe we should wait for the doctor to explain things to
you," and then, "Calm down, now, Miss, calm down. There's no
need for us to raise our voices, is there?" and finally, "I'm sorry
to tell you this, but your thumb has been amputated at the
knuckle." It took almost a full minute for Carol Ann to understand that the schools of fish swimming in slow spasms across
her vision meant that she was holding her breath. The nurse
opened a water bottle, placed a pair of the blue pills on her
tongue, and helped her swallow them. Then came the long hours
of careless assent and easy reminiscence she had dreamed about
while she was sitting behind her desk at work. Memory after
memory leafed open in her mind like buds on a tree. The time she
found her babysitter rubbing one of her mother's bras against
his cheek. The night she spilled her popcorn on the usher at the
movie theater. The Matisse and Duchamp posters with which
her college roommate had decorated their dorm room. The fountain outside the library where someone had arranged the coins to
spell *Mike Rules!* Her recovery suite had a single bed this time,
and she could run the lamp or change the position of her mattress
without fear of disturbing anyone. She did not recall turning the

television on, but on it certainly was, and she watched two men in cheap suits debating how the Illumination had affected our duty toward animals, or "the lower creatures of the world," as they kept calling them. One of the men's ties was sending irritated little glimmers up his neck. An abscessed tooth was radiating from the other's mouth. Every so often there was a film clip of a stack of poultry pens in the bed of a trailer, the wire cages giving off innumerable white flashes; or a jockey hieing a horse around a track, its knees and shoulders burning with the strain of the race; or a gang of children flinging gravel at a stray dog, beads of light opening on its body as it tried to twist out of the way.

Dr. Alstadt must have gone home already, because the girl who came to replace her bandages that night could not have been older than twenty-five, fresh out of medical school, her hair held back with a pair of tortoiseshell barrettes. At first Carol Ann was too apprehensive to look at what remained of her thumb, and she kept her eyes fixed on the ceiling until the girl was finished, but a few hours later, when the same doctor returned to change the dressing again, a nurse had fortified her with a second dose of the blue pills and she was able to investigate the amputation. It was not as gruesome as she had imagined it would be. She had a neat little half-thumb now, homely but not repulsive, the crease along the center sewn so tightly together that the stitching looked like one continuous black thread. The injury shone like a penlight where the tendons had been sliced apart, and she was aware of the pain, but she did not mind it nearly as much as she suspected she should. The doctor swabbed her thumb with a clear, sharp-smelling liquid that evaporated almost immediately, then cushioned and rewrapped it. She was saying something about the importance of keeping the area disinfected when Carol Ann drifted off to sleep.

She woke with a start. It was three in the morning. For a moment she thought she had left the television on, but the flickering she saw from the corner of her eye turned out to be her own arm, flung haphazardly over the pillow. Waves of light were following each other all the way from her hand to her shoulder, a display she might have found hypnotic if it hadn't hurt so much. Her head ached, and so did her back. She was grinding her teeth, and there was an awful tightness in her stomach. Obviously, the pills had worn off, and with the sickness came the desperation—it had always been that way. The serenity she had accepted so naturally just a few hours before was gone now. She could hardly remember what it felt like. Here, in this place, her life seemed like one long litany of wounds, ending in these sweat-drenched sheets with half her thumb missing and stretching back through time in an unbroken sequence of bone fractures and muscle strains, sunburns and concussions, black eyes and canker sores. There was a light in her hand, and a light in her head, and doubtless a light in her memories, too. She had known days of happiness and beauty, rare moments of motionless wonder, but trying to relive them after they had vanished was like looking out the window at night from a partially lit room: no matter how interesting the view, there was always her own reflection, hovering over the landscape like a ghost. That face, it was the problem. Those eyes and that skin. She wished that she could throw the glass open for once and see things as they really were.

If she remained absolutely still, she thought, then maybe, just maybe, she would fall asleep again, and she lay on her side for a while watching the bands of light travel up her arm. When she realized the cause was hopeless, she got up to use the bathroom. After she was finished, she made the mistake of reaching for the faucet with her left hand and was hit by a jolt of pain so severe that her legs locked upright and she had to Frankenstein-walk back to her bed. It took a long time for her knees to loosen up, and even longer for the glow in them to subside.

Shortly after the sun rose, an orderly brought her a breakfast of orange juice and scrambled eggs. A nurse followed behind him with a chaser of blue pills. A few hours later, Dr. Alstadt found her staring out the window at the cars on the freeway, just sedated enough to be comfortable but just sober enough to be clear-headed. "Hello, Carol Ann," he said. He reached out as if to take the loop of hair that was dangling over her eye and brush it back with his fingers, then thought better of it and dropped his hand. "How are you holding up?"

"Where's Dr. Barrettes?"

"Dr. Barrettes?" He looked at her chart. "You mean Dr. Clovis. 'Dr. Barrettes'—that's good. Dr. Barrettes has gone home for the day. So, Carol Ann, I want to talk with you about what you said to me after the operation," which made no sense, none at all. She would have remembered if she had seen him after the operation, and she hadn't.

He gave her a quizzical look and pulled a chair up to her bed. "You don't remember, do you? That happens sometimes when you're still shaking off the effects of the anesthesia. Carol Ann, I sat here in this room with you for almost an hour yesterday. You were only half-awake, but you said something that implied your ex-husband had caused your injury. I'd like to know if that's true."

"What did I say?"

"Well, you were in kind of a daze. You kept talking to him about your alimony check. You said, 'You didn't love me. You didn't even like me,' and then, 'Are you happy now, you sad—?' You repeated the word *sad* a few times. I think you were trying to say *sadist*. 'Are you happy now, you sadist? It nearly lopped my thumb off.' "

She felt her face coloring—something that hardly ever happened to her now that she was an adult. She told him the story of the carving knife and the tape-sealed package and how she had found her alimony check buried beneath a pile of wood curls. "So I guess he did cause my injury, yes, in a roundabout way, but really it was my fault. One stupid mistake, and . . ." She made a sound she did not think she had ever made before, a sigh like the beginning of all sighs.

"Well, concerning that," Dr. Alstadt said. He told her about the physiotherapy she would need after her wound had healed— "not a lot, but some. The thumb is important. You can expect to lose about twenty percent of the function in your left hand. Twenty percent might not sound like much, but you'll probably have to learn a new way to tie your shoes, for instance. Brush your teeth. Trim your garden—do you garden? Hold a knife and fork."

The prospect of resuming her life after she left the hospital depressed her. Dr. Alstadt perched his glasses on his eyebrows and rubbed his eyes with his index fingers. He still wore a barely visible aura of emotional turmoil. She wondered where it came from. "Yesterday in the gas station you said you were having a bad day at work. You look like you're having another one."

"That's nothing you need to worry about. I'd rather talk about you."

"I've been learning how to tie my shoes and use a fork without my thumb for two weeks now, remember?"

He paused, made a decision, nodded. "Right. Well. The situation is that the hospital is facing a budget crunch. We either have to cut hours or cut jobs. I'm supposed to make the decision for the A&E."

"Arts and entertainment?"

"Pardon? Ah. No. Accident and emergency."

"So what are you going to do?"

"Make life a little harder for everyone, as opposed to a lot harder for someone. The staff won't be happy about it, but I've weighed all the options, and it seems like the one that will do the least harm. You know, 'First do no harm' and all."

"That sounds like the responsible choice."

"Yes. Well. Nobody can say I'm not conscientious. It might be my one shining virtue."

"What's your one shining vice?"

He amused her by pondering the question. "Nostalgia," he answered eventually, and a few seconds later, "Self-pity."

"I think we share a shining vice."

She spent another day lost in pain and reverie, staring at the patients bearing their light past her door and dozing off between outbursts of noise from the television. Every so often someone would arrive to feed her, medicate her, or change her bandages, and if she was sleeping she would rouse herself, and if she was hurting she would try to hide it. The tip of her thumb was gathered together in a smart little pucker around her stitches. She could only presume that, like a sausage, it had been hollowed out to make room for the skin to close. There was a fairy tale that had disturbed her when she was a child, too young for school, and she thought about it now, the one about the quarreling couple who waste all their wishes attaching sausages to each other's noses. Her mother used to read the story out loud to her, and whenever she reached the illustration of the poor wife tugging at the sausage on her nose, a look of cross-eyed fury on her face, Carol Ann insisted that she turn the page. She always rushed to put the book away the second the story was finished. There it would stand on its shelf, giving out an aura of indignation and menace, just as her teddy bear gave out an aura of sleepy affection, her toy box an aura of cheerful excitement, but the book was fixed against the backdrop of her room, and it had been for as long as she could remember, and it never occurred to her that she could simply get rid of it. She must have fallen asleep while the nurse was working over her because she seemed to spend the next few hours locked in a small stone house with her husband, the two of them trading wishes like insults. She woke up just in time to see the same orderly who had watched her claim the journal a couple of weeks ago take a few steps into the suite, shake his head as he realized who she was, and say, "Perfect. Just great. Wrong room."

That evening, before he left for home, Dr. Alstadt stopped by to ask her how her day had gone—and also, she could tell, to allow her to ask about his. Somehow, without trying, over a scant few conversations, they had transformed themselves in each other's eyes from doctor and patient to two fragile human beings, both afflicted by nostalgia and self-pity. When she asked him how everything had gone in the field of arts and entertainment, he said, "About how I expected it would. Everyone hates me a little, but no one hates me passionately." He reached up to grip his shoulder, rolling his head in a slow circle. She saw a dozen vines of light swaying on the back of his neck. They were thicker than the ones she had noticed before, and he said, "Ah, yes, my neck. It always gets like this by the end of the day."

"Turn around."

He must have thought she wanted to take a closer look at the spot because she surprised him by using her good hand to work the tension out of his muscles. Each white tendril grew brighter as she bore down on it with her fingers, then much softer as she eased away. When she was finished, Dr. Alstadt made a tiny halting sound of pleasure.

She was in the hospital two more nights before he allowed her to go home.

I love the photograph of you your parents keep by the front door, that little girl in her glasses and her Holly Hobbie dress. I love the way you kiss. I love the way you shake your head when you yawn. I love the "magically delicious" doodles you make when you're talking on the phone: stars, moons, hearts, and clovers. I love to look up and see you sitting beneath the lamp in the living room—reading a book, or staring out the window, or chewing the end of a ballpoint pen. I love how soft your hands are, even though hand lotion is disgusting goop and you'll never convince me it isn't. I love the way you line your brushes up on the vanity like silverware. I love knowing that if there's a restaurant I want to try, I'll get to try it with you; if there's a movie I want to see, I'll get to see it with you; if there's a story I want to tell, I'll get to tell it to you. I love your giggle fits. I love the names you've had picked out for 25 years: "Mira" if it's a girl, "Henry" if it's a boy.

The journal lay on the walnut table by Carol Ann's sofa, and though she had finished nearly a quarter of it, she still had to remind herself that it was not a continuous outpouring of unbroken passion, that every sentence represented a small, isolated profession of love, separated from the ones that came before and after it by the hard line of a night's sleep. The book was like the row of squares on a calendar: each piece held nothing more than the bare outline of a single day. It seemed to reveal the couple's marriage as fully as any diary, though, and the further she read, the more intimately she felt she knew them. The husband's name was Jason, and the wife's name was Patricia, and their relationship was as open and playfully chiding as it had been on their wedding day. They drove to the lake to picnic and swim, and they rented Woody Allen movies on the weekend, and though she liked spicy food and he did not, they took turns cooking meals for each other on their old gas stove. Carol Ann had seen the light fade from the woman's body but had failed to learn her name until she reached the journal's seventeenth page, when she came across the line, *I love sticking your name in songs where it doesn't fit the rhythm: "Patricia Williford, why don't you come to your senses?"* The fact that the two of them were no longer kissing each other's shoulders, or taking their rings off when they did the dishes, or dancing but only from the waist up—it seemed like a frightening mistake. And even if there was a Heaven, she thought, and even if they were together in it, that would not make it right.

She was finding it difficult to concentrate at work. In part it was the weather, a sudden string of gentle blue days that had lured thousands of birds into the air, but mostly it was her thumb, which still throbbed with pain, throwing up obstacles around even the easiest tasks. Answering the phone, punching the space bar on the keyboard, opening the window, retouching her makeup, maneuvering a bag of chips through the sliding gate of the vending machine—every hour presented her with another puzzle to solve. She knew she was in trouble the moment she got home from the hospital and found a pile of newspapers scattered on her welcome mat. Right away she realized she could not pitch them up to herself with one hand while she held on to her pocketbook with the other, as she ordinarily did, so she slipped off her shoes and spent an aggravating few minutes trying to kick them inside. The glass door kept swinging shut in the wind, though, and the papers came bounding back at her with a terrible banging noise, and finally she had to give up, put her purse on the accent table, and kneel down to collect them one by one. As soon as her wound finished healing, she knew she would be able to use her left hand again, but until then she would just have to keep bobbling through her days like a steel marble in a tilting maze game.

On Tuesdays and Fridays, she left work early for an appointment with her physical therapist, a briskly competent but slightly abstracted woman who seemed to view human beings as a simple collection of joints, muscles, and nerve bundles. At the beginning of each session, she would greet Carol Ann with a short conversation like—

"How are you doing this afternoon?"

"I'm all tangled up inside."

"Super! Now let's focus on that hand of yours."

—then lead her through a series of exercises designed to improve the strength and dexterity of her thumb, or what was left of it. There was the "thumb press," which involved flattening a barrel-shaped lump of clay into her palm. The "thumb abduction," a maneuver resembling a leg lift with her hand filling in for her body. The "isometric thumb extension," in which she made a hitchhiking gesture while her therapist applied pressure with an index finger. And then there was the "putty pinch" and the "prayer position" and half a dozen others. Her therapist had her repeat each of the exercises in three sets of ten, counting off the repetitions—*one, two, three, you're doing good, five, six*—while Carol Ann nodded along and pretended she thought it was helping. The glow that had been concentrated in her thumb would gradually spread across her entire hand, following the extensor in a long line up her forearm, and by the time the hour was over, anyone who saw her stealing through the back hallway to the parking lot, balancing her palm before her like a waiter carrying a bowl of soup, would know immediately how much her hand hurt. But then that was true of everyone now. Everyone, everyone, everyone, and all the time. The world had changed in the wake of the Illumination. No one could disguise his pain anymore. You could hardly step out in public without noticing the white blaze of someone's impacted heel showing through her slingbacks; and over there, hailing a taxi, a woman with shimmering pressure marks where her pants cut into her gut; and behind her, beneath the awning of the flower shop, a man lit all over in a glory of leukemia.

At work, Carol Ann took to scouring the Internet for images of political and business leaders with the angry flush of renal disease, the barbed-wire knot of a blocked artery, or any of the hundreds of other telltale patterns of resplendence she had learned to recognize. She included these pictures in her news packets without comment. And if her hand flared with pain while she was delivering a hard copy to her boss, and if the silver light of a toothache shone from his mouth as he said thank you, the two of them might make a small motion of their heads in sympathy, but they would not say a word. It was important that the workplace remain professional. They all tried their best not to acknowledge one another's suffering. Even when one of the receptionists came in with belt-strap bruises radiating through the front of her shirt, wincing each time she reached to open the filing cabinet, the rest of the staff avoided saying anything to her. It was almost noon that day before Carol Ann found the woman inspecting her stomach in the bathroom mirror and was forced to ask her if she was all right. She met Carol Ann's eyes in the glass, shook her head in disbelief, and repeated the question: "Am I all right? Am I all right? Am I *all right?*" It was like a chant or a song, four hard beats, and for the rest of the day, as Carol Ann sat hunched over her computer, surveying the leaders of the world, in all their wounds and illnesses, the phrase kept replaying itself in her mind: Was she all right? Was she all right? Was she all right?

Nearly a month had passed since she sliced through the tip of her thumb. One evening she arrived home to discover another package from her ex-husband waiting by the front door. This time the seams were covered by only a few strips of masking tape. Even with her good hand cramped from typing, she was able to steady the box against the kitchen counter and open it. Immediately beneath the lid was the front section of the *Financial Times*, and beneath that was a magazine called *How to Spend It*, and beneath that were hundreds of red plastic drinking straws. She knew how his mind worked, knew that wasting her time was a favorite mean little game of his, and right away she guessed what he had done. She still had to sort through forty or fifty straws, though, blowing into each of them with a hard blast of air, before she found the one into which he had rolled her alimony check. It shot out with the quiet *phut* of a spitball, landing upright between the ribs of the dish drainer. His usual petty degeneracy. She could picture him leaning back in a chair somewhere, grinning triumphantly, bowing his hands out to crack his knuckles. *I love the way your face falls whenever you see my handwriting on an envelope. I love how easy it is to aggravate you. I love waking up next to someone else in the morning.* For a moment she allowed herself to contemplate leaving an angry voice-mail message for him—she could threaten to file suit against him for her medical expenses, or for malicious wrongdoing—but the truth was she had injured her thumb by her own carelessness, she and no one else, and anyway he had changed his phone number, and she did not know the new one.

That Friday, she had an appointment to get her stitches removed. They were the dissolving kind, designed to be absorbed into her body, but her physical therapist had noticed that the tissue around the threads was inflamed and suggested that she look into having them taken out by a professional. On the highway a car had wrapped itself around a bridge stanchion, spilling blue cubes of windshield glass over the carpool lane. Carol Ann merged into the long line of drivers slowing to gape at the light show, creeping past the police cars, the ambulance, and the curve of orange cones, until her exit opened up and she could punch the gas and speed free of the fold. The hospital revealed itself through the flowing green of the pine trees. She parked and went inside. Soon an orderly in brown scrubs came to escort her into an examination room. The doctor who had lectured her about missing her follow-up appointments, Dr. Miss-Ann-Page, Dr. Misanthrope—she could not remember his real name—arrived to inspect her amputation. In a tone of weary reproach, he told her, "Fortunately for you, the wound has already sealed itself," and, "Some people have a negative reaction to the proteins in the suture. The result is a poor tissue response. That's all I'm seeing here, not the world coming to an end," and finally, as he braced her hand and picked at the knot with a pair of angled scissors, "Now I don't want any flinching from you, Miss, understand? This won't hurt a bit." Surprisingly it didn't. She watched the thread sinuate through her skin, flashing in and out of sight like a black snake moving through white sand. The first time a doctor ever took her blood, she was not yet three years old, and he had pacified her by telling her that her body was filled with red water, asking, "Did you know that? Would you like to see some?" She had sat there fascinated while he pricked her arm and his syringe filled with cherry Kool-Aid. She felt a similar fascination as she followed the surgical thread passing out of her thumb. Afterward, she was left with only a pale impression of stitches on her skin, barely glowing at all. A few lambent blood-vessel blotches traced the edges, and a checkmark of scar tissue rose above the knuckle. The whole procedure took less than ten minutes.

She was on her way out when Dr. Alstadt chased her down, placing a hand on her wrist. "So how did everything go with Dr. Kimberley?" he asked.

"*Kim*berley! That's it. I think he was angry with me about something."

"People always think that. He just has this manner. But your thumb is feeling better? You can get back to doing the things you love?"

"Like tying my shoes and brushing my teeth."

"Exactly."

She found herself adopting the pose of the woman she wished to be, someone coolly self-deprecating, confident, willing to puncture her own seriousness with a shrug and a wry remark. "My plan is to take it slow, start with one tooth and work my way up."

"Good idea," he said.

He smiled nervously, looking down at the chart in his hands. She could tell that he was mustering up the courage to continue.

"Is there something else, Doctor?"

"Actually, yes. We've transferred you over to primary care. Officially, you're no longer on the A&E registry, which means I'm not your doctor anymore. So I was wondering . . ." He cleared his throat. "We're not supposed to do this, but I was wondering if you would consider letting me take you out to dinner sometime."

"Doctor! I don't even know your first name!"

"It's Tom. Thomas. Dr. Thomas Alstadt."

"Dr. Thomas Alstadt." She indicated the file he was holding. "Is that me you've got there?"

He nodded.

"Does it have my phone number in it?"

He nodded again.

She tapped the chart and shifted on her heel and did not glance back until she had left the building. She happened to spy him at the exact moment he stopped watching her. He was turning his face away as an orderly in mocha-colored scrubs approached him with an outstretched hand, and so he did not see the call-me gesture she threw him. But it didn't matter—she was sure he had gotten the message.

Her legs carried her beneath the blue sky and the pine trees with that drifty roller-skating feeling she remembered from the sunlit summer Fridays of her childhood. She kept replaying the sound of his voice—*It's Tom, Thomas, Dr. Thomas Alstadt*—and laughing to herself. Sometimes they rose up inside her, these moments of fierce happiness, kindling out of their own substance like a spark igniting a mound of grass. It was a joy to be alive, a strange and savage joy, and she stood there in the warmth and destruction of it knowing it could not last.

That it was too big for her to contain.

That it would ebb as quickly as it had risen.

And sure enough, late that night, she woke to find that she had not yet finished healing. Her hair was pasted to her forehead, and her hand shone with a sharp pain. She was afraid that it was starting all over again, all the hurt and debility. She could hear the high sustained note of a fever in her ears. Her life was a waste and a failure, and she had never loved another human being, and she wanted nothing more than to escape the planes of her skin and appear in some other place. The world was unreliable. The world could turn on a dime. It was a joy to be alive when it was a joy to be alive, and it was a terror to be alive when it wasn't. What else had she ever learned?

It was several hours before the light subsided and she was able to fall back asleep. In the morning she drank an extra cup of coffee to clear her head. She did the dishes and watched a few hours of television, and at noon Dr. Alstadt—Thomas—called her to ask if she would be free for dinner that night. She had no other plans, and she started to give him her address, but he interrupted with, "Actually, I already have it. Your chart, remember. I hope that isn't creepy."

"I never want to hear from you again. So six-thirty, did we say?"

"Six-thirty."

That day, grocery shopping, her eye was caught by one of the newsweeklies in the checkout lane. The headline read, "History Is an Angel," and beneath that, in smaller print, "Bringing Light to the Past." She decided to buy it. When she got home, she sat down to read the cover story, a long essay about the pictorial history of the twentieth century and how it might have differed had the Illumination commenced a hundred years earlier. It was illustrated with a four-page foldout of famous photos, digitally altered to show new varieties of light emanating from them. A Spanish soldier reeling from a bullet strike, his head ringed in a silver corona. A man in a naval uniform crying as he played the accordion, a bright cloud of grief surrounding his face and fingers. The motorcade in Dealey Plaza, November 22, 1963: the president leaning into the eruption of light at his temple. A group of civil rights marchers hunching against the blast from a fire hose, the tightly contained spray of pain from their bodies matching the tightly contained spray of the water. A young girl with

napalm burns running naked in a dazzling aurora. A famine victim staring out of the radiance of her hunger. A dozen men in
fire helmets floating like lanterns in a field of smoke. There was
a terrible beauty to the images, and Carol Ann found it hard to
look away from them. Her job had made her a student of popular imagery. The pictures would be reprinted in all the papers
and on all the current affairs sites, she was sure of it, broadcast
again and again on all the cable news networks. She began to feel
uncomfortable with herself. Maybe she was just another driver
who couldn't stop gawking at a car crash. But then, in this case,
wasn't the car crash hers—or not hers alone, but hers in part,
hers along with everybody else's: the great shared car crash of
modern history?

Her thumb was still aching a little, but by that evening the
glow was weak enough that she could cover it with a Band-Aid
and ignore it. Dr. Alstadt arrived promptly at six-thirty. He was
wearing a green silk tie, a blue oxford shirt, and bull-nosed brown
shoes with a rolling pinprick pattern on top. With a comb and
water, he had attempted to flatten the lock of hair on his forehead, and though he had not quite succeeded, she found the
effort endearing.

She made a gesture that encompassed his entire outfit.
"Spiffy."

He wrinkled his lips. "Thank you very much. So are you ready
to go? I've made reservations for us at Jacques and Suzanne's."

"Just give me five more minutes."

She showed him into the living room and left to brush her
teeth and reapply her lipstick. She looked herself over in the full-
length mirror, kicking her leg up to tug a thread from her skirt,
then smoothing a ruck out of the fabric. It was years since she
had been on a date, and though he had already seen her at her

worst, or at least what he must have presumed was her worst, high on narcotics and stained with her own blood, she said a prayer that if she presented herself to him with enough poise and self-possession she might erase that other woman from his mind.

She returned to the living room just in time to see him taking the journal up from its spot on the walnut table. "What's this?" he said.

"That—it's not mine."

He let the book fall open and read aloud the first lines that met his eyes: *I love the concavities behind your knees, as soft as the skin of a peach. I love how disgusted you get by purées: "Who would do that to a poor defenseless soup?" I love waking up on a wintry morning, opening the curtains, then crawling back under the covers with you and watching the snow fall.* "I know what this is," he said. His voice quieted as he spoke. He shut the book and looked up at her. "An orderly told me you had this, but I told him it wasn't possible. Carol Ann, Mr. Williford has been looking everywhere for this book."

"Wait. Mr. Williford? *Jason* Williford? But he died. He died in the accident."

The prickliness in his voice made her stomach tighten. "Obviously he *didn't* die. Obviously if he had *died* he wouldn't be phoning the hospital all day long asking if we've found his wife's *book* yet."

"You don't understand."

"You're right about that."

"His wife asked me to take it. She said he was dead and she couldn't bear to read it again. That's what she said, those words exactly. I told her it wouldn't be right, but then *she* died, too. Right there in front of me. I watched her go, and I thought it was what she would have wanted."

"Well—" He shook his head. "All that may be true, but I still have to tell him we've found it. Excuse me a minute," and he tucked the journal protectively under his arm and flipped his phone open. Within seconds he was talking to someone at the hospital. "Hello, this is Dr. Alstadt. I need you to get a patient's number for me. His name is Jason Williford. That's Williford, spelled W-I-L-L . . . yes, that's right. Thank you." She tried hard to listen as he dialed the number, but the sound inside her head was so much louder than the sound outside that she could barely distinguish his voice. It was like a rainstorm beating against a tin roof, thousands of drops landing like little round stones, and by the time the storm faded, she was sitting next to him on the sofa and he was repeating her name, meeting her gaze while he cocked his head to the side. He waited until he was sure he had her attention before he said what he had to say.

"Mr. Williford wants to come over right away. I gave him your address. He's a mess, Carol Ann. I don't know whether he plans to build a shrine to this thing or burn it," he told her, brandishing the journal, "but one thing I'm sure of—if he's ever going to move on, he needs it back."

He was silent for so long that she thought he might have finished, but eventually, pausing to take the weight of his words, he continued. "I shouldn't have snapped at you. I'm sorry about that. I believe you when you say it was an accident, and I'm sure you never intended to hurt anyone. But you need to know that you've taken the most terrible month of this man's life and made it that much worse."

He gave her hand a consoling squeeze. She felt as if he had slapped her face.

For a while the two of them waited on the sofa. She thought, *This is not really happening,* and also, *In an hour this will already have happened,* the same phrases she had found herself repeating as the orderly wheeled her onto the elevator to have her hand disfigured.

Soon enough a taxi arrived in the driveway. Its motor halted, and she heard a pair of crutches tapping up the walk. A few seconds later the bell rang. She followed Dr. Alstadt down the front hall, rushing ahead of him at the last second to open the door. Outside there was the flexing coolness of a spring breeze. She stood there in it with her hand on her chest, the doctor beside her in his shirt and tie, before them a man with a look of breaking sadness in his eyes, all of them glowing in the darkness.

Jason Williford

The reality cuts across our minds like a wound whose edges crave to heal, but cannot. Thus, one of the great sins, perhaps *the* great sin, is to say: It will heal; it has healed; there is no wound; there is something more important than this wound. There is nothing more important than this wound.

—Whittaker Chambers

In the accident he had cracked his sternum and three of his ribs, dislocated his right shoulder, fractured his pelvis, and knocked identical wedge-shaped fragments out of his front teeth. The steering column had crushed his right knee. A ballpoint pen, flung loose from the coin tray, had perforated his stomach. The side-curtain airbag had bruised his left eye, and at first, after the swelling went down, he presumed that the light he saw leaking from his injuries was a result of the contact lens the doctor had prescribed, designed to keep the scab beneath his eyelid from scratching his cornea. Then someone told him about the Illumination, and he understood that the same thing was happening all over the world. Everywhere, everywhere, in bars, locker rooms, parks, and emergency wards, the wounded were burning with light.

He could see his own lesions shining through the bandages on his shoulder, the cotton compress on his abdomen, the pins and netting of his leg harness. He was aware of the pain, but ever since he woke from surgery, his senses had been buoyed up on a sea of narcotics, and as he lay there staring at the contours of his limbs, it seemed to him that he was watching a distant cloud bank flashing with lightning. Somewhere far away the rain was falling straight and hard. The sand was pockmarked with raindrops. It was all so lovely and mysterious. And yet for the nurses who came every few hours to change his dressing and adjust his drainage tubes he had only one question: "Can I see my wife? Will you check on her for me? Her name is Patricia. Patricia Williford. Patty."

"I'll have someone look into that for you, sir."

"She'll be worried about me. I need to let her know that I'm all right."

"For now, let's just concentrate on taking care of that body of yours, okay?"

It was like that every time he asked about her, as if his questions had slid through some invisible crack in the air and vanished into another world. Had they spoken to his wife yet? *I'm sure the doctor will be in to talk to you soon.* What was her condition? *Are you feeling any discomfort, Mr. Williford? How are those painkillers working for you?* Evidently a decision had been made that he was too fragile to know the truth. By the time his doctor finally sat down to explain what had happened to her, he was only waiting for someone to say the words out loud: "I'm sorry, Mr. Williford. We did everything we could, but your wife's injuries were too extensive. She didn't make it."

His twenty-three days in the hospital were spent watching his bones heal and his scars form, trying to forget who he was and what had happened to him. He couldn't cough, or even breathe too deeply, without feeling that his ribs were about to split open. Hiccups were a terror. The one time he sneezed, his vision blurred and he nearly passed out. Whenever he shifted his weight, he saw two long serrations of light opening through the thin blue cotton of his exam gown, one across his sternum, another over his left hip. The ballpoint pen had left a small round mark on the white field of his stomach, and he discovered that the seat belt had printed his torso with a crisply bordered bruise, like a soldier's bandolier, its ammunition sash glinting in the sunlight. Day by day he watched as it turned blue, then green, then spread over his skin in a grotesque yellow stain that gradually lost its shine and color. The radiance that had filtered from his mouth ceased to show as soon as his incisors were capped with porcelain. Suddenly, to his relief, he could pronounce his *f*'s and his *v*'s again.

It was his kneecap that took the longest time to mend. For nearly two weeks it sent an excruciating silver spike through his leg every time he moved in his harness. Just when it seemed the pain was beginning to abate, his physical therapist decided that the day had come for him to try walking again. She lowered his leg onto the bed and measured him for crutches. "They might be somewhat uncomfortable for you at first," she cautioned, "but won't it feel good to leave here on your own two feet? Now hold your horses until I come back," she said, and he lay there thinking about what it would be like to open his front door, to collect the mail and attempt to revive the plants. The name he had been struggling to ignore rose up inside him and pressed at his lips. *Her name is Patricia. Patricia Williford. Patty.* Only his long habit of silence and the abrasions lingering in his mouth kept him from repeating it out loud. Soon, the physical therapist returned with a pair of metal crutches. "Chromium," she said, "with gel polymer tips, the best we have." She insisted that he test them out. As he wobbled across the room, she carefully laid out her instructions, presenting them one by one like a waiter placing dishes on a table: "Nice and easy, that's right. Balance yourself on your left leg, your left leg. If it hurts, that means you're not letting the crutches do the work. You want to avoid placing any weight on that injured knee of yours." He found that if he ignored her advice, if instead he leaned into the pain when it came, his leg would flood with a glow so strong he was unaware of anything else. For a few seconds, he seemed to be nothing more than the light of that shattered bone, white and expansive, pulsing within its own radiance, and his wife's name faded entirely from his mind. The agony was nearly indistinguishable from bliss.

Over the days that followed, his pain became increasingly familiar to him. It would come over him when he was reaching for the push-buttons on his bed or crossing the floor to the bathroom, when he was watching the sun bounce off the TV, watching the rain leave its cat's paws on the window, a response he realized he had been waiting for all along, as if he and his wounds were simply having a conversation at bedtime, interrupted by long moments of insensibility. *Oh, yes. Where were we? You were asking me a question, weren't you?* He did not court the sensation, but he did not shrink away from it, either. Whenever he felt it diminishing, a brief feeling of regret settled over him. The fact that he was healing meant that he would be returning to his real life soon. The doctor had reduced his dose of sedatives. The nurse had removed his catheter. His knee had set inside its cage of pins and wires, and though he was still required to wear a brace, he was no longer confined to his harness. On his crutches he felt like an ape swaying across the African veldt, using his long arms to knuckle over the grass.

He was discharged from the hospital on one of those stern late-winter afternoons when a low blanket of rain clouds had turned the sky the color of a blackboard coated with chalk dust. He took a taxi home. As soon as he saw the walnut tree in his front yard slowing outside the window, he asked the driver to help him carry his small parcel of belongings inside. The house was dim and silent. Only a slight humming from the kitchen marked the stillness. He imagined himself pulling a chair across the floor and opening the refrigerator door, sitting in its tidy rectangle of light the way that pioneer families used to gather around a fireplace. It would be a source of comfort in the house, a place where nothing else mattered but his own momentary well-being. Instead, he paid the cabdriver and showed him back outside. He threw the junk mail in the trash and sorted his get-well-soon and sorry-for-your-loss cards into two separate stacks on his desk. He checked his e-mail, deleting the spam from his in-box. Finally he had just enough energy left to water the plants, rotate them, and pick their dead leaves loose before he took himself upstairs for a nap.

Shortly after midnight, he reached out to press his hand against his wife's back, feeling, as he always did, for the shallow rain-draw of her spinal crease. Then he remembered what had happened. He woke up thirsty and sweating in his blue jeans and went to the kitchen for a ginger ale. On the refrigerator he found the last Post-it note he had left her: *I love the spaghetti patterns you leave on the wall.* Long ago he had read somewhere that the best way to keep a marriage healthy was to find one new thing you loved about your partner every day. The notion had lingered with him, and so each morning before work he had paused on his way to the car to write her a mash note. There were thousands of them altogether, one for each day of their marriage. *I love the shape of your legs inside your brown leather skirt. I love how quietly you speak when you're catching a cold. I love hearing you tell the cockatoo story to people who don't know it yet. I love watching you step so carefully inside your footprints when it snows. I love the way you hunt for our names as the movie credits scroll by—"thirteen Jasons and not one Patricia."*

Usually, by the time the sun came up, he already knew what he was going to write, but on the morning of the accident he had run short of ideas and finally, standing over the stove, had allowed himself to resort to the spaghetti remark. There was one particular note he had been saving for their anniversary, a note he was sure she would like—*I love it when you wear my blue jeans, even if you do, too, drip chocolate sauce on them*—and if he had known it was their last morning together, the last time she would pad across the linoleum in her thick winter socks, the last time she would open the refrigerator looking for cream for her coffee or jelly for her toast, he would have used it a few months early. At the very least he would have written something more intimate than *I love the spaghetti patterns you leave on the wall.*

This was what she did: when she wanted to test the spaghetti she was cooking, she would fling a strand against the wall, and if it stuck, she knew it was ready, and if it didn't, she would try again a few seconds later. Sometimes, after the pot had finished boiling, she would throw an extra strand just for the pleasure of seeing it whip through the air and flatten so suddenly against the plaster. The next day he would find the pieces she had flung hanging over the stove, brittle and yellowed, clinging to the wall in precisely delineated loops and twists that left funny little abstract maps of themselves in the paint when he chipped them loose.

It was something he had always teased her about, that runelike series of curves and squiggles in the kitchen. *The pasta motif,* he had called it. And now, suddenly, the sight made his stomach clench. It took the best part of his life, the only part he had ever felt he understood, and consigned it to the past. Worse, it summoned up an image he had been trying to suppress ever since he woke with his injuries shining out of his skin.

Patricia's body as their car struck the bridge stanchion.

Her long hair whipping against the window.

Spaghetti patterns of blood on the dash.

He had always known that their time together would one day be spent. That it might be spent so soon, though, was a possibility he had never allowed himself to imagine. He was a fool. He crumpled the note up and tossed it in the trash. Then he fished it out and smoothed it flat against the counter. He couldn't bear to read it, but he couldn't bear to throw it away, either. He would have to put it in a file somewhere and try his best to forget about it.

That was when he remembered her journals—seven of them, each page filled from corner to corner with transcriptions of the notes he had left her. She kept them lined up on the glass and oak espresso table in the room where she exercised. Once or twice, hearing the springs of her equipment stop, he had peeked in to find her stretched out on her Nautilus or her rowing machine, paging through the journals as if they were old diaries she was investigating for traces of the thoughts that used to preoccupy her when she was young and brave, when she was unchanged. He attached the Post-it note to one of his crutches and carried himself across the house. Patricia's exercise room had always been a sanctuary for her, the one place in the house where she could play her music, burn her candles, and sort through her baskets of yarn and crochet hooks in privacy. Now it felt overwhelmingly empty. When he flipped the light on, the objects that greeted his eye had an unusual tidiness to them, a strange and frightening aura of completeness, as if the treadmill and the storage hutch, the stereo and the upright speakers, had all suddenly become imprisoned inside their own outlines. The silhouette of a beetle whisked its legs inside the ceiling fixture. One of the pipes gave a tug beneath the house. In the quiet, the noise made him shiver.

He went to press the Post-it note into Patricia's most recent journal, but beneath the window, on the table where it should have been, there was an empty slot with a boundary of dust around it. Where could it be? He tried to recall—had he seen the book in her hands the day of the accident? Maybe so. But when he went to the front hall and opened the box the hospital had labeled with her name, he found only her clothes, her shoes, and her pocketbook, along with a small plastic bag holding her wristwatch and jewelry.

She had definitely taken the journal into the car with her. He was sure of it now. He remembered her clutching it to her hip as they left to meet their reservation at the restaurant. "What if I get bored and need something to read?" she had joked, whispering to him with her hand alongside her mouth, "I'll let you in on a little secret—the guy I'm dining with today is a real snooze." But if it wasn't in the box, then where was it? Who would lose a dead woman's handwritten journal? Who would steal it?

Who, as it developed, but the woman who had shared her recovery room. The hospital spent a week or more attempting to track it down before discovering that she had taken it. Apparently, she had adopted it as some sort of charm or talisman, a sad, sick symbol of God-knew-what illness or unhappiness. She had actually been reading it—*reading it!*—as if it were her own cache of personal letters. She had spoken with Patricia, had watched her die, had believed he was dead, too—or at least so she said. But none of that excused her, none of it healed him, none of it made his life one bit easier or brought his wife back from the dead. When she finally placed the journal in his hands, apologizing for what she called "this misunderstanding," he felt himself shaking with relief and exhaustion. Absurdly, he found that he was afraid of dropping the book. The idea came to him that it was Patricia herself he was holding, that she had fallen and twisted her ankle, maybe, and given him her hand, and he was bearing her up as she limped through the snow. Soon they would both be inside again. He would place a pillow beneath her foot and kiss her toes one by one, starting with the pinky, and they would drink half a bottle of red wine, then wipe the stains from each other's lips with their thumbs, and she would make a happy little upsy-daisy noise as he carried her upstairs to bed.

Instead, he brought the journal home, took it into the living room, and set it on his lap. His fingers flipped backward from the endpapers, watching as the pages filled with her handwriting. He had no need to leave the Post-it note inside, since she had already written it down. There it was in her own precise script, facing him one more time, the last sentence on a half-empty page, *I love the spaghetti patterns you leave on the wall,* ending with that oddly turned period of hers, like a toppled *v* or a bird's beak.

One morning, some six weeks after the accident, his editor woke him from a sound sleep to ask if he knew when he would be returning to work. "I realize you're going through a rough patch, Jason. Grieving—check. Convalescing—check. I get it, I'm with you, I understand. By all means, you should take as much time as you need. But I'm telling you, you're missing out on some of the greatest shots of your life right now. Have you seen the stuff Dawes has been producing? Or Laskowski? Even Christman gave us a front-pager yesterday! Christman for Jesus' sake! I'm telling you, this Illumination thing is really big. Don't just sit there in that house of yours and turn to stone on us. I can't believe that's what she would want, Patricia."

He felt like the priest of some ancient blood religion, incensed to hear her name spoken out loud. "How do *you* know what she would want? Maybe this is *exactly* what she would want."

"You don't mean that."

From down the block came the mosquito-like drone of someone operating a lawn mower. Mysteriously, his anger evaporated.

"I don't, you're right. Tell you what, Paul—I'll try to have some images for you by the end of the week, okay?"

"Sounds good. Whenever you're ready. No pressure from me on this end. Take all the time you need."

Jason snapped the phone shut and went to the mirror, where he stripped off his pajamas and embarked on his customary preshower ritual, stretching his limbs and tensing his muscles to see how much light they gave off. His eye and his cheek had healed completely, as had his shoulder and his hip, his gums and incisors. One of his ribs still shone with a filmy incandescence, and a new abrasion on his elbow, tacky from scraping against the supermarket meat freezer, glittered like the mica in the sidewalk. Since his discharge from the hospital, he had been dining mainly on microwave dinners and cheap delivered pizza—salty, greasy foods that upset his digestion—and when he turned too forcefully to the side, he could see a pair of bright rectal fissures opening up behind him. Then there was the scar on his abdomen, a small red fold tattooed with a pucker of blue ink. The wound still wept with light occasionally, but only if he distended his belly. It was his knee that continued to worry him, maintaining a constant twilight glow that was run through by cruel white flares whenever he took it out of its brace, sank his weight onto it, or attempted to rotate it laterally. In short, he was still recuperating from the accident. The pain was not as bad as before, though, and he thought he could risk a walk through the neighborhood.

After he had showered and eaten breakfast, he got his camera and set off on his crutches. He wanted to see what images the world would present to him, whether his eye had been altered by sorrow, whether he had any skill left, any talent, and that was how he came to meet the cutters.

He had spent the morning framing the pictures he saw in his

lens, capturing them one by one—although he hated that word, *capture;* hated its suggestion that with a camera you could seize any sight that presented itself to you, stuff it in a cage, and point to it as it jammed its nose through the bars. Better to say that he preserved them, then. He preserved the sight of an old man sitting on a motionless merry-go-round, a long strand of angina shining through his shirt. The sight of a mother smacking the seat of her son's pants, the burning corona of a bite mark on her arm. A street cop with a gleaming herpes infection on his lip. A rail-thin window-dresser, her sides lit up by shingles. The sight of a girl afflicted with acne, staring down at herself in a fountain, her face fluorescing up at her from the steel mirror of the water. He was pleased to discover that he had not lost his facility for composition, that the lines and curves of things still sought out their counterparts in the air, their colors laying their shapes out in polychromatic blocks. His camerawork had always been a product of habit and instinct, tilting toward craftsmanship rather than artistry, and maybe that had made him a second-rate photographer—he didn't know—but there was one thing to be said for habit and instinct, for plain old humble craftsmanship, and that was that it wasn't so easy to snuff out.

He had shouldered his camera and was preparing to head back home when one last image presented itself to him: a pack of adolescents, seventeen or eighteen years old, smoking cigarettes beneath the bus shelter. Their arms and legs were patterned with dozens of freshly inflicted injuries. The glowing lines and tiny luminescent planets on their skin resembled the pits and notches carved into the bus bench. His gaze was drawn to their deliberate, almost sculptural quality. He found it hard to look away.

Surreptitiously, he returned his camera to his eye, moving his head a few inches to the left to compose a shot. Before he could release the shutter, though, a boy with a chain of burn blisters reaching up his arm shouted, "Hey! Dude with the camera! C'mere!"

Jason looped the strap around his neck and crossed the street, steadying himself on his crutches when he reached the shelter.

"What's your name, man?" the boy asked him.

"Jason Williford. I'm a photojournalist for the *Gazette*. You guys don't mind if I snap a few pictures, do you?"

"Ten dollars."

"What?"

"Ten dollars, and you can take our picture. Apiece."

"I can't offer you any money. I'm a journalist."

"Ten dollars in cigarettes then. There's a gas station over there on the corner. Call them a gift."

He thought it over. There was a specific shot he kept envisioning, one that would allow the wounds engraved on their skin to flow across the borders of their bodies into the pocks and slashes on the bus bench, like hanging lights echoed in a polished tabletop.

"Two packs. Two packs for the lot of you. That's the best I can do."

"Deal," the boy agreed. Jason was halfway to the corner when a girl perched on the backrest of the bench, her shoes beating out a two-four rhythm, called after him. "Salem Black Labels!"

As soon as he returned with the cigarettes, a boy in a red T-shirt tore the cellophane from one of the packs, knocked a cigarette loose, and replaced it upside-down. Then he tweezed a second one out with his small, knuckly fingers and lit it. "I heard these things are bad for you," he said. "Did you know that quitting smoking now greatly reduces serious risks to your health?"

One of the other kids said, "Huh-I-did-not-know-that. Did

you know that smoking by pregnant women may result in fetal injury, premature birth, and low birth weight?"

Hardly a beat had passed before someone added, "Did you know that quitting your health now greatly reduces serious risks to your smoking?" And then they were all working at it together, jockeying to extend the thread of the joke. They passed the cigarettes around with a plastic lighter. Jason took advantage of their inattention and began snapping pictures. There was a panel ad on the back of the bus shelter that kept disrupting the balance of the shots, announcing in bold black letters PERSONAL INJURY, MEDICAL NEGLIGENCE, BIG TRUCKS, and time after time he had to find a perspective that would obscure the words. Ordinarily he would have crouched or stood on his toes, maybe climbed over the bench for a better angle, but the brace on his leg had turned such maneuvers into elaborate feats of acrobatics.

In the end, though he wasn't quite able to achieve the image he had envisioned, he found one that came close: the dazzling white stroke of the recent incision on a girl's exposed waist beside a scythelike mark on the fiberglass bench, the one extending into the other in a perfect curve. Quickly, before the girl could move, he released the shutter.

The other girl, the lovely pale fashion-model-type sitting atop the bench, the one who had shouted for Salem Black Labels, gestured to him. "Hey, Jason Williford, photojournalist. I've got a picture for you. Are you ready?" She took three quick drags on her cigarette to make the emberhead glow, then, on the inside of her wrist where the blue vein beat, extinguished it. A powerful smell overtook the air, like the whiff of salt and char at a burger joint. The cigarette sizzled, and the smoke changed color, and a magnificent wave of light came bloating out of the burn. Through Jason's camera, it resembled the great fanning loop of a solar flare. The aurora borealis was dancing over Greenland. Radios everywhere were filling with static. He couldn't help himself: he took the shot.

Within seconds the light had subsided, throwing off a few last sparks as it fell to the surface of the girl's wrist, where it continued to twitch and flutter. A smile was locked on her face. The bays of skin beneath her eyes were moist with tears. He took a shot of that, as well.

Enough, he decided. Laskowski and Christman be damned.

He capped the camera and returned it to his shoulder. "So all those cuts on your bodies—you guys did those to yourself?"

The kids exchanged a glance and broke up laughing.

That evening he was sorting through the pictures he had taken, selecting the ones to submit to his editor, when he realized something: during his long afternoon in the processing room, not once had he thought about Patricia. He had become lost in the familiar beaverish activity of enlarging, fixing, and scanning his photos, and his memories of her had vanished, along with his awareness of the pain in his leg. The little system of injuries that was his body and the one immense injury that was his life—he had forgotten about them both, and when he thought back on the contentment he had felt, a terrific surge of guilt passed through him. He had accepted that he would forget Patricia in his suffering sometimes, but to forget her in his pleasure? It seemed monstrous, inexcusable. He forced himself to picture her: the freckles on her back and shoulders, the soft, swelling veins that ran along her ankle, the dimple that appeared on her cheek whenever she tried not to smile, all of it swimming in the blood of the car accident.

He bore down on his knee until the joint spasmed with light. His breathing quickened, and his teeth ground together. He would not allow his pain to forsake him.

Two days later he had an appointment with his physical therapist. The routine was familiar by now. She gripped his shoulder as he executed a slow windmill with his arm—a simple matter of form, since his collarbone had already healed—then had him straighten his back and twist his torso around, inspecting his hip for signs of stiffness or discomfort. She examined his stomach as he performed a sit-up. The scar on his abdomen shone in the glare from the overhead lamp, and she had to switch it off to make sure the source was not internal. Finally she came to his leg, guiding him through a battery of stretches, lifts, and pivots that made his face break out in a hard sweat.

"I have to admit," she said when they were finished, "I'm still concerned about your knee. We ought to have switched you over to the forearm crutches by now. You're behind schedule. Have you been doing your leg extensions?"

He had discovered that when he removed his brace, bending his knee until the ligaments tightened, then jerking his leg rigid, the joint would pop with a violent paroxysm of light. The lacerating sensation would last for several minutes. He could not stop testing it.

"Not regularly, no."

She jotted something down in his folder. Then, contemplatively, she asked, "Did anyone ever tell you you were dead when the paramedics brought you in?"

"No. Wait. I was?"

"You were. The doctors revived you on the operating table. It's a miracle you're alive today. You should have some respect for that miracle and take better care of yourself." She clicked her pen shut with a flourish, as if punctuating the remark. "Okay. Lecture over. Like I said, I'm not ready to switch your crutches out just yet, but I think we can get rid of that brace you've been wearing. You have to promise me you won't test your limits, though. If your knee flares up, you'll lie back and rest awhile. Can you promise me that? Can you? Mr. Williford? Hello?"

So he had died, but what did that mean? Had his heart stopped beating? Had his brain shut down? Of the hours following the accident not one memory remained to him: no flash of images, no luminous white tunnel, only the sight of the bridge whirling smoothly, even elegantly, above him, like the long arm of a wind-mill, and then, some time later, the speckled yellow ceiling of the recovery room. His therapist wrote out a prescription for him. He left with an appointment to return in seven days. As his crutches conveyed him past the staircase and the admissions counter, past the bank of ferns twitching their fingertips in the air, it occurred to him that he had, quite literally, been resur-rected. But resurrected into what? he wondered. His life had become unfamiliar to him, cold and disquieting. He felt as if time as he knew it had flickered to a close. The world had ended. The oceans had climbed their shores, the buildings had burst out of their windows, and all the old meanings had fallen away. It turned out that the world at the end of time was just like the world at the beginning: a single set of footsteps printing the grass, everything lit with its own newness, a brighter and much, much emptier place.

He was passing a newspaper box when the front section of the *Gazette* caught his eye. Positioned above the fold, filling a quarter-page, was his photo of the girl in the bus shelter. The light from her cigarette burn was not as crisp in the paper's min-eral ink as it had been in his own emulsions, but the wound's dis-play of pain, that curved lily blooming so magnificently into the air, was no less remarkable for that. The girl's arm plunged across the frame in a lovely white slash. The cigarette seemed to pierce her wrist like a nail. Behind it one could just make out the blurred fabric of her blue jeans and, in the upper left-hand corner of the shot, the braided green vines of a small tattoo. The photo was a stand-alone, with no companion article. The caption read, "Melissa Wallumrod, 17, practices bodily mutilation with her friends Monday morning near Allsopp Park. *Gazette* Staff Photo/Jason Williford."

He took out his phone and dialed his editor, who answered, "Jason! How does it feel to be back in the land of the living?"

"It feels fine. But—"

"Well, you earned it, my friend. That's one first-class shot you took. What we need now is to get you out on assignment somewhere. The Middle East. South Central. Name your war zone. Someplace where you can really exercise your skills."

"Paul, listen, I have a question for you. How did you trace the girl's name?"

"Girl?"

"The one in the picture. The one with the cigarette."

"Oh, that was easy," he said. "What happened was I sent one of the interns over to the park and, well, okay, no luck there, but then I sent him to the high school during their lunch hour, that one over by the new Target, and bam!—someone recognized her tattoo. The intern found her out behind the building with her friends. Said she was cagey at first, wouldn't give him her name, but that cigarette burn was there on her wrist, all tacky and glowing around the rim. We looked her up in the yearbook. She's definitely the one."

"Thanks, Paul. That's all I needed to know. I'll have another batch of pictures for you by Friday."

Jason hung up and bought a copy of the newspaper, riffling through it to see if any more of his pictures had made it to press. On the back of the City Section, squeezed into a twenty-eighth of a page, was his image of the old man on the merry-go-round, his scalp mottled with liver spots, the cloth of his shirt fissured with arteriosclerosis. There was a Dawes photo on A-2, a Laskowski on A-8, and a second Dawes on B-1, plus the usual dozen or so from the Associated Press. Jason folded the paper and tucked it behind his crutch. A scrim of clouds drifted over the sun. There were days when everything seemed to have a beautiful underwater lucidity to it, the banks and the traffic lights, the billboards and parking meters, all of them tilting through their planes until something bent or contorted inside them and they shimmered back together. He watched a homeless man with small misshapen sores shining out of his beard sifting through a trash barrel. He watched a woman in a thin linen dress stepping out of a French salon, her freshly waxed pubis phosphorescing through her skirt. There was an ache inside people that seemed so wonderful sometimes. He wished he had brought his camera with him.

His brace and crutches had made it impossible for him to drive, and anyway his car was still in the impound lot awaiting destruction, the right side crimped around an invisible concrete pillar, so he hailed a taxi and rode back home. He paid the driver and climbed out onto the curb. From his front door, he collected a religious leaflet signed, "Sorry we missed you, will try again later. 'For the Lord God will illumine them.'—Rev 22:5." Inside, the silence of the house was broken only by the wooden table clock in the hallway, the one Patricia had picked up at last year's summer arts festival, making its elaborate *tap-TAP-t-t-tap-TAP* noise as it clattered through its numbers. She had always said that it reminded her of the walnuts that came tumbling down their roof every October. To him, though, it sounded uncannily like fingers traveling over a computer keyboard, and for an instant, as he rounded the corner, he truly expected to see her sitting there at her desk in the next room, her eyes following the cursor as it flashed at the bottom of the screen. The sun would be falling in scraps against her back, a hundred fragments of light opening and closing through the shadows of the philodendron. The shampoo she had used that morning would be perfuming the air. He was sure of it.

He had such memory lapses several times a day, but they never lasted for long. Soon enough he would begin thinking about her half-finished diary of love notes, and the way he kept asking after her in the hospital, and the smooth expanse of sheets on her side of the bed, and he would have to wrench his knee to distract himself from where his thoughts had taken him.

He was walking through the living room when he spotted someone peering in the window—a small round head, cut off at its shoulders like the ornamental sphere on a newel post. It was the boy from down the block, the one with the pale blue eyes who never spoke to anyone. He was staring hard into the room, his hands cupped around his face like a diving mask. He was so absorbed in whatever he was looking at that Jason remained invisible to him until he drummed his fingers on the glass, a sound that startled the boy and sent him tripping out of the bushes and across the lawn, then curving down the street until he vanished into the darkness of his garage. What had captured his attention? Jason wondered. The couch and the coffee table, the armchair and the television—everything was in its place, none of it at all unusual. For a moment, he entertained the notion that the boy was some sort of tormented mystic, able to see the spirits of the dead. It was a floating little Hollywood fantasy in which Patricia had returned to the house as a ghost, and the boy could see the dead, but he could not hear them. Why couldn't he hear them?

Because the dead had no voices—maybe that was it. Or because his talents were too small. Or because he was only a kid and he had not yet grown into them. Whatever the reason, he had been watching Patricia's lips as they formed the words she wished to say. There was something she needed to communicate before she faded into the next world, a message she wanted to leave for her husband.

Tell him that . . .

Tell him I . . .

But he did not know how to finish the sentence.

He found himself wandering into the room where she used to exercise. There was still a CD in her stereo, he noticed, and, out of habit, he pressed PLAY to see what she had been listening to. *Sometimes I feel like I can't even sing, I'm very scared for this world.* He recognized the song right away, with the shrilling of the crickets, that plaintive voice arching out over the mandolin. *Eviscerate your memory.* Before the chorus took hold, he was overcome with a sense of dread and had to press the STOP button. He shook his head involuntarily, like a dog throwing off crests of water. He sat down on the stationary bicycle. He had known the song for twenty years, longer than he had known Patricia, longer than he had known how to drive or write a check. Its meaning in his life ought to have been incorruptible. It was about his own mind when he was thirteen, the endless afternoons he spent lying on the carpet with his headphones on, the yard work he needed to finish and the girlfriends he wished he had, the innocent freedom and sadness of it all, but now somehow it had become blighted with the knowledge that Patricia had been listening to it the day of the accident, or the day before, or she had been preparing to listen to it the day after. Every note was a note she knew by heart, every word a word she used to sing, and she was gone now, and he had killed her, and he felt like a criminal presented with the evidence that would put him away. All these weeks, he had been telling himself it was only a matter of time before everything would return to normal. But it never would return to normal, would it?

He got back up and forwarded to the next song on the CD, but stopped it before the lyrics began, just as the guitar was interrupting the organ. He switched trays and played a few seconds of a classic R&B song, *If you ever change your mind, / About leaving, leaving me behind,* and then a few seconds of a pop tune the two of them had always loved, *With you in that dress, my thoughts, I confess, / Verge on dirty,* and then the opening lines of an old jazz standard, *A tinkling piano in the next apartment, / Those stumbling words that told you what my heart meant.* He saw how they had all been transformed into something much smaller and grayer. It seemed that every song he knew had been hollowed out, scraped clean of its associations, and refilled with memories of Patricia: the smell of her shampoo; the way she rested her hand on his lap; the sound of her gasping his name as the ice took the wheels of the car, then repeating it as they flipped over and spun toward the concrete pillar. It was all too unfair.

When the doorbell rang, he left his crutches lying on the floor and hobbled over to the foyer. It would be a UPS driver delivering a package, he presumed, or maybe a neighborhood activist canvassing the block with a petition, someone he could send away with a thank-you and a signature, but when he opened the door, the face that greeted him belonged to the girl from the bus shelter, the willowy one with the burn rings on her arms and legs, Melissa Wallumrod.

He said her name. "What are you doing here?"

"Oh, I bet you can figure it out if you really try."

"Yes, well, about that, I didn't know who you were myself until this morning. That was my editor's initiative."

"Your editor's initiative got me kicked out of my house." She was carrying a green canvas duffel bag that was padded out like a bolster. She swung it onto her feet. "My parents made me pack up and leave."

"I see. How did you find me?"

She took the front section of the newspaper out of her back pocket and read from the caption beneath the picture. "Melissa Wallumrod *dot dot dot* bodily mutilation *dot dot dot*. Here we are: '*Gazette* Staff Photo, Jason Williford.' You're in the phone book. After that, it was a piece of cake." She looked him up and down— his head cocked, his arms tucked close to his sides, one knee slightly raised—and said, "So, Flamingo, are you going to let me in or what?" Then she shouldered past him, disrupting his balance. A thrill of pain flashed through his leg as his foot struck the floor. By the time he caught up with the girl, she had already dropped her duffel bag on the carpet and set herself on the arm of the couch, apprehensively, experimentally, like a cat seeking a high place from which to avoid being startled.

"Make yourself at home, why don't you."

"I intend to."

And she meant it.

He asked her the obvious question. "What are you doing here?"

"I need a place to stay," she confessed. Apparently, she had decided that his house would do. Nothing he said could dissuade her. Maybe if she apologized to her parents . . . he was certain they would . . . "Ha. Obviously you don't know Tom and Doris." Why didn't she try one of her friends? "Um, hello? I guess you missed the paper this morning. I'm a bad influence—'the girl who practices bodily mutilation near Allsopp Park.' " But why on earth should he allow her into his home? Didn't she think that was asking too much? "Hmm, I don't know, let's see. Maybe because you're the one who came prying into my life and stirred everything up. Can you honestly tell me you don't bear some responsibility for that?" Well, then, what made her so sure she could trust him?

She scoffed. "Please. Look at you. You're in even worse shape than I am."

Finally, out of exhaustion, and because she had played on his highly reactive sense of culpability, he gave in. "One night."

She smiled. "So where's the guest room?"

He did not know what to do with a teenage girl, how to look after her or keep her entertained, so he left her alone to read her manga and listen to her iPod. Late that afternoon, he went to the playground at the end of the block to snap a few pictures. Afterward, he stopped at the mini-mart to buy something for dinner. When he got home, she was still there and had not stolen anything, so he made her a meal of spaghetti and meat sauce with a salad of iceberg lettuce and shredded carrots, the kind that came in a transparent plastic pouch. It was the best he could do. That night, he sat down with her to watch TV, a game show she liked about a dozen couples who raced each other around the world to win a million dollars. It had begun to thunder and rain. The house felt close around them. She excused herself during a commercial, and when she came back, she had a new burn mark on her ankle, glowing like a heating coil. A sheen of clear tissue fluid wept from the center.

"You must love this shit," she said, falling onto the couch beside him.

"Excuse me?"

"The Illumination." She gestured at the TV screen, where

one of the contestants had fallen off a camel, scraping a radiant stroke of red war paint across his forehead. Behind him the beast was chewing its tongue and swatting its tail. Its knees presented a constellation of distinct silver points. "For a photographer, this must be like Heaven."

"Heaven? No, I wouldn't say that." He was thinking of all the times he and Patricia had sat on the couch sharing popcorn while they watched a movie, his hand hovering solicitously at the rim of the bowl as hers reached inside, then hers hovering there as his did. That was his Heaven, and it had come and it had gone. What this was, he didn't know. Heaven-plus. Heaven-minus. "Why don't we call it purgatory?"

She must have interpreted the remark as a joke, because she answered, "Very funny, Jason Williford," and jabbed him in the gut. His scar began to send out circles, a slow wave of them, traveling across his chest and stomach as his wound throbbed with pain. Fascinated, she pressed her palm to the spot and watched the light radiate past her fingers.

That night, in his room, he lay awake listening to the girl across the hall drumming her nails against the headboard of her bed. He imagined her stepping through his door, her cuts and burns sketching faint traces in the air as she knelt beside him and stroked his brow, saying, "Very funny, Jason Williford. Very, very funny," and for what reason? There was another body in the house, another voice, another set of hands enacting their own private ceremonies. He was not used to it. But then it was temporary, and he supposed he would not have to get used to it.

The next morning, around ten o'clock, when the girl woke, he asked her whether she was planning to go to school that day. She shook her head listlessly and padded off to the kitchen in her pajamas. When she came back with a soda, he asked her why not, and she popped the can open, sipped at the overflow, and answered, "Senior Skip Day." That seemed plausible enough, but the next day she said the same thing, and then it was the weekend, and still she had not gone to school, and still she was sleeping in the guest room.

Each afternoon she went out for a few hours with her hand-bag and her iPod, but she always returned before he chained the door for the night. On Monday, she said to him, "I hope you don't mind, but I borrowed the key from that hook in your office. I thought it would be simpler if I made myself a copy." On Tuesday, she said, "You know, most of the time you walk around here like your best friend just died, and then it's like this wind blows over you and you're perfectly happy all of a sudden. Why are you that way?" On Wednesday, she said, "So what kind of a person was she? Did she have any hobbies? You know, like tennis or something?" On Thursday, she said, "What the fuck happened to the paint on your kitchen wall?" And on Friday, she said, "Why didn't you two have any children?"

"We were talking about it. She wasn't ready yet."

"Jesus." She accented the word in the Irish way: *Jay*-sus. "I'm sorry."

"Why be sorry?"

"I don't know. I guess I just mean that it might be easier if you had some little half-version of her running around."

But would it have been? In the year leading up to the accident, he had hinted as often as he thought he could get away with it that he was ready to have a child, but Patricia had always just smiled foggily at the suggestion, saying, "You'll be a good father," or, "Snips and snails and puppy dog tails," some amiably circum-spect remark which made it clear that she felt no urgency about the matter and that if there was a clock ticking, it was not hers.

He had wanted a child so persistently back then, so powerfully, or at least he had believed he did. When Patricia ran the bathroom faucet in the morning to wash her face, in his ears the sound disguised itself as the babbling of an infant, and late at night, when the wind chimes touched pendants on the back porch, the bells were like a dream of tinkling mobile music. Now, though, it was obvious to him that what he had really wanted was a family, not a child. He was grateful—relieved—that there was no "little half-version of her running around," no face that looked more like its mother's every day, no vessel for all his grief and contrition. There were more than enough children in the world already. He saw them every day in grocery stores and fast-food restaurants and the playground at the end of the block, laughing and shouting at one another, so careless and daring. They played slapping games that left luminous blotches on the backs of one another's hands. They climbed fences and tackled one another, fell off bicycles and rolled down hills, until their bodies were resplendent with bruises. They held races on busy sidewalks, dashing past grown men and women lit all over with injuries of their own. Everyone had his own portion of pain to carry. At first, when you were young, you imposed it on yourself. Then, when you were older, the world stepped in to impose it for you. You might be given a few years of rest between the pain you caused yourself and the pain the world made you suffer, but only a few, and only if you were lucky.

One night, Jason took his camera to the pedestrian mall, where a local hardcore band was performing on the summer stage. It was a softly glowing June evening, with a ghostly moon hanging in the treetops. The sky was the kind of barely shadowed pink he had noticed before in the linings of seashells. Fifty or sixty teenagers were huddled together on the plaza, leaping at one another and hurling their shoulders around as the band went charging through its songs, two or three minutes at a stretch.

Jason found a spot on the brick curb surrounding a pumpkin ash. He was close enough to the mosh pit that occasionally, when some poor kid was expelled from the scrum like a watermelon seed, he had to hold his crutches out for protection. He aimed his camera into the audience and began shooting. The motion of the crowd was too frenetic for him to select his images with any care, so instead he relied on instinct and chance, taking picture after picture as the dancers slammed into one another's bodies. He found the crossed metal struts of the stage and tried to keep them centered in his lens. As the sun faded from the sky, the dancers and their thousand little traumas became more prominent. The bruised faces and wrenched elbows. The muscle strains. The split fingernails. The chipped smiles. The gashes they opened in one another's calves and ankles with their steel-toed boots. He would end up with a time-lapse study of teenage recklessness, he imagined, the kids' bodies slowly disappearing into the darkness until nothing was visible but a bright field of lesions, a Muybridge series of scratches and contusions. He stayed there snapping pictures until the band finished its set and someone in the audience shouted, "Break your guitars," and the singer said, "Only rich assholes destroy their instruments," and then the crowd came apart in a few last halfhearted scuffles.

Jason was looking forward to printing the photographs, spreading them out on his table and selecting a few to submit to the paper. For the first time since he had returned to work, he did not know what he would find. The mystery had roused his curiosity. When he got home, though, the front window was casting a quadrangle of light across the yard. Inside he found Melissa lounging in the living room with seven or eight of her friends.

He recognized a few of them from the bus shelter—the boy who had bartered with him for cigarettes, the girl with the curved incision on her waist. His house had been occupied by strangers. The air had that strangely saturated quality peculiar to places that have suddenly fallen silent, as after a dirty joke or an argument, and the tension was strong enough to stifle any irritation he might have felt. He began telling the kids about the concert and the mosh pit, the floating star map of injuries. "I'm surprised you guys weren't there."

A boy lying on the floor said, "Not our kind of music, man." He had folded one of Jason's throw pillows across the middle and was using it to prop up his head.

"What is your kind of music?"

"We're into show tunes."

"Shut up, Bryce."

The boy began singing "Memory."

"Hey, I *like* that song."

"Bryce, cut it out."

"I can smile at the old days. I was beautiful then."

"Dude, nobody wants to hear you sing."

Jason swung a few steps closer on his crutches. "So what were you all doing when I came in?"

That silence again—it was extraordinary. No one would meet his eye. A girl in a college T-shirt shielded her mouth behind her palm. Melissa scratched her neck, leaving a small area of coruscation that vanished like a firefly's mating flash. He looked around for a knife, a matchbook, a pack of cigarettes. That was when he spotted Patricia's journal, the one she had been carrying the day of the accident, the day she died, the day he did. It was jammed between two of the couch cushions. Had he neglected to return it to the exercise room? Or had they found it while he was gone? He pictured them prowling around the house looking for ways to amuse themselves. *Hey, guys, you have to check this out. It's some kind of long-ass love letter.* He let his crutches topple away from him. Something happened as he sank to the floor. It was several seconds before he realized, and then only dimly, that he had scraped a layer of skin from his knuckle on the edge of the coffee table.

The journal was in his hands now. It smelled of nicotine and potato chips, and also, faintly, of the shea butter that Melissa or her friends or the woman who had taken it from the hospital must have used. Patricia's own scent was gone, exhausted, just as it was gone from the bed, the towel rack, her favorite chair, as it would soon be gone from every corner of the house except a few well-hidden sanctuaries, some drawer or jewelry box he had never had occasion to open and that would steal the breath from him when he did.

"All of you need to leave."

Though he felt frail, his voice had a surprising full-bloodedness to it. The kids stood up from the furniture almost as one. There was the sound of springs extending, of clothing brushing against itself. Someone tried to speak to him. "We didn't mean anyth—"

"Leave! Right now!"

He waited for their steps to shuffle across the hardwood, then lifted his head. Melissa was standing between the living room and the front hall, her body sliced in two by the doorway.

"You, too. This isn't your home. Out."

She let her foot sway back and forth until the floor interrupted it with a squeak. "You know, for what it's worth, no one was laughing at you. I thought the diary was beautiful, and so did they. That's why I wanted to show it to them. I just thought you should know that. Have you ever seen the movie *Ghost World*?" she asked.

She was stalling for some reason, hoping perhaps that he would tell her he understood, that there was nothing to forgive. The corroded rubber of her shoe had left a gray mark on the white pine boards.

"Never mind. Okay. Anyway. I'm sorry. I'm not a decent person. No big surprise, right?"

She closed the door behind her as she left.

He sat down in one of the padded chairs by the bookcase. His knee flared a little as he straightened his leg, but the bone had almost healed, and the luster of the wound was too faint to distract him anymore. This life of his—he was no good at it. He had seen photographs of people whose tragedies had turned their faces to transparent glass, had even taken a few: survivors of house fires and hunting accidents whose grief was distinguished by a wide-open compassion that extended outward in every direction. Not so his own, which had a miserly inward-looking quality that embarrassed him. Sadness had made him smaller than he used to be, less caring. It was his joy that had been distinguished by compassion. *I love listening to you pick out a song you don't know on the piano. I love the way you'll try to point out a star to me over and over again sometimes: "That one. Right there. Can't you see it? Just follow my finger." I love the lines that radiate from the corners of your eyes when you smile, and I'll love them even more when they're permanent, honey. I love how you roll your eyes but can't help smiling whenever I call you "honey."*

The skin he had stripped from his knuckle was buckled against itself, a loose tag of flesh that hung from the middle of his index finger, thick enough that he could still make out its natural color. He bit it off and spat it into his hand. Then, because he did not know what to do with it, he set it on the coffee table. The new layer of tissue on his finger smarted as it touched the air. When he pressed it with his thumb, the light seemed to surge around it, a wobbling crown of silver tinsel. He sat there toying with it as the wooden clock made its keyboard noise. Was he increasing the sting or merely concentrating it? He couldn't tell. But the flesh took on a crimson tone as he worked his nail into it, the light became a more fixed silver, and for a while the feeling absorbed all his attention. Then he heard a click that sounded like something settling behind the wall, and he turned to see the boy who never spoke to anyone, the scrawny, blue-eyed kid from down the block, staring into the house again. His eyeglasses were touched to the window, and Jason thought, *The little spy, the dirty little voyeur, what right did he have, what right did any of them have, to treat his home like a TV show, tuning in whenever they felt like a bit of entertainment?* He rose to his feet and hurled Patricia's journal. It clanged off the window and landed facedown on the rug, its pages flexed into a sort of oxbow. The twigs of the bushes rustled outside, and when he looked again, the boy was gone.

Within seconds, his anger had turned to embarrassment. He had let his frustration get the better of him. Patricia would have been ashamed. He sat back down and put the knuckle of his index finger to his mouth, moistening the barked spot with his tongue. Some time later, he felt a hand on his shoulder and realized he had fallen asleep. His neck was stiff, and the light was making him squint, but he saw that Melissa was back, and no wonder, since as far as he could remember, he had not bothered to chain the door.

"Is it all right if I get my things?" she asked.

"Wait. Do you have somewhere to go?"

"In two months I do. August the twentieth. Until then I can just bum around on other people's couches."

"What's August the twentieth?"

"First semester of college."

"College? Your whole high school career was nothing but senior skip days."

"Yeah, at the end it was, but by then what was the point? I already had my acceptance letters. My GPA was like 3.85. I figured I could miss the rest of the semester and still end up with B's and C's. I'm not stupid, you know, just self-abusive." She glanced to the side as if addressing a court reporter. "Not like that," she said, rolling her eyes. Then she noticed the discoloration on Jason's finger. "Jesus, you really got yourself, didn't you? Hold on."

She left the room. A car coasted down the street with a sizzling noise. The crickets were offering their midnight chorus. Jason wondered if it had rained while he was asleep.

He noticed that Melissa had picked the journal up and replaced it on the coffee table. The binding was scuffed away at one corner, exposing the brown strata of the boards, and though she had tried to smooth the pages flat, there was still a kink to them. She returned with her backpack and took out a bottle of peroxide, a cotton ball, and a Band-Aid.

"You don't want this thing to pus over, believe me."

She held his finger up to the lamp and began disinfecting it. On the back of her leg he saw a fresh cut stretching all the way from her heel to the cove of her knee. It gleamed like a river of pristine water on a clear summer morning. "Why do you do that? Burn yourself. Cut yourself like that."

Her lips gave an amused slant. "Tell me, Jason Williford— how do you feel right now?"

"Honestly? Miserable."

She gave his finger a motherly kiss. "There. Is that better?"

"No. No, not really. Very sweet, though."

"What about this?"

She took the wound between her lips and bit. A darting sensation engulfed his hand, flashing along his wrist in a series of tiny pulses. She bore down until her teeth pierced the skin. A deluge of light poured out of his finger, so bright that it shone through her cheek. He could see the delta of blood vessels reaching across her face. When she bore down once more, slowly increasing the pressure, the shape seemed to resolve itself into the outline of a fallen tree, and then the room filled with a hazy pink radiance, and he lost all awareness of it. A hard spasm gripped his radial flexor. His body tightened in a wondrous surge of pain.

He opened his eyes to find her cleaning his knuckle again, dabbing it one last time with peroxide, covering it with a Band-Aid. "There," she said. "All better now."

It was nearly one o'clock, far too late for him to send her away, so he told her she could stay the night. She went to her bed in the guest room, and he went to his own across the hall, where he could see his injury filtering through the covers like a night light.

The next morning he woke early. He still needed to develop the photos he had taken at the concert. He selected a few to submit to the *Gazette* and set out for the office. When he returned home, Melissa was sitting at the kitchen table, eating leftover pizza from a take-out container. He poured himself a glass of water, chose a slice of mushroom-pepperoni, and sat down beside her. It was at that moment, without so much as a word, that they came to their understanding: he would allow her to live with him until she left for college, and in exchange she would teach him how to manipulate his body, inflicting those small, perfect impairments that rid him of his entire history.

The lessons began easily enough, with a straight pin and the edge of one of his fingernails. Melissa showed him how to slide the point slowly into the quick, creating a thin tunnel of steel that separated the nail plate from the connective tissue. It was a minor trauma, and yet it hurt, it hurt, and the light blazed out of it in an acute silver line. Sitting at the table after he removed the pin, he felt nothing but relief, pure relief, as gratifying as any he had known since he was a boy, when he would suddenly, for no reason at all, run as far and as fast as he could until he was completely out of breath, sinking onto the grass and watching the trees twitch blissfully in the breeze. The blood welled onto his fingertip. His mind sailed along in a dreamlike vesper. In the days that followed, Melissa guided him into greater and more pleasurable forms of injury, assisting him through each procedure step-by-step. She plucked the hairs from his stomach with a pair of tweezers, patiently and deliberately, so that each one generated a ring-shaped lambent spot that spread open and disappeared like a raindrop striking a puddle. She removed his shoe and his sock, crossing his big toe over his second to bring on a foot cramp. She gave him a pocketknife and coaxed him into making a series of cuts on his body, beginning with the least sensitive areas and progressing to the most: first the elbow, then the shoulder, then the back of the hand, the chest, the inner curve of the thigh. She offered him instructions on his technique: "Next time you don't want to go so deep. FYI, once you pass the first like *millimeter*, it doesn't hurt any more, it just does more damage. In fact, it hurts less, because the shock mechanism kicks in. At least that's been my experience. Now, if we're talking about matches or cigarettes, that's something else altogether. Burn pain and cut pain are two totally different things." By the end of the week, he could lay down knife wounds as easily as if he were quartering an apple, but still he could not bring himself to apply a cigarette to his skin. It was not the heat that frightened him but the ember. She taught him how to use a butane lighter instead, running the flame until the flint wheel was uncomfortably hot, then damping the gas and immediately pressing the metal to his flesh. In a single afternoon, he left half a dozen identical burn marks on his arms. They throbbed with light for a while before they fell cold. Afterward they looked like the badges of some strange new plague, their raised red welts like ridged tire tracks. The hair he had singed from his skin filled the house with a smell like sulfur and charcoal. When he opened the windows to let the rooms ventilate, he could hear a dog barking, an insect chirring, a door slamming, a car honking, a sprinkler ratcheting around in circles. The wooden clock typed four-thirty in the hallway. It was all so beautiful. The next step, Melissa said, was for him to re-address the injuries he had already formed. Most of his wounds from the car accident had healed completely, and those that hadn't were cushioned behind too much fat and muscle for him to damage them any further. There was still his knee, which con-tinued to give off little twinges from deep inside the joint—and would occasionally, before a storm, when the barometric pres-sure dropped, emit a lustrous ache that even Melissa agreed was impressive—but it, too, had largely mended, and he couldn't count on it to bring him the kind of pain it used to. That left his more recent injuries. Melissa showed him the best way to reopen his cuts: tracing their seams with a knife, then lifting and peel-ing the skin away. It felt as if he were trying to unseal the flap of an envelope without tearing the paper. There was blood, of course, but never as much as he was afraid there would be, and on her own arm Melissa demonstrated how to stanch it using a styptic pencil. He tried the same remedy and found that it brought a short-lived sting to his skin that was nearly as brilliant as the wounds themselves. He knew so little about the ways his body could be made to suffer, and yet already he had learned more than he ever thought possible. Never before had he endured so many varieties of injury—burns, punctures, bruises, lacerations. And always with the pain came a kind of ecstasy, the feeling that he had crested a hill and lifted free of his expectations. His future was behind him now. He no longer needed to struggle. Nothing could hurt him as much as he had already been hurt.

From three to five, starting in July and lasting until mid-September, the front wall of his house was turned directly toward the sun, and the light flowed in through the windows. The living room and the bedrooms became needlessly hot, even when he shut the blinds and ran the air-conditioner, and he took to spending those late afternoons with Melissa and her friends, sometimes at the bookstore or the movie theater, sometimes in one of the pavilions by the reservoir. In the old days, when he saw men such as himself—older guys who had attached themselves to a group of teenagers, paying for their meals, cracking the occasional dated joke—he thought exactly what everyone else did: *Look at that poor deluded sap trying to recapture his faded youth.* But he was not trying to recapture a thing. He was only trying to endure the heat for a while. If he could have recaptured his youth, his youth as it actually was, with the pattern of the next twenty years intact and waiting for him, would he have? Maybe so. But a whole new youth, with its own set of dreams and uncertainties, would only have exhausted him. People often talked about wishing they could return to the moment just before a tragedy and begin again, repairing the rupture in their lives, setting off down a different path, the right path, the path that should have been theirs all along, but then, as time passed, they healed and moved forward in ways that depended upon exactly that rupture, and it became harder and harder to justify abandoning what they had gained for the sake of what they had lost. Jason knew, though, he knew without question, that if he could have returned to the day of the accident and prevented it *(don't leave home, don't leave home)*, he would have. He would have taken everything he had learned since then, every moment of the life he had created, and destroyed it. It was his gift to Patricia, his tribute—to create the kind of life he would be willing to burn to ashes.

Often it was nearly dark by the time he got home. He would find the answering machine winking up at him with its red eye. He had stopped returning the calls he received, but he continued to listen to his messages.

"Mr. Williford, this is Karen at Dr. Sutter's office. We're phoning to see why you've missed your last two appointments. Is anything wrong?"

His crutches were propped against the wardrobe in his bedroom, but he no longer bothered to use them. He would not be keeping any more of his appointments.

Beep. "Hey, dude, where you been? The whole crew is getting together for the game this weekend. Tim reserved a skybox at the stadium. We wanted to see if you could come along. No need to chip in, it'll be on us. Just give me a call."

He had friends—of course he did—but he presumed that if he kept ignoring their entreaties, they would eventually forget about him. He would be free of their kindness, of their pity. He was tired of jokes that stopped short in his presence, gazes that remembered the way he used to be.

Beep. "Jason. Paul here. We're flying Trieschmann out on assignment to the West Bank, and we need a camera to accompany him. You've been shooting some good stuff for us lately, and I wanted to see if you would be up for the job. Should get you a lot of attention, if you can do it. They're dropping like dominoes over there."

The truth was that the entire Middle East might have vanished in a single gleaming detonation, and he would not have noticed. Every morning he forced himself to leave the house and take a picture or two for the *Gazette*. That was all the scrutiny he could bear to give the world. No matter where he looked, he saw nothing but pain. An evangelist handing out pocket editions of the New Testament, a star-shaped kidney stone illuminating his urinary tract. An old woman whose arthritic fingers looked like brown twigs coated in ice. A horse trailer hauling a single young Appaloosa, its left eye glowing white as a Ping-Pong ball. In spite of everything, his instincts had not abandoned him.

He looked forward to the hours he spent with Melissa and her friends. With them he visited parts of the city that he had never seen before: the undersides of bridges, the pine chases behind housing developments. One afternoon, they were loitering in the playground of an elementary school when he saw Christman, from the paper, taking pictures of the bare flagpole. God only knew what he found interesting about the subject. There he was in the courtyard, though, firing off shot after shot, standing beneath the aluminum rod in a circle of compressed dirt.

He noticed Jason sitting on one of the climbing platforms and came over. "Williford," he said. "What are you doing here?"

"Oh, I don't know, I was just thinking of photographing that flagpole over there fourteen or fifteen times."

It took Christman a second to realize Jason was kidding. He clutched his camera protectively to his chest, then gave a little *ah!,* as if to say that he had been in on the joke all along.

"But seriously, man, what's with you and the kids? And Jesus, what happened to your—to *all* of you guys' arms and legs? That's not still from the car accident, is it?"

Someone said, "Leave Jesus out of it," and the others struck up their usual chorus of one-liners.

"Define 'accident.' "

"A bus is more like it."

"What's with you and the flagpole?"

" 'We're not creating wounds. We're uncovering the wounds that are already there.' "

"Shut up, Bryce."

Jason waited for their voices to simmer down before he told Christman the truth.

Christman was skeptical. "*Knives* and *fire*. Right. Uh-huh. Seriously, man—"

"I am serious. Would you like to see for yourself?" Jason opened the largest blade on his pocketknife and ran it along the edge of his arm, watching the skin separate from his wrist to his elbow. It was the longest cut he had ever permitted himself to make. The noise that came out of him was barely human, a slow, strained creak that rose into its own sound like some ancient tree tightening in the cold.

Christman brought his camera to his eye. Jason let him take the picture. He could already imagine the caption: "Jason Williford, 35, practices bodily mutilation with several young friends outside Oak Grove Elementary School. *Gazette* Staff Photo/Glen Christman." He listened to the shutter snap and felt the blood streaming out of him, and he didn't care, he didn't care. This was how he would waste the rest of his life, he thought, sitting in the heat of the sun and carving light into his flesh. When Christman made his excuses and left, he seemed to bob across the playground like a balloon. A car floated slowly down the street, and the kids' bodies swam between the bars of the climbing tower. The color had been wicked out of the grass. A bird offered a glorious caw. Jason tried to stand up, but his legs wouldn't support him.

A voice he recognized said, "You guys, I forgot to bring my stuff. I better take him somewhere and get him fixed up." Then the girl who was staying with him, the beautiful one who liked to cut herself—Melissa: that was her name—put her arms around him and lifted him to his feet. Together they set off across the schoolyard.

At the end of the street, she stopped at a convenience store and bought him a bottle of water. "Here, drink this," she said. His head cleared once he did. He felt a little better. They arrived home to find the front door hanging open. Had he forgotten to lock it? Had she? He didn't think so.

At first, he was sure they had been robbed, but after Melissa had cleaned and bandaged the cut on his arm, the two of them walked through the house taking inventory. Nothing appeared to be missing, or at least nothing important, though the wind had scattered a pile of receipts across the foyer, and the wooden clock had fallen from the table in the front hall. When he bent over to retrieve it, a mahogany cog came rattling out of the case and rolled across the boards, dead-ending against the wall. He put the clock to his ear. It was no longer ticking, so he set it down on the floor again, nudging the corner with his toe.

"It's okay," he heard Melissa saying, and he wondered why he could feel her voice against his neck, and then she was brushing his cheek with the back of her hand and they were kissing. He had a body, and so did she, and they sank into each other, their wounds irrigated with an exquisite light. As she parted his lips with her fingers, he experienced a gradual sliding and turning sensation. He felt as if he were in a plane banking out over the ocean. His life was passing below him like the distant creases of the waves. The white triangles of a hundred sails dotted the water. He could not remember where he was going.

Chuck Carter

The world was beginning to flower into wounds.

—J. G. Ballard

Chuck Carter lived in dozens of different places every day. Sometimes he lived in a house with dark green carpets. Sometimes he lived in a school that smelled like milk. He lived in a run-down car with his parents sometimes. They drove it everywhere, his mom and his pretend dad. The door was spotted with giant pumpkins of orange rust. The seat belt slanted across his chest like a sash. Chuck's whole body vibrated with the engine, even his bones. He liked to watch the power lines swooping past outside. They rose and fell in a beautiful, slow, hypnotizing way. It looked like they were taking turns bouncing on trampolines.

One time, Chuck rode in an elevator with glass walls. This was the single best place he had ever lived. He remembered sailing into the enormous blue sky like Superman. Below him, all the people had turned into moving dots. He felt tall and brave and powerful, nothing like himself. The ride lasted three minutes, and then it was over. He still dreamed about it once or twice a week. It was the best and happiest of all his dreams. His other favorite place to live was under the clotheslines. There were two of them, twins, stretching across his backyard. He liked to live between them while the sheets dried. It felt like camping out in an airy white tent. Sometimes he wished he could stay there and never leave.

Mostly, though, Chuck lived either at home or at school. It

took him a while to learn the exact rules. Rules were extremely important, and the more exact the better. Rules kept the world from turning into a vicious trap. There were dangers everywhere, a thousand tripwires in the grass. People had to watch their step, even in the sunlight. When he was little, Chuck had rehearsed the rules tirelessly. The house was where he lived when it got dark. He also lived there on weekends, plus during snowy weather. He lived in the school for eight hours a day. He wasn't allowed to sleep there, only in the house. The school had three separate times: class-, lunch-, and recess-. The house had five: chore-, play-, meal-, bath-, and bed-. Both the school and the house were two stories tall. Both had time-out corners, and both had magnolias around them. They were different from each other in one big way. The school had kids who shouted and knocked Chuck over. In the house there was only him and his parents.

To Chuck, the house resembled a stack of yellow rectangles. The rectangles were bricks, and they glistened after it rained. Though they looked delicious, he wasn't supposed to taste them. That was another rule, but a hard one to remember. He was a crazy little retard, always licking the house. What was wrong with him that he was so stupid? How many times did he have to be told "no"? Those were the questions his pretend dad hissed at him. There were real dads, and then there were pretend dads. It was only pretend dads who called their kids retards. Chuck's hair curled softly at the nape of his neck. No real dad would grab a handful and twist it. No real dad would laugh and say, "Indian torture ritual. Go ahead, run and tell your mom, you little twerp." A real dad would never, ever do such a thing. It seemed obvious as soon as you thought about it.

———

It was easy for Chuck to recognize other people's pain. When you hit people, or pushed them, something terrible happened. Their bodies changed underneath the skin, straining, tightening like ropes. Cats and dogs and horses reacted exactly the same way. It looked like something inside them was trying to escape. It looked like a ghost wanted out of their bones. The difference was real and physical, not in Chuck's imagination. He had seen it happen at least a million times. Over the years, he had almost gotten used to it. People confused him usually, but not people who were hurting. So when the light came, he wasn't surprised one bit. Suddenly, everywhere he looked, people began glowing from their wounds.

This time he wasn't the only one who noticed it. His teacher saw it, his mom, even his pretend dad. He and his parents were watching TV when it started. There was a gymnastics competition happening on the sports channel. Girls in leotards were tucking and whirling like amazing machines. They hopped lightly, toe by toe, along a balance beam. They ran leaping onto a springboard and flipped over backwards. Then one of them broke her leg doing a cartwheel. She fell down, and a gasp spread through the audience. Her shinbone glittered like a mirror full of camera flashes. The couch springs creaked noisily as Chuck's parents leaned forward. At that moment, he realized they could see it, too.

Later, he watched as his mom bit a hangnail loose. Right away, her cuticle began to sparkle along the curve. (That was the white horseshoe around her fingernail: a cuticle.) His pretend dad nicked himself shaving, and the cut shimmered. And when Chuck pinched himself, a test, it worked perfectly. A cloud of light danced and quivered over his skin.

On Monday, his teacher, Mr. Kaczmarek, was late to school. Rushing inside, he accidentally banged his hand on the door. The whole class watched it flicker like a slow fire. Later, at recess, Mr. Kaczmarek divided them into Bombardment teams. Todd Rosenthal stalked Chuck with one of the red balls. He said, "Let's see you dodge this, you dumb bastard." The ball hit Chuck hard and square on the forehead. The other kids gathered around, watching the light spread open. Every single one of them reacted exactly the same way. They began running and hurling their dodgeballs at one another. When the recess bell rang, they all filed back inside. Everyone's skin was printed with glowing white plates of light. It took almost the whole day for them to disappear. The last one winked out just before the buses arrived.

As usual, Chuck sat at his desk and never spoke. Technically, a "dumb" person was just someone who stayed quiet. Chuck *was* dumb, and everybody knew it, including Mr. Kaczmarek. But he gave Todd Rosenthal two checkmarks for saying "bastard."

A week passed, and still nothing had returned to normal. The president appeared on the news to give a speech. He used words like *no obvious harm* and *further study*. An awful bright silver cavity kept flashing from his mouth.

Chuck got bored and wandered outside while he was talking. A black sports car was tilted forward onto the street. The car's front tire had gotten wedged inside a manhole. It was lodged underground, smoking and wailing as it spun. The driver was punching the window and screaming curse words. His nose was leaking blood, shining onto his upper lip. Some of Chuck's neighbors stood on their lawns watching him. A man in gray sweatpants shouted, "Put it in reverse!" Someone else said, "Want me to go get my winch?" The car's engine just kept howling like a wounded animal.

There were similar accidents, similar horrible scenes, all the time. Chuck saw stories about them on the TV at night. A bus might tip over speeding around a steep curve. The passengers would stumble from the wreck like gleaming torches. A chef might slice her hand open carving a turkey. The wound would cast a bright light over the counter. A model in high heels might fall on the runway. Her face would come up glittering from the wooden floor. Light kept pouring out of people whenever they hurt themselves.

At first, all the grown-ups were upset by these accidents. Car crashes and mistakes with kitchen knives were nothing new. The strange glow—that was what bothered them so much. Nobody knew what to call the thing that was happening. Soon, though, within days, people began talking about "the Illumination." The name was everywhere suddenly, a kind of secret agreement. It made the changes in the world seem less frightening.

Chuck heard two strangers gossiping about it in the supermarket. They were old men with thick glasses and rubbery ear-lobes. He liked the way their teeth clacked in their mouths.

"That war injury of mine's lit up like Independence Day."

"You should've seen my Emmy with the arth-a-ritis this morning."

"And look at my trick knee shining—the damnedest thing."

"She can't hardly make the coffee her hands clench so."

"It's this Illumination is what it is, don't you know."

One of them picked up a jar of peanut butter. "Five big ones!" he complained, and slammed it back down. Nobody but Chuck seemed to notice the way it glowed. Even objects felt pain if you struck or ignored them. Jars of peanut butter could be hurt just like people. Dirt bikes, toys, shopping carts, cereal boxes: they all could. Chuck knew—and had always known—that it was true.

Once, at age five, he had kicked his toy train. He remembered how it hit the wall and flipped over. The chimney, made of plastic, broke off with a crack. The train looked like a hand with a missing finger. It looked like an empty shack standing in brown dirt. Chuck sat down and tried his best to repair it. The face on the front stared up at him sadly. The very worst part was the way it kept smiling. Chuck could tell that it had not stopped trusting him. It still liked him and wanted to be his friend. He had to pat its head and say, "There, there." His mom found him crying and jamming the pieces together. How could he explain the horrible thing he had done?

That was the day he began treating everything so gently. He never threw his toys or knocked them together anymore. He made sure that both his shoes were always tied. (The right one was a boy, the left a girl.) Once a week, he washed and dried his rock collection. He used all sixty-four crayons when it was coloring time. The trees he drew might be blue, black, or yellow. It didn't matter, as long as every color was happy. Chuck had eight stuffed animals—mostly bears, plus one elephant. At night, he arranged them all carefully on his bedspread. He stroked the animals softly and smoothly on their backs. Then he slipped his body delicately into place beneath them. He wished them eight separate goodnights before closing his eyes.

Wherever he looked, he could see the light in things. Everything looked silver when you saw it in a mirror. Everything was helpless and needed to be saved from harm. There was the big plastic upside-down water jug at school. There was the stone birdbath in his next-door neighbor's yard. There were metal coins and the chrome handlebars on motorcycles. Trees gleamed with sap, and rocks sparkled with hidden crystals. Some tennis balls glowed bright green in the ordinary sunlight. Lamps, clocks, and televisions all shone with an inner light. Was it impossible that what they shone from was pain?

Chuck's duty, he believed, was to watch over it all. He was big, strong, noble—the Superman of lifeless objects. Objects did not understand how dangerous the world could be. They were simple, childlike, and they could not protect themselves. He hated to see them hurt, hated it beyond words. And that was why he had to steal the book.

It belonged to the man who lived down the street. According to Chuck's parents, he had undergone a terrible accident. One rainy day his car had slid into a pillar. He survived the crash, barely, but his wife did not. Afterward, he spent a whole month recovering in the hospital. He came home oozing light from his knees and stomach. He was like a thin white skeleton on his crutches. "The poor son of a bitch," Chuck's pretend dad said.

One night Chuck noticed the man carrying a book inside. The book ached with the hard light of something broken. Chuck could see its unhappiness melting straight through the covers. It was like a little sun shining across the street. The man walked past a window into his living room. Then he stopped and sat down and the light vanished. The next day, Chuck decided to get a closer look. He waited until his parents were arguing and went outside. The sky was the watery blue of a robin's egg. A dragonfly landed on the rim of a Coke bottle. The bottle captured the sunlight, firing it into the air. It was an afternoon for coasting downhill on a bicycle.

Chuck looked both ways, paused, and ran across the street. He followed the stepping-stones through the man's front yard. He slipped sideways through the bendy twigs of his bushes.

Then he pressed his forehead to the wide cool window. He spotted the book right away, sitting on a table. Its pages were a thick stack of brilliantly glowing squares. The whole house shimmered, but the book was something special. Chuck wished he could tell what was wrong with it.

Later, at home, he could not stop thinking about it. His curiosity grew stronger and stronger as the day passed. Eventually, he returned to the window to look at it. The next day, and the next, he went there again. He began living behind the bushes as often as possible. He lived there secretly, usually in ten- or fifteen-minute stretches. Week by week, the book shone with its secret pain. Chuck was amazed it didn't set the table on fire. Every so often, the man drifted past like a sailboat. Twice he caught Chuck standing outside peeking in at him. The first time, Chuck didn't think he was even home. Suddenly he just appeared, walked over, and touched the glass. His fingers landed with a *rat-a-tat-tat*, and Chuck ran away.

The second time was a warm, dark, breezy midsummer night. Chuck watched the man shout at a group of teenagers. One of them, a girl, was living with the man. Chuck was almost completely sure she was not his daughter. She had glinting cigarette burns on her arms and legs. They looked like the holes in Swiss cheese, but silver. Once, outside walking, she had called Chuck her "main man." She had mussed his hair and given him a Whatchamacallit. "Chin up, little guy," she'd said, blowing him a kiss. That was a whole month before, minus a few days. Now the teenagers, the whole skinny crowd, left the house. The girl was the last of them to step outside. Afterward, the man sat on the couch, motionless, breathing hard. He was clutching the book shakily in his slender hands. When he spotted Chuck, he hurled it at the window. Light came whipping out of it in long white ribbons. As Chuck took flight, the bush's twigs scraped his face.

That night, he lay in bed watching the scratches flicker. He kept picturing the book twisting wildly through the air. He wondered what it thought as its pages skittered open. Whether it imagined it was being punished for its mistakes. How it felt without a good solid table underneath it. If it believed the world would always be so frightening. Right then and there, he decided he would rescue it.

Another month went by before the chance came his way. He knew the man's habits, and knew the girl's, too. He had spent the summer watching them like a detective. They both left the house for several hours every afternoon. At night they usually ordered a pizza and watched TV. They slept late most mornings and ate leftovers for breakfast. The man took pictures of the girl with his camera. The girl posed with her arms crossed over her head. Occasionally she rubbed the man's back through his polo shirt. She taught him how to use a knife against himself. Their bodies were both marked with hundreds of narrow cuts. The wounds covered their skin, every inch, in glittering ladders.

One day, shortly after two-thirty, Chuck snuck across the street. He was feeling courageous, invincible (which meant unbeatable, not see-through). He crept into place and waited behind the tall bushes. Around three, the sun turned the window into a mirror. The sight of Chuck's eyes staring into themselves surprised him. He was blinking the image away when the man exited. The girl came with him and off they walked together. Neither of them noticed Chuck standing against the bricks, fortunately. After their footsteps faded away, he crept out of hiding.

He took the spare key from beneath the fake rock. He opened the door—first one lock, then the other. The house smelled like bread dough mixed with tennis shoes. The floor was a glossy white with scattered black knots. Chuck made it a rule to tiptoe between the lines. He passed a table with a wooden clock on it. He turned a corner and went into the living room. The book was sandwiched between some magazines by the couch. The pages were buckled, the cover scuffed, the letters faded. When Chuck gripped it, his bones showed through his fingers.

Chuck bumped the table in the hallway as he left. The clock teetered and fell with an awful splintering noise. Immediately, it lit up inside, its pieces throbbing with pain. He wanted to hold it to his forehead and cry. But he was scared of getting caught there, scared crazy. He held the book to his chest and ran home. No matter how Chuck tried, he just kept hurting things. That was how the world worked—he couldn't change it.

His mom was mixing cookies and burning a plain candle. A wax-and-sugar smell like birthday cakes hung in the air. Big important things always happened to Chuck on his birthday. On his second birthday, for instance, he finally started walking. On his seventh birthday, he got sick with chicken pox. He used to have a cat named Alley Cat Abra. On his fifth birthday, she was killed by a car. On his ninth birthday, Chuck decided he would stop talking. He never said anything right, so what was the use? He hadn't spoken since, and it wasn't—*wasn't*—a phase. On his fifth birthday, he went to Chuck E. Cheese's. Chuck E. Cheese shared Chuck's name, which made them alike. Chuck decided he was his friend, his smiling buck-toothed friend. One was Chuck the Boy, the other Chuck the Mouse. Chuck the Mouse handed Chuck the Boy some gold tokens. Chuck the Boy followed Chuck the Mouse into the kitchen. Chuck the Mouse carried him back outside by the armpits. His giant head bobbed around like something inflated with helium. Later, Chuck the Boy got trapped inside the crawling tubes. His pretend dad yelled, "Climb the hell out!" at him. He coaxed him slowly through the maze, pointing and shouting. "To the car!" he demanded, and Chuck's birthday was over.

Now he was ten: ten years and seven months old. His last birthday party was already a whole half-year ago. He thought about the presents his parents had given him. His favorite was the picture box with the multicolored pegs. His second favorite was the tic-tac-toe game with the beanbags. His least favorite was the robot with missiles for arms. He remembered kneeling on the dark green living room carpet. He remembered clapping his hands during "Happy Birthday to You." Then his mom set down a cake with burning candles. "How does it feel to be another year old, Chuckie?"

His pretend dad touched the softest part of his neck. "Your mom and me paid serious money for this cake. That means no throwing up this time, you hear me?" He turned and smacked Chuck's mom playfully on the butt. "Things sure were different ten years ago—weren't they, honey? We had a lot more money before *that* little accident."

"Frank!" she said and gave Chuck a little nervous glance. She looked away, and after that everything came in tens. There were ten flames that disappeared in threads of smoke. There were ten fingers squeezing Chuck's shoulder as he swallowed. There were ten pictures on the wall in the hallway. There were ten steps between his bed and his dresser. There were ten birdcalls from the trees, then another ten. There were ten houses on each side of the street. There were ten boys in his class, and ten girls. There were ten checkmarks by his name on the chalkboard. There were ten words in every sentence—yet another rule. There were ten soft beats in every moment of time.

Chuck took the book and hid it in his dresser. That night, he leafed through it quietly in his bedroom. It seemed to be a diary of miniature love notes. Each one was a single sentence written in blue ink. They all began with the same two words: *I love. I love the smell of your perfume on my shirts. I love the way you curl up against my body. I love watching the sunset from the roof with you. I love seeing your number appear on my cell phone.* The notes stopped suddenly in the middle of a page. The blue ink threw a glare up from the paper. It danced on the ceiling like sunbeams reflecting from water. The man must have been writing to some- one very special. Were they for the girl with all the cigarette burns? The one who had been teaching him to cut himself? No, no, they were for his wife, his dead wife. The one who had passed away in the car accident. The one who went away and left him all alone. Who turned him into a poor son of a bitch. The answer was obvious once Chuck gave it some thought.

All summer long, he read the book bit by bit. After a while, he felt like he knew the man. The night he finished, he started again from the beginning. He got a Magic Marker and highlighted his favorite sentences. *I love the poems you wrote in junior high school. I love how you fumble for words when you're angry. I love holding you tight when you ask me to. I love knowing exactly how crazy I am about you. I love sensing you beside me on long road trips. I love the idea of growing old and forgetful together. I love how skillfully you use a pair of scissors. I love watching TV and shelling sunflower seeds with you. I love your "Cousin Cephus and his pet raccoon Shirley." I love the mess I made of braiding your hair. I love your ten fingers and love your ten toes.*

Chuck liked the sound of the words in his head. Not every

sentence made good sense, or not right away. Some of them were bizarre or mysterious, some downright baffling. It was fun trying to figure out what they meant.

I love your terrible puns: "Miró, Miró, on the wall." What was a "Miró," Chuck wondered, or a "Miró, Miró"? Were there really supposed to be two on the wall? Or were they like tom toms or yo-yos or BBs? Were they a single thing that had a double name?

I love the "carpet angels" you make after I vacuum. Chuck decided that carpet angels must be like snow angels. He tried to make one with his arms and legs. He lay down, scissored them open, then stood back up. The carpet looked just the same—green, without any angels. Maybe the trick only worked right after someone had vacuumed.

I love that little outfit you wore on my birthday. Chuck pictured a cowboy outfit: hat, gun, bandana, and all. Once, in kindergarten, Todd Rosenthal had worn one to school. He kept pretending to fire his gun at Mariellen Chase. Finally, Ms. Derryberry had to send him to the office.

There were many other strange, confusing sentences in the book. Yet it seemed gentle to Chuck, not sad or angry. He wished he could understand why it shone so brightly.

At the beginning of September, he started the fifth grade. He went to the normal school, not the special one. Both his psychiatrists had 100 percent agreed: Chuck was normal. He was normal, not special, and definitely not a retard. His pretend dad was just plain wrong about some things. Chuck was five when he began seeing his first psychiatrist. His name was Dr. Diehl, and he called Chuck "Charles." Chuck liked him anyway because of his glass octopus bowl. Inside it he kept lollipops with gum in the middle. He always let Chuck take one before they began talking. Chuck would suck the lollipop, rolling it over his tongue. The hard globe of candy would become thin and pitted. Sometimes it would taste like strawberry, sometimes like root beer. Eventually, he would crunch through it with his back teeth. Then came the part where he would chew the gum. Sandlike grains of candy would crack open in his mouth. A sweet powder would coat the insides of his cheeks. Eating the lollipop was the best part of Wednesday afternoons. He truly missed it when he stopped visiting Dr. Diehl.

Chuck started seeing his second psychiatrist after he quit talking. They still met once a week, every Monday after school. He was a tall, skinny, gray-haired man called Dr. Finkelstein. Dr. Finkelstein, whose name was almost the same as Frankenstein. Dr. Finkelstein, whose forehead had a triangle of red sunspots. Dr. Finkelstein, with his pencil jar and stack of notecards.

He might ask Chuck, "Care to use your voice today?"

Chuck would take one of the notecards from the stack. *No, sorry, I don't feel like talking aloud right now.*

"Why do you think that is?" Dr. Finkelstein would say.

Chuck would tap the pencil against his knuckles awhile. *Did you know New Mexico's state bird is the roadrunner?*

Dr. Finkelstein would read the card and ask, "Beep, beep?"

Chuck didn't know why the doctor said such strange things. He would lean forward, smiling, waiting for Chuck to respond. Chuck would gesture at him to return the little card. He would shade in all the *a*'s, *o*'s, and *e*'s. Then he would move on to the *b*'s and *d*'s. He would fill the rest of the hour drawing roadrunners. Chuck was good with eyes but terrible—hopeless—with bodies. His roadrunners looked like feather dusters attached to gardening rakes.

———

Chuck's fifth-grade teacher, Ms. Mount, was nicer than Mr. Kaczmarek. She was teaching them about the states and their birds. That was how Chuck knew about New Mexico and road-runners. The state bird of Delaware was the blue hen chicken. The state bird of New Hampshire was the purple finch. The state bird of South Dakota was the ring-necked pheasant. "Why would Della wear a blue chicken on her head? That new ham you brought me sure is purple, Finchie. Dakota, I'm going to wring your neck," she would say. This was her way of helping them remember the facts. The circle of her hands tightened around an imaginary neck. She made a choking noise and stuck out her tongue. A sore glistened on the tip like a white crater.

The routine made Chuck laugh with a great big "Ha!" All the other kids turned around to stare at him. First, he was weird, and second, he never said anything. Those were the thoughts he could see on their faces.

That was the morning Todd Rosenthal pushed Chuck during recess. Chuck was waiting in the seesaw line when it happened. He fell forward, landing on the rubbery green Nerf-like foam. Todd hoisted him back onto his feet by the elbow. He said, "I'm going to wring *your* neck, Chuckie boy."

Todd Rosenthal had been bossing Chuck around ever since kindergarten. Kicking his desk chair and snapping his pencils in two. Firing spit wads at him with a flat popping noise. At lunch, he would sit across the table from Chuck. Chuck never quite knew how he was going to behave. Sometimes he would just eat his Doritos, ignoring Chuck completely. Sometimes he would crush Chuck's sandwich inside its Ziploc bag. Chuck felt bad for his crushed sandwiches—horrible, in fact. They became swirling oil slicks of peanut butter and jelly. They were marked with the dents of Todd Rosenthal's fingers. He wished he knew how to put them back together. Todd usually stood behind Chuck in the recess line, too. He liked to bump into him while they filed outside. Or step on his ankle so his shoe came loose. Or whisper, "Will you be my gay boyfriend, Chuck Carter?" But why would Todd Rosenthal want to wring his neck? Chuck had never understood him, not for a single minute. Chuck was weaker than Todd, smaller, a lot less threatening. He kept waiting for all his little meannesses to end.

That day on the playground was like every other day. After Todd said "Chuckie boy," he said, "Count on it." He said, "I'll wring that scrawny neck like a chicken's." He said, "When you least expect it, there I'll be." Then he slapped Chuck, softly, like a gangster, and left.

For the rest of the day, Chuck's elbow felt tight. He kept stretching his arm, hoping the joint would pop. The skin rippled slightly where Todd Rosenthal had grabbed him. It was nearly impossible for him to scratch his back.

That afternoon it rained and then gave way to sunlight. The parking lot reflected the sky from a thousand puddles. The basketball hoops dripped onto the pavement like shining halos. At three-thirty, Chuck's mom picked him up in the car. She took the fast way home, speeding along the highway. The road was drenched with sheets of blue and white. At fifty miles per hour, the seats began to shake. Chuck's teeth chattered in his mouth like a wind-up toy. His mom honked and shouted "Moron!" at the other drivers. Her voice shivered as she sang along with the radio. They stopped for gas, then groceries, then finished the drive. The rain had washed the dust out of the gutters. The bricks of Chuck's house were dyed dark with water. They were stacked together like crispy double vanilla sugar wafers. He had not been caught licking them in several months. That was back in February, before the Illumination began. His pretend dad had come storming across the yard, furious. He had promised to whip Chuck, hard, unless he stopped. He couldn't keep sticking crap like that in his mouth. Seriously, was he that messed up in the goddamned head? He needed to grow the hell up and quit it. Chuck knew the rule by heart: no tasting the bricks. But sometimes, rule or no rule, he still wanted to. It was one more problem he could not figure out.

Chuck left his mom alone to unpack the grocery bags. He dropped his backpack on the floor of his bedroom. A bullfrog mirror hung on the back of his door. Chuck saw himself staring out from inside its shining mouth. The finger-shaped bruises on his elbow were purple and silver. There were five of them—one, two, three, four, five. Five times two was ten, so everything still fit together. He sat at his desk and took out his notebook. The stories he had heard about fifth grade were true. He had lots of homework—too much, in his opinion. Nearly every day he had some new assignment to complete. One night he might have to draw a plant cell. The next he might have to answer questions about Ethiopia. Or color and label the four chambers of the heart. Or fill out the tiny squares of the multiplication table. Or write a paragraph about Benjamin Franklin flying a kite. Today it was time to study for his vocabulary quiz. He would have to spell the words, then define them. *Evaporate, illiteracy, physician, membrane, diminutive, fragile, majestic, chandelier, sabotage, approximately.* They were longer than most of the words he knew. He practiced using them in a sentence to memorize them.

As soon as the sun rises, the water will evaporate.

I was sick, so I went to see the physician.

There is nothing good about illiteracy, so learn to read.

Fridays and Saturdays were like a diminutive summer or Christmas. For approximately two days, Chuck could do whatever he wanted. His parents usually let him stay up late with them. They sat side by side in the fragile TV light. They slurped beer and whispered and flirted with each other. They let their fingers walk quietly up each other's legs. Meanwhile, Chuck colored pictures, ate honey-roasted peanuts, and drank soda. A membrane of Cherry Coke trembled above the glass's rim.

One Friday, he decided he would draw a majestic rainbow. An actor was on TV accepting a lifetime achievement award. His lungs shone with cancer through his tuxedo like chandeliers. Chuck looked down and tried to concentrate on his drawing. One by one, he used all sixty-four of his crayons. He was getting ready to shade in the last section. He took his favorite color, cornflower blue, from the box. But his pretend dad snatched the sheet of paper away. He waved it in the air like an American flag. He said, "Bedtime for Bonzo!" and made a chimpanzee noise.

There was that feeling of miniature needles in Chuck's eyes. He hated crying so easily, but he couldn't help it. His rainbow was only one curve short of being finished. His pretend dad had ruined the drawing with his sabotage. Now, like always, he was angry at Chuck for crying. Underneath his breath, he said, "For the love of God."

Chuck tried to stop sniffling, but it did no good. His bears and his elephant were waiting on their bench. They were frightened and lonely and wondering where he was. He ran to his bedroom in his socks and pajamas. After he shut the door, he heard his parents whispering. His pretend dad said, "What's the use in me trying? I could be Mr. Perfect, and it still wouldn't matter."

He said, "Face it, we've raised one Grade A brat."

He said, "You try to make a single monkey joke—"

Chuck's mom sighed and cleared her throat to interrupt him. "If you really attempted to figure him out, you could. It's not like you have to be Sherlock-frigging-Holmes. You want to know how to put him to bed? There are three different ways to do it," she said. Chuck pictured her extending her fingers as she listed them. " 'Chuck Carter, Chuck Carter, it's time to sleep till morning.' 'Your stuffed animals are waiting for you to say goodnight.' And then, if he absolutely won't listen, there's another one. 'I want your head on that pillow in five minutes.' "

His pretend dad smacked the table and asked, "But why?"

"I can't explain why, honey—I just know it works."

"You're saying he'll cry whenever he doesn't get his way."

"I'm saying what harm does it do to humor him?"

"The world will eat him alive when he grows up."

"That doesn't mean that we should eat him alive, too."

Chuck put himself to bed and listened to them argue. He lay there for a long time before falling asleep. He dreamed he was riding the glass elevator into space. The Earth disappeared beneath the clouds and a billion stars. He was either Superman or Batman or the Green Lantern.

The diary Chuck took still shone like a wounded animal. Sometimes he liked to sleep with it under his pillow. The light was sad and bright and comforting to him. In the morning, he would wake up inside its glow. Some of the book's pages were bent into a wave. Chuck tried everything he could imagine to press them flat. He took his shoes off and stood on the cover. He put it beneath the leg of his dresser overnight. He piled all his other books on top of it. He even ran it under the heat of an iron. He thought he felt the curve loosening beneath the weight. Then his nose prickled with the smell of something burning. A fishing line of black smoke lifted into the air. An orange spark crawled over the paper like a ladybug. When he blew, it turned into a dozen smaller sparks. They smoked and vanished, leaving brown pinholes in the page. Chuck was worried that he had only made things worse. The book was still kinked, even after all his work. He had stepped on it, scorched it, weighted it down. What if it believed he was angry—was *punishing* it? He picked it up and hugged it to his chest. He thought, *I didn't mean it, I didn't mean it.* The light was as bright as it had ever been.

It was a cool, cloudless day in October: jacket weather. The sheets drying in the backyard were rippling and swaying. Some cardinals were chasing each other through the magnolia's branches. Shortly after lunch, Chuck took the diary outside with him. The sheets were like a narrow room without a ceiling. He lay there thinking and teasing the grass into threads. He could see a gray squirrel twitching its bushy tail. He could see airplanes drawing white chalk-lines in the sky.

He kept remembering something about his kindergarten teacher, Ms. Derryberry. Ms. Derryberry had kept an unusual toy on her desk. It was a row of metal balls on V-shaped threads. The balls worked like a grandfather clock or a teeter-totter. She would let the first one swing into the others. The ball at the end of the row would jump. When it fell back, the first ball would jump again. Then the last ball would jump, then the first again. Those two balls, the first and last, took turns swinging. Each would land back where it started with a clack. The five or six in the middle stayed perfectly still. After a while, the toy would run out of energy. The noise would stop, and everyone would return to work.

Like Chuck, Ms. Derryberry had believed in having many rules. There were rules about talking and playing and sitting down. There were rules about gum-chewing and lining up for recess. There was even a rule about going to the bathroom. It was rule number seven on the list: Restroom Privileges.

ONE BOY, ONE GIRL, YOU MUST TAKE THE HALL PASS!!

She gave gold stars to everyone who followed the rules. Twenty gold stars were enough to earn you a reward. The reward might be a piece of hard cinnamon candy. It might be the chance to lead the recess line. Sometimes Ms. Derryberry let you hand out the art supplies. And sometimes she invited you to sit at her desk. You got to climb like a king into her chair. She let you play with the little swinging silver balls. It didn't matter how hard you slung the first one. Soon they slowed down and began tapping against one another. They quickly found their rhythm, going *clack clack clack clack*. They were like circus acrobats doing graceful tricks in midair. They rocked and tilted, side to side, back and forth. Each collision was a little quieter than the one before. (That was the word for things knocking together: a collision.) Finally a ball would fall so softly that it stopped. All of them would sway slightly on their V-shaped threads. And you would get up and return to your seat.

Just thinking about the desk toy could calm Chuck down. The clacking sound, those seesawing silver globes—they were wonderful. It was true then, and it was still true now.

On hard days, he would remember watching the toy operate. He imagined another toy just like it inside his head. His heart seemed to thump along with the clacking noise. He had the peculiar feeling of being suspended by strings. It gave him a soothing sort of rocking chair sensation.

The sheets billowed in the wind, and Chuck sat up. He had no idea how long he had been outside. He opened the diary to a page in the middle. The man across the street loved his wife's morning ritual. He loved the way she saved the comics for last. He loved how the smoke followed her around a fire. The walls of the room suddenly began to fall away. Chuck's mom was taking the sheets down from their clothespins. "Well, hello there, Buster," she said when she spotted him. "Don't forget we're getting that hair of yours cut today." Chuck leaped up and ran back inside with the diary.

That afternoon, his pretend dad stayed home cleaning the garage. It was just Chuck and his mom in the car. Chuck sat in the front seat, behind the rustiest door. Metal flakes drizzled to the ground when he slammed it. His whole life, he had loved riding in the car. He loved how the tires floated sideways on wet roads. He loved the soft fabric that sagged from the ceiling. He used to laugh whenever his parents honked the horn. It sounded like that *Sesame Street* monster bopping its nose. That was years and years ago, when Chuck was little. Back then, he sat in an egglike cushioned plastic seat. His mom would buckle him in and shut the door. It would open, like magic, in a completely different place. The grocery store, the park, the church—he never knew. He would've stayed there all the time if he could.

At the barbershop, Chuck sat between two big silver mirrors. One was in front of him, the other behind him. The mirrors kept reflecting each other across the open floor. Their frames became smaller and smaller, shrinking into the distance. He could see thousands of Chucks inside the long tunnel. Every time he moved sideways, so did all the others. He nodded so that the barber could trim his neck. The other Chucks nodded, too, at exactly the same time. He shook the hair from his gown—so did they. He stretched his arms out like wings—so did they. The barber told Chuck, "No more squirming around, young man. You don't want me lopping off one of your ears."

Chuck pictured his ear hitting the floor like heavy fruit.

The barber paused and said, "Whoa there, no crying now." He gave Chuck a reassuring little pat on the shoulder. "You have my word, your ears are safe with me."

Slowly and carefully, he clipped the hair behind Chuck's ears. His scissoring hand glowed white from every joint and muscle. Chuck stopped sniffling as he watched it open and close. It was like looking at an X-ray of a hand. Behind him a skeleton was sawing and fluttering its fingers. It was making chopping gestures—a strange dance of bones. And then, before Chuck knew it, his haircut was finished.

The barber cleaned his neck, dusting it with baby powder. He unsnapped Chuck's gown, and hair sprinkled to the floor. Chuck's chair sank onto its pole with a hissing noise. He got up and followed his mom to the counter. Not until then did he catch sight of Todd Rosenthal. The other barber was shaving his hair down to bristles. He was saying words like *head lice* and *nasty buggers*. He lectured Todd's parents: his mom and his real dad. "Really it's gotta be your best option with these things." He mowed a stripe in Todd's hair with the clippers. "You can comb or you can cut is about it. I had one guy tried to drown them with gasoline. Now that works, but you'd better not light any matches. You'll have yourself a bonfire is what you'll have yourself. No, when the lice get this bad, it's shaving time."

A thousand Todd Rosenthals glared at Chuck from the mirror. "Say one word and you're dead," they mouthed to him.

On Monday, at school, Todd came in wearing a hat. Ms. Mount told him he would have to remove it. He handed her a note, and she read it silently. She nodded *okay, he had permission to wear his hat*. Todd kicked Chuck's chair as he walked to his desk. Then he sat by the window, which rippled with rain. A car slid past, and the water separated its headlights. The red dots of its brakes shone from the glass. Then they vanished, and the rain was just rain again. Todd gripped his cap by the edges, tugging it down. Chuck noticed how snugly it fit, but didn't say anything.

Everyone began trading whispers—everyone but Chuck, that is. One by one they turned to peek at Todd Rosenthal. They all spent the morning wondering the exact same thing. Why in the world was he wearing that stupid thing? What was he hiding that he refused to show them? Someone wrote Todd a note during the American history lesson. Chuck glanced at it before passing it to Nathan Chowdhury. It read, "Do you have cancer (check yes or no)?"

Todd returned it with an extra box checked SCREW YOU. He sat high in his seat like a long-necked bird. He stared straight ahead at the writing on the chalkboard.

At lunch, Matthew Berry revealed the answer to the mystery. He crossed behind Todd Rosenthal and flipped his cap loose. A field of tiny lice marks shone from Todd's scalp. They looked like stars on the dome of a planetarium. A party noise rose up from the fifth grade table. The lunchroom became loud with the overlapping bubbles of conversations.

"Did you see I think spots yeah must be bugs."

And, "Man can you totally Todd-Rosenthal-believe head lice."

And, "Hat-on-comb gag me contagious is this kindergarten?"

Matthew Berry gave a shudder and said, "Dude, that's nasty." Todd middle-fingered him, jamming his hat back on his head. He saw Chuck watching him quietly from a faraway seat. "What the hell are you looking at, Chuckles?" he growled. "You've got maybe three seconds to wipe that face off—"

The lunch monitor shouted, "Fifth grade table, quiet down immediately!"

There was a brief silence before the whispering began again. Todd Rosenthal filled eight minutes flicking French fries at Chuck. The fries blossomed with light as they broke into pieces. Food fights were against the rules, but Todd didn't care. When the bell rang, everyone filed back to the classroom.

That afternoon, the rain cleared, and they had recess outside. The sun shone through the limbs of the big magnolias. Chuck looked for a spot where he could play alone. The green foam that carpeted the playground was still damp. He imagined his footsteps leaving dry peanut shapes behind him. Instead, they filled with water, then slowly emptied back out. Chuck stopped by the wooden tower and watched them disappear. He noticed Todd Rosenthal glancing over his shoulder at him. Todd turned and said something to Craig and Oscar Poissant. The two Poissant brothers were sixth-graders—twins, but not identical. The three of them were standing on the steep hillside. Their own footprints were pressed like stitches into the grass.

Chuck was living beneath the slide when they came over. Craig Poissant let his meaty arm rest on Chuck's shoulder. "We were over there talking and had this crazy idea. We thought it would be fun to kick your ass."

"Doesn't that sound like fun to you?" Todd Rosenthal asked. "If it doesn't, you only have to tell us so."

"We only beat kids up if they really want it."

"Yep, we're nice that way, us three," Todd Rosenthal said. "So what's it going to be—ass-kicking or no ass-kicking?"

At first Chuck thought they were kidding around with him. They showed him their teeth, and he showed them his. They were four friends sharing a joke on the playground. Chuck didn't get the joke, but he almost never did. Then the other Poissant brother, Oscar, said, "Kid's not talking."

"No, he doesn't have a word to say for himself."

"That must mean he wants us to beat him up."

"Well, if that's what he really wants," Craig Poissant said.

Todd Rosenthal brought his palms out to push Chuck down. He leaned in so that Chuck could smell his breath. Chuck ducked and ran away as fast as he could. He could hear Todd and both the Poissants chasing him. He went tearing through the crowd of kids playing basketball. Some of them stopped and stared, some just kept shooting. Chuck curved away, sprinting behind a row of parked cars. Oscar Poissant dashed around the side to cut him off. Chuck avoided him by sliding between a pair of SUVs. He wriggled under the chunky mirrors and past the bumpers. Before he knew it, he was back on the playground. He crossed in front of the swings, dodging someone's feet. Then he darted beneath the tower and the monkey bars. Suddenly he came face-to-face with the wooden fence.

He heard the drumbeat of sneakers landing on the foam. He barely had time to turn around before it happened. Todd lunged at him, landing a punch on his stomach. The second hit his neck, and the third his chest. The boards rattled as Todd shoved Chuck against the fence. A hard kick swept his legs out from under him. He found himself lying facedown, Todd squatting on his back. Todd didn't say anything, just kept punching Chuck, smacking him.

The teachers came running with their strong arms and whistles.

Someone shouted, "Get off of Chuck Carter *right this instant!*"

Someone else shouted, "All right, break it up, you two!"

Todd Rosenthal's cap slipped off as the teachers grabbed him. His scalp looked like a firework that had burst open. He said, "There, punk," and gripped Chuck with his knees. "There it goes, and what do you think of *that*?"

Then Chuck felt himself losing a hundred pounds of weight. He was too shaken to stand up on his own. A green-shelled bug was crawling toward him, twitching its feelers. Its face was like a face from some other planet. Chuck wondered how long it would remember staring at him.

That afternoon, when he got home, he ached all over. He went to his room and took his clothes off. His bruises shone in the mouth of the bullfrog mirror. There were bunches of them, so sore that they glittered. A bruise below his ear and another on his shoulder. A bruise the size of an apple on his back. A row of small knuckle-shaped bruises above his belly button. Where he didn't have bruises, he had cuts and scratches. He twisted his neck and listened to the joints pop. He wiggled one of his front teeth with his tongue. Falling down, he had scraped a patch from his chin. There was a crust of dried blood around the edges. The school nurse had put a Scooby-Doo Band-Aid on it. When he peeled it loose, it tugged at his skin. For a few seconds, the light poured out like water. It hurt just a little too much to be beautiful.

His body felt uncomfortable and strange, like someone else's clothing. It seemed too small around him, or maybe too big. He collapsed in bed with his elephant and his bears. On TV, cops and detectives didn't mind getting beaten up. They just brushed themselves off and began smoking a cigarette. In real life, getting punched made you tired and queasy. Chuck only wanted to lie there staring at the ceiling. Unfortunately, he had chores to do and homework to finish. His mom made him get dressed and sweep the driveway. The concrete was still wet from the hard morning rain. The water foamed and bubbled beneath the broom like soda. After he finished sweeping, he threw away the soggy leaves. He hauled the big green trash can to the curb. Then he went to his desk and did math problems. He read chapter nineteen from *The Story of America*. He studied the next ten words for his vocabulary quiz. *Exasperation, paradise, fraying, infected, temporary, candid, camouflage, indignant, animated, cuticle*. He knew the last word already, but not its spelling. The quizzes were actually working, he thought, improving his vocabulary. He wouldn't have guessed they would work, but they did.

That evening, after dinner, his pretend dad called him outside. "What's this I hear about you and the Rosenthal boy?"

Chuck bowed his head and looked down at his knees.

His pretend dad sighed and took hold of his chin. "It's high time I taught you how to fight, son. Every man's gotta know how to defend himself," he insisted. "Now put up your fists," and he thumped Chuck's forehead. "You have one job: to keep me from doing that. Understand?" he asked, and though Chuck's head hurt, he nodded.

Chuck moved his hands around in front of his face. He imagined that he was the Flash and had super-speed. He imagined that he was a robot with steel hands. It didn't matter—his pretend dad kept thumping his forehead. He was a lot faster than Chuck, a lot stronger. Sometimes he came from the left, sometimes from the right. He used his index finger and also his middle finger. "Show some muscle," he told Chuck, and, "Stop jellyfishing around." "Come on," he said, and, "What's the matter with you?" "Dodge and parry!" he shouted, but what did that mean?

After a while, Chuck quit believing he could stop him. This was just what the world was like, he thought. This was how the rest of his life would be. He was the boy who couldn't learn to defend himself. The boy who stood outside waving his tiny fists around. The boy whose pretend dad would not stop poking him.

The wind was moving across the yard, swirling, then resting. The leaves on the grass were all glossy and speckled. They kept lifting onto their edges, then slowly toppling over. It happened thirty or fifty times, too many to count. He was reminded of waves rolling gently onto a beach.

Eventually he realized that the poking and shouting had stopped. His pretend dad was gone, and he was alone again. His forehead hurt with the sting of a hundred taps. His bruises were glowing, beating like hearts through his clothing.

The sun vanished in a pool of thick red light. He went back inside, and he slipped into his bedroom. The diary he had taken was lying on his dresser. He sat down and opened the cover and began reading.

I love the way chocolate makes your eyes light up.

I love hearing you try to defend Hall and Oates.

I love your compassionate heart—your big, sloppy, sentimental heart.

The pages looked just as sensitive as they always had. They were like a giant mosquito bite, infected from scratching. Chuck closed the diary and tucked it under his pillow. He lay down, patting the sad square lump it made. He wanted to heal the book, to make it better. If he tried hard enough, maybe he could do it.

In the morning, when he woke, his muscles were sore. The light of his wounds had spread across his body. His bruised places were dimmer and hurt a little less. The rest of him was what hurt a little more. He had a hard time waking up and getting dressed. His mom had to yell his name three different times. His pretend dad had to throw a shoe at him. The shoe thunked against the wall, leaving a black scuff.

Chuck decided to take the diary to school with him. He spent the day petting its cover under his desk. He massaged the wave, smoothing it down with his hand. Maybe he was imagining things, but it seemed to help. The pages still shone, but not as brightly, he thought. Not as brightly and not with the same awful pain. The book rested a little more comfortably in his hands. He began carrying it around with him wherever he went. People whispered about it for a while and then stopped. It was one of the many weird things Chuck did. He never said anything, and he laughed at stupid jokes. He couldn't reach the basket when he threw the basketball. Now he liked to stroke a book under his desk. No surprise, and who cared, and what else was new?

Todd Rosenthal had been suspended from school for the week. On Monday, when he returned, he avoided looking at Chuck. He stomped past his chair without even kicking the legs. His hair had grown up in a soft-looking brown fuzz. He kept rubbing it with the palm of his hand. Chuck bet it would feel the way a peach felt. Or slightly fuzzy, but also firm, like a tennis ball. Or prickly like Velcro, the side with the plastic bristles. He wanted to run his fingers over it but didn't. Some things were so obvious that they weren't even rules.

For the next two weeks, everything was good for Chuck. School was a paradise where no one noticed he existed. His bruises went away, and his scabs began to peel. Todd Rosenthal ignored him, sitting quietly next to the window. He did not step on Chuck's shoes in the recess line. He did not ask him to be his gay boyfriend.

Then one morning Ms. Mount stayed home with a cold. They found a substitute—a man—sitting at her desk. He was Mr. Brady, he said, "but call me Felix." He was skinny like Chuck, and short, and wore glasses. He forgot to collect their homework after he took roll. He didn't understand what the bell meant when it rang. Worse, he began allowing the class to vote on everything. "Who votes we line up by height today?" he asked. "Who votes that we read out loud from the textbook?" "What would you like to study next: science or history?"

At the noon bell, Mariellen Chase asked him a question. "Is it okay if we eat lunch in class today?"

"Let's put it to a vote," Mr. Brady—Felix—said. "All in favor of eating in class, raise your hands."

Fifteen hands shot up immediately, and only five stayed down.

"Okay, then," he said, dropping his fist like a hammer. "By a count of fifteen to five, eating here wins."

He spent the next half hour working on a crossword puzzle. He kept rolling a cough drop around in his mouth. Now and then he looked up, saying, "Quiet down, guys." But everybody was too busy talking, and no one listened.

Chuck finished his bologna sandwich and his pack of Twinkies. He put his lunch box away and took out the diary. He stroked the cover, trying to brush its pain away. He pretended it was a cat, purring in his lap. He wished that he could feed it a cat treat.

Lunchtime was nearly over when Nathan Chowdhury grabbed the book. He caressed it and kissed it, murmuring, "Oh, baby, baby."

Todd Rosenthal said to him, "Nathan, man, chuck it here." Chuck's heart beat faster at the sound of his name. (It wasn't really his name—he knew that—but still . . .) He watched the diary's pages flutter apart in the air. Todd caught it, smiled at Chuck, and cracked it open. Right away, without a thought, he tore a page out. The light was terrible and made Chuck's stomach go tight. His mouth tasted bitter, and his hands began to sweat. To see all that love and sadness destroyed was agonizing. Todd Rosenthal noticed his reaction, laughed, and tore another page. The whole class turned around to watch what was happening. The sound of ripping paper was louder than their conversations. They looked at Chuck, at Todd, then at Chuck again. They wanted to see if he had started crying yet.

"Hey, what's going on back there?" the substitute teacher asked. Suddenly he crossed the room, stopping next to Todd Rosenthal. "That's enough monkey business," he said, and took the diary. He handed it back to Chuck, torn pages and all. Then he brought him the Scotch tape from his desk. "It could be worse, right?" he said, squeezing Chuck's shoulder. "Tape it back together and it'll be good as new."

Apparently, Mr. Brady didn't know that he should punish Todd. He didn't seem to understand how the check system worked.

Carefully, Chuck repaired the book, ignoring the whispers he heard. He slid the loose pages into place, squaring their edges. He fastened them together with long strips of invisible tape. He made sure all the broken words lined up correctly. When he was finished, he let the book fall shut.

It *wasn't* as good as new—it was nowhere close. It shone like a man whose bones had been broken.

The rest of the afternoon passed slowly for Chuck, hazily. At recess, he spotted Todd Rosenthal climbing the wooden tower. It was freezing cold, and everyone had a sore throat. A few kids were playing soccer in the parking lot. A pale light flickered over their tongues as they shouted. Chuck saw the light but did not hear the words. He approached the tower and went up the ladder. It seemed that he was riding the glass elevator again. He felt tall and powerful and nothing whatsoever like himself. He rose quietly into the clear blue sky like Superman. Far below him, the kids turned into little moving dots.

He found Todd Rosenthal standing at the platform's open edge. He was dangling a cord of spit from his mouth. Chuck shoved him and watched his body hit the ground.

In seconds, everything was over, and the teachers came running. The fall had wrenched Todd's shoulder out of its socket. His arm had snapped with a sound like breaking chalk. His teeth had pierced the flesh of his lower lip. Blood, thick and shining, was already spilling from the wound.

The teachers bent down over him, trying to soothe him.

"Don't worry," they said, and, "Cry it all out, honey."

"Mr. Kaczmarek is calling the doctor for you right now."

"Your mom and dad will meet you at the hospital."

Todd rolled onto his back and twisted his eyes shut. He moaned, "Why does this shit always happen to me?" No one said anything to him about the curse word.

The teachers were trying hard not to look at Chuck. They seemed embarrassed by him—even the substitute, Mr. Brady. He marched Chuck inside, leaving him in the secretary's office. Chuck sat on the couch listening to the clock tick. After a while, the principal summoned him to her desk. He could see the ambulance pulling away through the window. Its flashing red lights dipped like fish across the wall. The principal kept snapping her fingers and saying, "Pay attention." And, "I must say your behavior surprises me, Mr. Carter." And, "You realize this will go on your permanent record." Her lipstick had leaked into the cracks between her teeth. Finally, she shook her head and turned away from him. She picked up the phone to call his pretend dad. And then it was Chuck's turn to be in trouble.

The school punished him with two full weeks of suspension.

His parents punished him by taking away his stuffed animals. "Plus no Cokes, TV, or comic books," his mom said. His pretend dad even got her permission to spank him. He gave Chuck ten whacks with a wooden cutting board. Afterward, Chuck noticed him smothering the expression on his face. He looked like he did after he mowed the lawn. He was satisfied with the hard work he had done.

"This was for your own good now," he told Chuck. "It's a lesson I can just about guarantee you'll remember."

"This family doesn't even believe in spanking," his mom added. "You have no idea how disappointed I am in you. I always said I would never hit my child: *ever.* But this—oh, Chuckie, you broke that poor boy's arm."

She was standing at the kitchen counter tapping her feet. The heels of her shoes stabbed the floor like knives.

The days of Chuck's suspension passed like a long dream. Because both his parents had jobs, he stayed home alone. He imagined he was an orphan without the sad parts. Over and over again, he walked through the empty house. He made little teepees—dominoes—out of his playing cards. He spent a while tossing beanbags at his tic-tac-toe game. (The spotted beanbags were his, the solid ones Todd Rosenthal's.) He stood at the window looking out over the yard. Cars and trucks and bicycles drifted slowly down the street. Squirrels crossed the grass, their tails jerking on invisible wires. He could see the yellow bricks that lined the porch. As usual, they looked like something he would enjoy tasting. If he was a retard, then he was a retard. He had become too old to do anything about it.

Chuck began visiting Dr. Finkelstein on both Mondays and Thursdays. His mom said she was having concerns about his psychology. (That was a big word for his personality: his psychology.) The doctor kept rubbing his forehead, his three red sunspots. He wondered what Todd Rosenthal could have done to Chuck. Why had Chuck gotten angry enough to break his leg?

Chuck took out a note card and wrote his answer down. *Who told you I broke his leg, because I didn't.*

"But why did you push the boy off the tower?"

He did something bad, Chuck began, then crossed it out. *He tore something of mine apart and hurt its feelings.*

"But only people have feelings," Dr. Finkelstein said, "not objects."

This was the most ridiculous thing Chuck had ever heard. Objects were quieter than people, maybe, but no less sensitive. The one big difference was that objects could not move. They weren't able to fake their feelings or hide them. It was people who could lie, people who could pretend. People could laugh like friends and then beat you up. People could say they were your dad and hit you. Sometimes the faces of people seemed unreal to Chuck, inhuman. They were like masks they wore over their real faces. Masks to show how old or how young they were. Masks to show how healthy or how sick they were. People could cry out of sadness or happiness or anger. But then they could smile for the exact same reasons. The strangeness of people went on and on and on. Objects, on the other hand, were mostly simple and good. Chuck was always kind to them—it was a rule. They needed his help to make it in the world. They had no one else to look out for them. That was why he was so upset about the book. He had tried fixing it and had let it down. It gave off more light now than it had before. Why, then, had he taken it at all, he wondered? He was no more than a thief and a kidnapper. The book would be better off with anyone but him. He might as well give it away to a stranger.

A week into his suspension, someone knocked on the door. Chuck was not supposed to answer it, but he did. A tall man in church clothes stood on the porch. He stooped over the way that grown-ups without kids do. "Why, hello there," he said, his hands on his knees. "Can you tell me if your parents are at home?"

Chuck shook his head no and began shutting the door.

"Wait," the man said, and reached into his leather satchel. "Will you give them this flyer when you see them?" He passed Chuck a slip of paper, yellow like butter. The paper read, "For the Lord God will illumine them." Beneath that was the name and address of a church. And beneath that was a cross surrounded by tiny lines. And beneath that were Chuck's fingers reaching from his hand. And beneath that was his hand sticking from his sleeve. He was reading the flyer when he had an idea. He held up his palms to say, *Wait right here.* Then he went to his bedroom and got the diary. He came running back across the living room with it. He turned it over to the man in the suit.

Aloud, the man wondered, "What's this you have for me?" He looked slightly confused, but fanned through the book's pages. He tried to return it, smiling encouragingly, his hand outstretched. Chuck backed away, and the man's smile tightened in confusion. He was about to speak when Chuck shut the door.

The man wasted a few minutes knocking and shouting hello. The doorbell rang nine times, though Chuck imagined a tenth. Finally the noise fell away, and he looked outside again. There was only the empty porch and a fraying spiderweb. The man must have moved on to the next house. Chuck had been worried he would leave the book behind. But no—his worries aside, it was no longer there. It wasn't on the doormat, wasn't poking from the mailbox. It wasn't leaning against the stairs or the brick wall. Obviously, he had given up and taken it with him. Chuck hoped that he would give it a loving home.

It was a Thursday, which meant one thing: Dr. Finkelstein. Chuck's appointment was supposed to last from four to five. His pretend dad had to drive him to the office. "I'm missing two hours' pay for this crap," he complained. "That's two hours of food coming straight from our refrigerator. Two hours of working lights, two hours of running water. Two hours of goddamned gasoline for the goddamned Plymouth Reliant." He kept honking the horn and shouting "Jerk!" at people.

The doctor was still in another session when they arrived. They lived in the waiting room for a few minutes. Both of them sat down, Chuck and his pretend dad. Chuck skimmed a news magazine he found on the table. Someone, a Chinese soldier, had been shot in the head. Light was gushing from his temple in a sideways fountain. Some children were starving, their stomachs glimmering like crystal balls. Their pain had made them simple, honest, candid, like objects. Chuck had seen it happen many times in his life.

A patient came out, and Dr. Finkelstein called Chuck's name. He asked Chuck to join him in his office, please. A surprise was waiting on top of the doctor's desk. He had gotten one of those clacking metal desk toys. It looked exactly like the one Ms. Derryberry had owned.

The doctor set it in motion, and Chuck immediately relaxed. The V-shaped threads rocked back and forth, back and forth. Again and again the silver balls fell tapping into place. The sound filled Chuck with a gentle, swaying, hammocky feeling. "A neat little gadget, this, isn't it?" Dr. Finkelstein said. He cracked his knuckles and continued. "So let's get started. On Monday we were talking about your chores at home. Will you write down your least favorite chore for me?"

The only one I really hate is cleaning the tub.

"The tub!" Dr. Finkelstein said, rolling his eyes in exasperation. "Yes, there's nothing worse than having to clean the tub. Is there anything else you dislike about living at home?"

When my pretend dad yells at me or my mom.

The doctor's face became animated as he read the note. He was interested, but he tried to pretend he wasn't. Unless he was only pretending to be pretending he wasn't. Sometimes people played elaborate games to hide their true feelings. The doctor jotted something down on his pad of paper. "Your pretend dad?" he prompted, reaching for the desk toy. He pinched hold of one of the hanging metal balls. When he let it go, the toy rediscovered its rhythm.

Chuck explained the difference between real dads and pretend dads. He wrote down some of the clues he had uncovered. How real dads never filled the house with their shouting. How they didn't twist the hair on their sons' necks. How they ate dinner without flicking their food at anyone. How they didn't secretly wish that their sons were dead. Or not dead, exactly, but that they'd never been born. Chuck filled card after card explaining things to Dr. Finkelstein. Most dads were real dads, but Chuck's dad was pretend. The clues, though small, all came together to prove it. The doctor kept reaching for the toy and restarting it. Before Chuck knew it, he'd used up the whole hour.

"We'll have to stop now, I'm afraid," Dr. Finkelstein said. "Can you send your mom in alone for a minute? I need to discuss something with her, something having to—"

Chuck finished his note while the doctor was still speaking. *My mom couldn't take time off from work this afternoon.*

"Oh, then your dad—your pretend dad—then he's here? That's fine, just fine," the doctor said, twisting his shoulders. There was a popping noise and a button of light. The light flashed open where his spine joined his neck. "Ask him to step inside for a second, would you?"

Chuck left the office and sat down on the couch. He waited while his pretend dad talked to Dr. Finkelstein. The door, a bulky oak, let hardly any sound through. Chuck heard his pretend dad shouting two words: "completely ridiculous."

He came out brushing the doctor's hand from his arm. His teeth were set so firmly his jaw was shaking. "Move," he said, stomping past, and Chuck followed him outside.

They sped home in a thick smell of burning gasoline. His pretend dad left the car slanting across the driveway. The engine continued to run after he removed the key. It rattled and coughed and then sputtered to a halt. He said, "So I understand I'm not your real dad. Imagine my surprise," and he pulled the car's emergency brake. "I guess that means you're not my real son, either."

He yanked Chuck across the bench seat by his elbow. With long, angry strides, he hauled him toward the house. He was as indignant as Chuck had ever seen him. Chuck tried to keep up, but it was too hard. His shoes kept leaving scars of dirt in the grass. The scars didn't glow, which meant the grass wasn't hurt. A root made Chuck stumble, and he tripped and fell. He became a plant, dirt, a fish in a puddle. There were bits of leaves stuck to his blue jeans. He had grass in his hair and between his lips. His pretend dad lifted him to his feet, armpits first. Chuck was sure—pretty sure—he intended to kill him. He realized it was something he had always seen coming. He wanted to have one last Coke, one last cookie. He wanted to hug his elephant and all his bears. He wanted to say good-bye to everything that loved him.

His pretend dad opened the door and shoved him inside. There was his mom, standing wide-eyed and gaping at them. She was opening the mail with a miniature wooden sword. Someone must have given her a ride home from work. "What's all the ruckus, you guys?" she said to them. "Good lord, Chuck, you're covered head to toe in dirt! That's it, into the tub with you right now—chop-chop!"

Reluctantly, his pretend dad's fingers loosened their grip on him. Chuck had little doubt his mom had saved his life. He felt like he was waking from a bad dream. Miles of jagged rocks had been rushing up at him. The wind was beating like a flag in his ears. The ground was going to separate him from his skeleton. Then he was lying in bed, eyes open, wide awake.

He went to the bathroom and took off his clothes. The chafed skin of his armpits shone in the mirror. He filled the tub with water and heaps of bubbles. He could hear his parents arguing, that awful tumbling noise. The running water made it impossible to recognize the words.

In the tub, the bubbles shifted every time Chuck moved. They were like clouds changing their shape in the sky. A little rhinoceros rose up inside them, then knelt over. It seemed to lift its horn before it was overwhelmed. Its life was short, temporary, just a few seconds long. There were flies that hatched and died in a day. Chuck had seen a program about them on TV once. He turned the faucet off and heard his parents shouting. His pretend dad was saying, "Don't give me that business. He gets it into his head to push some kid—"

"Who was picking on him, don't forget," his mom interrupted.

"And we get stuck with a thousand-dollar hospital bill."

"Which means you get to knock him around *why* again?"

There was a pause while his pretend dad punched something. "You cannot—*cannot*—ask me to justify myself to you."

Chuck turned the faucet back on to muffle their argument. It was just him and the water and the bubbles. Blowing on the bubbles made a cave appear inside them. Waving his feet made the heat roll through the tub. Eventually, his parents' voices grew too loud to be camouflaged. His mom's came first, sharp and full, like a siren. "If that's the way you feel, why don't you leave?"

Then he heard his pretend dad saying, "Maybe I will!"

Finally the door slammed shut like a paper bag exploding.

Chuck stayed in the warm water for a long time. The bubbles slowly swallowed one another, sinking and spreading open. Eventually, they were just a few islands of white film.

After the heat vanished, he climbed out of the tub. The house was so still he heard the air conditioner ticking. The silence seemed too big, too eerie, and he shivered. He wasn't sure he wanted to open the bathroom door. The thought of what he might find made him afraid. He pictured his mom lying in a pool of light. A pool of white light, a pool of red blood. He imagined his pretend dad speeding away in the car. Chuck would be an orphan with the sad parts included.

He ran to his bedroom and crawled under the covers. He wished his mom had given his stuffed animals back. At last, though he wasn't sure when, he fell asleep.

He woke much later, in the darkness of early morning. It was 5:52, according to the clock, and then 5:53. He got up and walked quietly into the living room. Both his parents were there, lying senseless on the couch. They were hugging, their bodies curled together like two tadpoles. His pretend dad must've come home while Chuck was sleeping. He must have kissed his mom and apologized to her. How had Chuck ever convinced himself that anything would change? He tiptoed back to his room, but he wasn't sleepy. He lay on his side, his hand beneath the pillow. Soon, bit by bit, the dawn began filling the curtains. He thought that his heart would stop beating from sadness. There it was, the sun, coming up just like always.

Ryan Shifrin

As one has to learn to read or to practice a trade, so one must learn to feel in all things, first and almost solely, the obedience of the universe to God. It is really an apprenticeship. Like every apprenticeship, it requires time and effort. He who has reached the end of his training realizes that the differences between things or between events are no more important than those recognized by someone who knows how to read, when he has before him the same sentence, reproduced several times, written in red ink and blue, and printed in this, that, or the other kind of lettering. He who does not know how to read only sees the differences. For him who knows how to read, it all comes to the same thing, since the sentence is identical. Whoever has finished his apprenticeship recognizes things and events, everywhere and always, as vibrations of the same divine and infinitely sweet word. This does not mean that he will not suffer. Pain is the color of certain events. When a man who can and a man who cannot read look at a sentence written in red ink, they both see the same red color, but this color is not so important for the one as for the other.

—Simone Weil

Judy was coughing up blood again. He held a tissue to her mouth, watched it darken, then replaced it with another. For a moment, as her stomach rose and fell beneath the covers, everything was quiet. From out of the lull she asked, "Is it May already?" and then, "Who brought the garden inside?" and in a sunburst of intuition he realized that she saw the seven stained tissues on her bedside table as roses, the same lustrous red as the apothecaries their mother used to cultivate when they were kids. It was another five minutes, another handful of roses, before one of the tissues came out speckled a watery pink. At last she was able to close her eyes and rest. He left her to her garden dreams, slipping out into the daylight.

A half hour later, distributing his leaflets, he came to a house where a dog began to bark, its chest concussing against a frosted glass door. For an instant he was eight years old again and Judy nine, facing the old bull mastiff that used to lunge at them from behind Mr. Castillo's chain-link fence, listening as he called out, "Max! Leave those children alone! Heel!" Except that Mr. Castillo's dog's name was not Max, it was Duke, maybe, or Buster.

Was there anyone else who had been there and might remember, anyone but him and Judy?

He backed away and continued down the block.

Every day was the same: young parents and vacationing students, the elderly and the unemployed, all answering their doors to him with open stances and quizzical eyes, as if he might be delivering something they would only then realize they had always secretly desired. Then he would ask them if they had heard the Good News, and their postures would stiffen, their features grow hard. *God* was a word that embarrassed people. He knew missionaries who were able to use it without sounding pushy or insincere, letting it shine in their voices like some small, familiar object, not the sun but a nail head, a key ring, a strand of silk—something that reflected its light rather than generated it. But he was not one of them. He had seen too many people retreat behind their faces as he spoke, and now he found it nearly impossible to open his mouth without steeling himself for rejection. *God*—his timidity had stripped all the grace from the word. So instead it was *Good News* he said. And he smiled like he thought a man filled with peace might smile. And though most of the people he met were polite enough to accept a leaflet from him, he had learned not to expect anything more.

Only twice that day did someone actually engage him in conversation. The first was a woman who saw the Bible he was carrying and asked, "Jehovah's Witness?" and when he shook his head asked, "Mormon?" and when he shook his head again asked, "Methodist?" When he told her the name of his church, Fellowship Bible, she pointed to herself and repeated, "Methodist," shutting the door. The second was a man who took a flyer and read it out loud: " '1 John 1:5: This then is the message which we have heard of him, and declare unto you, that God is light, and in him is no darkness at all.' " He was one of those people who did not fold or crumple the page but laid it gently on a table, as if he were attempting to balance a coin on the surface of a puddle.

"What's your name, son?" the man asked.

"Ryan Shifrin, sir."

"Ryan Shifrin. I want you to promise me something. Can you do that?"

"I think so."

"I want you to promise me that you'll never darken my door again. And I want you to promise me that you'll tell your buddies to stay away, too."

It was not the promise Ryan had been hoping for, and at the end of a long day of *no thank you*'s and *not interested*'s, he had just enough billy-goat tenacity to ask why.

"Because you're making a grand mystery out of total horse-shit," the man answered, "and don't get me wrong, that's your constitutional right as an American, but I resent you bringing it into my home."

What could Ryan say? That he apologized? That he understood? It was Judy who had always been the diehard, the true believer, praying that it would not snow on her birthday, that Wheaton College would pluck her from its waiting list, that the cancer would not spread to her lungs and afterward, when it did, that her suffering would be bearable, but always and only if it be God's will. Their shared childhood of bedtime prayers and family devotionals had carried Ryan to church nearly every Sunday of his life, but it had carried Judy much further, into a world of praise music, revival meetings, and mission work. She was a Christian by constitution, whereas Ryan was merely a Christian by inertia. Or he very nearly was, he would have been, if not for the occasional moment waiting at a stoplight or pushing a shopping cart with a floating front wheel through the supermarket when, despite the fact that everyone was in pain and everyone was dying and no one knew what they were or where they came from, an inexplicable sense that it would all be okay washed over him like a wave. It was the same feeling that Wittgenstein had found so curious, the one that had convinced him of the existence of God. A hint, a clue. Not a burning bush or a disembodied hand marking out letters in plaster, but the slight breeze He left as He brushed past the world.

That evening, when Ryan got home, Judy was still sleeping. A new stain had appeared on her pillow, a spatter of blood, already dried to rust along the edges. He could hardly bear to see it there, grazing her lip like the plume of a long red feather.

He cradled her head while he replaced the pillow, trying not to disturb her, but she woke anyway. She blinked and recognized him, gave a teetering smile. "Ryan," she said, "you're back."

"That's right. Home again."

He pressed his hand to her cheek. This simple moment of ordinary respiration, with her breath warming the backs of his fingers—he knew that it would not last.

She asked, "How were the leaflets today?" and when he groaned, she laughed, a thin puff of air she expelled through her nostrils to keep herself from coughing. The attempt did not work. It was as if she reserved all her energy for these explosive hacking noises that left her completely exhausted. Quietly, between coughs, she said, "Well, thank you for doing it anyway, going to all those houses for me."

"A promise is a promise."

"Oh, poor Rye-rye. Just look how it wears you out."

"It's your life, I'm just keeping it warm for you."

This was how they spoke to each other these days, not like brother and sister but newlyweds pretending they had already grown old together. *It was a beautiful service, wasn't it, dear? The finest. You and your suit and me in my dress. Yes, you never looked lovelier than you did in that dress of yours.* It had started when their parents died, their father barely a year after their mother, and settled into habit once Judy got sick. Soon, Ryan went to the kitchen to prepare some of the vegetable broth that was the only food she could stomach anymore. He fed her with one of the antique silver spoons they had inherited from the family. Afterward he cleaned her face and neck with a damp washcloth he heated in the microwave. She was already drifting back to sleep by the time he finished.

"Hey, Judy?"

"Mmm?"

"Mr. Castillo, do you remember? The old guy who lived next door. What was his dog's name?"

She thought about it for a second and murmured, "Trinket."

That was the night he woke at two o'clock to the sound of retching. He rushed to Judy's bedroom. She was coughing once more but with her lips closed this time, her cheeks bloating out again and again, as if she were blowing up a balloon, and when finally she opened her mouth, he saw that on her tongue she had produced something the size of a strawberry. Her face exhibited a look of astonishment and humiliation. *Is this normal?* she seemed to be asking. *This can't be normal.* She spat the lump out of her mouth, and Ryan left to pack it in a bag of ice. For the rest of his life, whenever he remembered the night she died, he would wonder why he had believed he should preserve it. What befuddled reflex was he obeying? Why didn't he phone the hospital first?

The paramedics who arrived not ten minutes later kept calling Judy "the crit." "We're on scene with the crit," they said into their radios. "The crit is not responding to verbal stimuli. The crit's pupils are fixed, pulse slow and even." They picked her up, harnessed her to a stretcher, and told Ryan he should follow them to Mercy General. No, he could not ride in the back of the ambulance. They were sorry. Regulations. So he grabbed his keys from the dresser and ran outside and started the car. The ambulance seemed to float through the streets like a toy, a die-cast racer propelled along a plastic track. Gradually he fell behind, watching the blue lights lend their flicker to more and more distant buildings, until, abruptly and inexplicably, at the corner of Burlington and Court, the driver began obeying the traffic laws. By the time the hospital came into view, Ryan was no more than half a minute behind them, but when he pulled into the emergency room's entrance bay, the paramedics were already sitting on the ambulance's back fender as if they had been there all night. One was scuffing the pavement with his shoe, the other upending a thermos into his mouth. When Ryan got out of his car, they met his eyes and shook their heads at him. And so the first part was over, and he could begin teaching himself not to remember.

It was a year later that the light began.

Ryan was scorekeeping for a youth basketball game at the church the night it started, operating the board from a table at mid-court. In the last seconds of the fourth quarter, one of Fellowship's boys attempted to dunk the ball and dashed his hand against the rim, a blow so violent that the backboard clanged on its springs. The noise continued to reverberate even after the final buzzer sounded. Beneath the basket the boy was hunched over. Inquisitively, as if the pain had simply made him curious, he bent his wrist, and from inside, where the tendons fanned apart, it began to shine, a hard surge of light that turned his glasses into vacant white disks. He winced and said, "Aw, Christ."

At first Ryan assumed the glare from one of the lamps in the parking lot must be sliding through the stained-glass window, casting a peculiar incandescence over the boy, one that just happened to be concentrated on his injury, but the brightness followed him as he staggered across the floor to the sidelines, crumpling like an animal onto the bench. A few of the other players, Ryan noticed, had glowing white bruises on their arms and legs. The visiting team's coach wore a circle of light around his left knee, the bad one, the knee with the wraparound brace. Ryan thought something must be wrong with his vision. He blinked and rubbed his eyes, opening them to see dozens of other people, in the bleachers and on the court, blinking and rubbing their own. What was going on?

Driving home he passed a traffic accident on the highway. A car had flipped over onto its roof, and in the front two bodies were hanging from their safety belts, glowing like pillars of fire. The light was no illusion. Ryan stopped his MP3 player and dialed through the broadcast band. The first few channels were following their programming guidelines, airing music or commercials, sermons or station ID stingers, but eventually he found a community radio show that occupied the thin sliver of airspace between an oldies station and the local public radio affiliate. "And I'm sorry," the host was saying, "but, you know, this is some weird business we've got going on here at the Reggae Hour. For those of you who've just tuned in, Tony, my engineer, has this toothache on it looks like—what?—his right incisor. Right incisor, Tony? His right incisor. And it's shining like a lightbulb, a bite-size effing lightbulb. A Christmas light! I do not lie to you, ladies and gentlemen. I do not lie."

So Ryan was not crazy.

At home, he immediately turned on the television and sat watching the news until he fell asleep, and then again when he woke up. He could hardly do anything else.

The Illumination: who had coined the term, which pundit or editorial writer, no one knew, but soon enough—within hours, it seemed—that was what people were calling it. The same thing was happening all over the world. In hospitals and prison yards, nursing homes and battered women's shelters, wherever the sick and the injured were found, a light could be seen flowing from their bodies. Their wounds were filled with it, brimming. The cable news channels showed clip after clip to illustrate the phenomenon. There was the footage, endlessly rebroadcast, of the New York City mugging victim saying, "It hurts right here, and right here, and right here," touching the three radiant marks on her neck, shoulder, and breastbone. There was the free-for-all at the hockey match, one lightning flash after another bursting from the cluster of sticks and uniforms. There was the fraternity party at which the pledges had taken turns punching through sheets of glass, leaving their hands sliced open with glittering, perfectly shaped gashes. And those were just the images Ryan could not shake, the ones that haunted him when he closed his eyes in the shower to wash the shampoo from his hair. Over and over again he watched soldiers burning out of their injuries, footballers flickering through their pads and jerseys. He watched children with sacklike bellies basking in a glow of hunger. Occasionally, the light seemed to arrive from a distinct direction, like the sun slanting through a gap in a curtain, but often it simply infused whatever aches or traumas afflicted people. At such times, it had the appearance of a strange luminescent paint layered directly over their skin. They might have been angels in an El Greco painting.

That was the beginning. For a few months, church attendance spiked. Some of the seats at Fellowship Bible were taken by visitors, some by the Christmas-and-Easter set. It didn't matter—

each new face showed the guilt, fright, or confusion of someone confronted by a game whose rules had suddenly changed. After a while, though, when it became clear that the world was not ending, or not ending soon, and everyone began to accept that pain now came coupled together with light, the congregation diminished. Each Sunday, fewer and fewer people were required to sit in the folding chairs the ushers had arranged behind the pews, until finally the chairs were taken up and put away, wheeled into the closet on their long metal platforms. Again the church directory was crowded with photos of people who turned up only once or twice a year.

Ryan wished he could permit himself to be one of them, but it was impossible. There was someone who was watching him, who needed him there in her stead, someone who whispered an almost imperceptible *thank you* each time he walked through the door, her voice no louder than a breath, scarcely strong enough to make a candle flicker. It was for her sake that he was still distributing the leaflets. He devoted a few hours a day to the job, circulating from one neighborhood to the next so that he walked down every block on his route at least once a month. The church paid him for it—not much but enough, or enough for now. Enough along with the insurance settlement. Enough along with his investments and the money he had saved during his brokerage days. "For the Lord God will illumine them," the new leaflets read, from the final chapter of Revelation, singular, *The Revelation of St. John the Divine,* and he marched from house to house with a sheaf of them in his leather satchel. When no one was home, he would take a leaflet from the *sorry-we-missed-you* stack, scroll it shut, and tuck it into the doorjamb, next to the campaign flyers and the pizza offers. When someone answered, he would smile as if he understood why he was smiling and ask the ques-

tion he always asked: "Tell me, have you heard the Good News?"
He abided by business hours, which meant that there were always
more *sorry-we-missed-you* houses than *have-you-heard-the-Good-
News?* houses. In the summer it was mainly schoolkids he saw, in
the winter retirees and homemakers. And there were the invalids,
too, of course, a surprising number of cripples and terminal
cases, as if on every block two or three houses had been seized in
the jaws of some great machine and reduced to stone and timber.
The old men with prostate conditions. The diabetes patients with
ulcerated feet. The arthritis sufferers with swollen joints. All of
them were illuminated with the telltale signs of their own infir-
mity. "Sorry about your heart," Ryan wanted to say, or, "Sorry
about your legs," but he was still getting used to the etiquette of
the situation. Was it discourteous to admit that you could see a
person's sickness playing out on the surface of his body? What if
it was a form of sickness that had always previously been hidden?

One afternoon, at a yellow brick house with a lopsided magnolia dropping its leaves in the yard, a boy who had clearly been
beaten opened the door. The collar of his shirt was frayed, and a
scab was beginning to heal on his chin. He wore his glasses too
close to his eyes, which gave him the downcast look of a dog in a
trench. Ryan had the impulse to pick him up and carry him away.
No, no, this won't do, he wanted to say. *This won't do at all,* but
instead he smiled at the boy and asked him if his parents were
home. The boy held up a finger—*just one second*—and sprinted
into the darkness of the house. A bruise with squared-off edges
radiated through the seat of his pants.

Ryan switched the satchel to his other shoulder and looked
around as he stretched his muscles. A chain of roots arched across
the lawn, appearing every so often as a ropey brown bulge in the
overgrown grass. A patch of concrete was crumbling at the end

of the porch. When the boy reappeared—alone—he handed Ryan a book. Ryan had never become a father, had never even done any babysitting, and talking to children, he always felt a strange and powerful foreignness emanating from their delicate little skulls, as if he were trying to communicate with someone who was secretly much cleverer and more intuitive than he was, attuned like the elephants to the hum of some mysterious subsonic tone. He riffled through the book's pages.

"What's this you've got for me?"

The boy waved him away.

"Yes, this is a nice book. A nice book indeed. Here, you can have it back now."

The boy recoiled. Barely a second had passed before he slammed the door.

When Ryan knocked, no one responded. It seemed to him that a choice had been made on his behalf. For some reason, the boy had given him the book; for some reason, he wanted Ryan to keep it. He put it in his satchel.

Later, at home, skimming through the pages, he discovered a long sequence of tiny handwritten love notes, each one printed in the same slanting blue ink. *I love watching you sit and crochet while I'm doing the bills or clearing the photo banks. I love those old yearbook pictures of you. I love it when you watch me shave and laugh at the faces I make. I love how, when we come home from a bar, you'll hang the clothes you wore in the garage until the cigarette stink evaporates.*

Shaving and cigarettes and old yearbook photos—so obviously the notes had not been written by the boy himself. Maybe the journal belonged to his parents. Or maybe he had found it at a flea market or garage sale. One thing was certain: it had not been treated with any particular care. The cover was scuffed, the fly-leaf spotted with coffee or Coca-Cola. There were scorch marks on a few of the pages, as if it had been plucked from a bed of embers just before it could ignite.

I love sitting outside on a blanket with you, my bare foot brushing against yours. I love how embarrassing you find your middle name. I love your Free Cell addiction. I love how irritated you get at smiley face icons, or, as I know you love to call them, "emoticons." I love the way you'll hold a new book up to your face and fan through the pages to inhale the scent. I love wasting an afternoon tossing stones off the pier with you. I love seeing your body turn into a mosaic through the frosted glass of the hotel shower. I love the fact that you know all the lyrics to "The Fresh Prince of Bel-Air." I love it when you fall asleep while I'm driving, because it lets me feel like I'm protecting you. I love the way you'll call me in the middle of the day to apologize for the littlest things.

That was all there was to the book, page after page of *I love you*'s, yet something about it was curiously beguiling. It was like the yellow window of a house casting its glow into the darkness as Ryan took one of his two-in-the-morning insomnia walks, a mystery oriented around the simplest of questions. Who was that family moving around behind the glass? How long would they remain awake? Would their love for each other ever sour into indifference, into hostility? And would anyone even notice if it did? How many times could you repeat the same three words before they tumbled over and began to mean the opposite of what they said?

I love you.

The Good News.

Oh Heavenly Father.

After Ryan finished reading the journal, he set it on the sideboard. He could always return the book to the boy's house later, he thought, but somehow, as the months passed, he never did.

He kept working for the church, knocking on doors with his satchel and his flyers. He would walk for blocks and blocks sometimes with the shadows of the clouds coasting over him as if he were an open pasture where a puddle pierced with grass had formed beside a leaning fencepost. The rhythm of his stride made it easy to lose himself in meditation. Over and over again he found himself waking from reveries whose course he could barely follow. He was thinking about how rarely his body had failed him, how different two lives could be. He had always been healthy, had never been accident-prone, and aside from a poison ivy rash when he was in Boy Scouts and an abscessed tooth when he was twenty-three, the debilitations of sickness and injury were something he barely knew. It was not until Judy got cancer that he came to understand how illness could diminish a person and reveal her as she truly was. Sometimes he would dream that she was dying again, that he had heard her choking, had run to her bedside and watched her bring up that horrible strawberry of blood, except that the Illumination had already begun this time and her body was washed in a pitiless white light. Her pain was intermittent, like the sun flaring through a stand of trees seen from the window of a moving car, and when he finally came back to himself, he was surprised to find that it was not a dazzling spring day when he was six and she was seven, and they were not buckled into their dad's old Bronco as it whisked them down a wooded highway.

One morning, he was collecting another batch of leaflets from the church when Pastor Bradley took him aside and suggested he think about volunteering for their next mission trip. "Hear me out," he said. "Don't dismiss the idea so quickly. You're perfect for the job," and then came the words that made Ryan feel as if he were tipping over inside himself, falling through the unbearable emptiness of his years. "A forty-five-year-old man.

Never married. No kids, no parents, no siblings. It seems to me you have very little to lose."

There he stood with the heat rising slowly to his face. "I'm forty-two."

"Mmm–hmm, mmm-hmm," the pastor said, and he rested a hand on Ryan's shoulder. "Tell me, don't you think it's time you gave your life over to something bigger than yourself?"

At first, Ryan found mission work difficult. The hotel rooms with their loamy beds and broken thermostats. The hospitality houses with their pet dander and overbuttered food. The forced camaraderie and the lack of solitude. After a few years, though, he grew accustomed to the food and the company, if never to the hotel rooms, and began to take pleasure in his duties. Gradually he developed a reputation for his thoroughgoing nature, his quiet sense of responsibility. The other missionaries noticed his reluctance to testify during prayer meetings but attributed it to the modesty of his character and the hushed power of his faith. They failed to see the truth, which was that he had—or seemed to have—the religious instinct but not the religious mind-set: his intuition told him that everything mattered, everything was significant, and yet nothing was so clear to him as that life presented a riddle to which no one knew the answer. But ultimately, to his surprise, evangelism was a job like so many others, where it did not matter what you believed, only what you did. A good thing, since he had never been exactly sure what he believed. He believed in holding on. He believed in keeping up. He believed in causing as little trouble as possible, which meant, he supposed, that he believed in squeaking by. He believed in English Breakfast tea and egg-white omelettes. He believed in pocket watches and comfortable shoes. He believed in going to bed at a reasonable hour. He believed in exercising three times a week. He believed there was a mystery at the center of the great big *why-is-there-anything* called the universe, and that it did not speak to us, or not in any language we could understand, and that it was an insult to the mystery to pretend that it did. He believed nevertheless that his sister was watching him from somewhere just out of sight, that even if her affection for him had died along with her body, her attention—her interest—had not. He believed that his life would make sense to him one day. He believed there was more light, more pain, in the world than ever before. He believed that the past was better than the future would be.

For his rookie post he had been sent to Seattle, the kind of safe, prosperous city, with a healthy network of ministries and outreach programs, to which the church assigned people who needed to be eased into the work. From there he moved on to Chicago, and then to New Swanzy, Michigan. After that, every six months or so, he would find himself being transferred yet again, sometimes to the most blighted area of a large city—East St. Louis, North Philadelphia, Hunters Point in San Francisco—sometimes to a fading farm town in the Plains or the Mississippi Delta, some small cluster of fields and houses strung together by a single-pump gas station and a couple of local businesses, one a grocery store with a sign that read STORE, the other a restaurant with a sign that read RESTAURANT.

The pastor would call him aside and say, "Shifrin, you know where we could use a man of your skills?"

"Where's that?"

Seeley Lake, Montana. Or the Vine City neighborhood of Atlanta. Or Barlow, Mississippi.

And off Ryan would go, packing his bags and leaving his forwarding address with the secretary at Fellowship Bible. He knew evangelists who liked to talk about their feeling of backward homesickness, that overpowering sense of estrangement that alienated them from their friends and families and drove them into the world to spread the Gospel. Maybe, Ryan thought, he had developed his own variation of the disorder. No, he was not troubled by homesickness, of either the backward or the forward sort. He had grown used to the itinerant life, though, and no longer missed his old rootedness. What was home to him? What did it have to offer? If he had a home at all anymore, it was not a where but a when. Home was thirty-five years ago, when his parents and his sister were alive, and his bedroom walls were plastered with football posters, and his days were marked by triumph or defeat according to whether or not Becca Yeager had spoken to him at school.

He sensed that the church was grooming him for something. Seven years had passed since Pastor Bradley coaxed him into volunteering. Seven years of reflection, seven years of wandering. Seven years of trying to look through the sickness he could see in people's bodies to the sickness the Bible said lay in their souls. Every few months he was posted to a new city where his colleagues would ask him to try his hand at a different brand of missionary work. The radio ministry, the literature ministry, the church-planting ministry. It was obvious to everyone where his talents lay—he was suited to literature, not to church-planting, and certainly not to radio. No matter how chancy the neighborhood, he could walk its streets with a stack of pamphlets and spend the day safely emptying them from his hands. He could explain the messages they contained in words that were, if not convincing, then at least clear and precisely shaded. And when they had fallen out-of-date, he could rewrite them, a task he found intimidating until he realized that preparing a religious pamphlet was simply a form of collage—splice a few Bible verses together with a story or two of sin and salvation and voilà: a lesson in scripture. His true gift, it turned out, was for titles. One night he happened to hear a discussion on public radio about great works of literature and their failed early titles, and though he was listening with only half an ear, he caught the speaker saying how poorly *Gone With the Wind* would have been received if Margaret Mitchell had allowed it to remain *Tote the Weary Load*, or *A Farewell to Arms* if Hemingway had persisted in calling it *They Who Get Shot*. He examined the pamphlets that were cataloged on the church computer. The first one to meet his eye was "The Power of Prayer." Not bad, he thought, but what if it were "God's Line Is Always Open"? Next came "You Can Be Free from the Bondage to Offenses," which was—let's face it—awful. He changed it to "Which Cheek? The *Other* Cheek." And then there was "Salvation: The 5 Most Asked Questions," which, after some thought, he recast as "Go to Hell! (and How Not To)." He had done enough tampering for one night, he decided. He printed fifty copies of each pamphlet and added them the next morning to the church's literature stand.

That Wednesday, after the evening service, he discovered that the pamphlets were all gone, every last one of them. This was in Miami, at a busy Cuban church housed in the back of a thrift shop. It seemed possible that someone had simply stolen them for scrap paper. But the next day a team of missionaries took a boxful to distribute in the Art Deco district and returned to Ryan's room in less than an hour. They had already given out the entire assortment, they reported, and afterward, walking home, had found fewer than half of them in the trash cans lining Ocean Drive. "What we've got here is the milk chocolate—no, the crack cocaine—of religious tracts," someone said to Ryan. "I'm telling you, man, you should have gone into advertising."

For the next three weeks, until another call came and he was appointed to Boxholm, Iowa, everyone called him the Ad Man.

He had traveled the entire country during his seven years of service. He had visited tiny clapboard houses exiled at the ends of wooded roads. He had picked his way through hivelike clusters of bars and apartment buildings. He had driven through the countless nameless suburbs that went snowflaking out from big Midwestern cities, giant recurring patterns of green grass and smooth black asphalt. He must have been witness to tens of thousands of people, and over time he had formed an interest in the varieties of injury they displayed. He could have put together a book sorting their traumas into two separate lists on the basis of where they lived, one for the city and one for the country. *A Comparative Taxonomy of Wounds.* On any city street you could spot the pulse flares of impacted heels, in any city hospital the elongated *V*'s of stab wounds, while at any country fair, any minor-league baseball game, you would find skin cancer pocks like small clusters of stars, sprained knees like forks of lightning, dislocated shoulders like the torchlit rooms of ancient houses. People in the city exhibited the sickly luster of pollution rashes and the silver sparks of carpal tunnel syndrome, while in the country they wore the shimmering waves of home tattoo infections, the glowing white zippers of ligature abrasions. In the city you had your lungs and your stomach to distress you, in the country your skin and your liver, and everywhere, everywhere, there were the agonies of your head and your heart.

And yet somehow Ryan had escaped with barely a scratch.

He was convinced he had seen every disease imaginable, but one day he was in Brinkley, Arkansas, buying a bottle of water from a convenience store, when the girl at the cash register closed her eyes, planting her palms on the counter, and the entire armature of her skeleton showed blazing through her skin. Her lips shaped the numbers *one, two, three,* to the count of seventeen, until the pain had run its course and the light diminished.

She let the air out of her lungs and finished scanning his water bottle. Her eyes had the clarity of ice thawing in a silver tray. Nonchalantly she said, "That'll be a dollar seventeen."

Ryan was shaken. "Are you all right? Give me just a second—" The girl's full name was printed on her badge: Felenthia Lipkins. "Give me just a second, Felenthia, and I'll call the hospital."

"It's Fuh-*lin*-thia. Like Cynthia."

"Fuh-lin-thia. Would you like me to call a doctor?"

"*You* said *Felon*-thia. Black girl working at the Superstop so I've gotta be a *felon*. Is that it?"

Her voice was salted with the cheerful testiness of someone who was merely pretending to be angry, and though he was relieved that she was feeling well enough to badger him, he never knew how to react in such situations. It was as if the claim that he had offended someone, no matter how spurious, tripped a set of switches in his head. Even if he realized he was being teased and that the appropriate response was to do some teasing of his own, he could only answer squarely, with gravity and embarrassment. "Look. I'm sorry. I didn't mean to imply . . . or to infer . . . to suggest that—"

"Relax, man. I'm just funnin' with you."

"Oh. Oh, all right then."

The hot dogs revolved in their metal carousel. The drums of the frozen Coke machine made their ocean-in-a-seashell noise. Everything was spinning.

Ryan collected his water and headed for the door.

"Hey, what about that dollar seventeen?" Felenthia Lipkins called after him, and when he did an about-face she added, "Who's the felon now?"

A week or so later, he was distributing leaflets in the parking lot of a cafeteria, watching the windshield wipers snap into place like flyswatters and fix the papers to the glass, when from behind him a voice said, "Excuse me." He presumed the remark was addressed to someone else. As a rule, people avoided him while he was working. Some overburdened mother could walk outside with an armload of leftovers and three crying children at her legs, and still, if she spotted him near her car, she would linger by the building until he had moved on.

"Oh, *I* see how it is. Black girl says excuse me, and the white man won't even answer."

He swung around. It was her, Felenthia Lipkins, pronounced *fuh-lin*, not *felon*, the girl whose bones showed through her skin. She was standing with a little boy, no older than two, rubbing the luminescent blotch at the corner of his eye and repeating, "Yo, yo, what's up?" to himself, as if he had just learned the phrase and didn't want to forget it.

Felenthia cut her eyes at Ryan. "You're the guy who thought he could leave without paying for his water, aren't you?"

"And you're the girl who hates white people."

She nodded, impressed. "Touché. What are you doing with the flyers?" He handed her one from his satchel, and she read the verse printed at the top. " 'Truly the light is sweet, and a pleasant thing it is for the eyes to behold the sun. Ecclesiastes 11:7.' Well, that's fine and all," Felenthia said, "but you're forgetting Ecclesiastes 11:8: 'If a man lives many years, let him rejoice in them all, but let him remember the days of darkness, for they shall be many. All that comes is vanity.' "

"Wow. You know your scripture."

"Preacher's daughter," Felenthia admitted, and she gave the kind of speedy little dilatory curtsey that could not be mistaken for anything but a joke. "*You*, though, I wouldn't have guessed for a Christian type. Tan slacks, aftershave, gray hair in a side-cut. I was thinking businessman."

"Well, in an earlier life, I was a stockbroker."

"Uh-huh. And you made a billion dollars and stashed it away in the Cayman Islands and realized the hollowness of money so you resigned to devote yourself to—"

Which was when it happened again. She gasped, shutting her eyes, and her bones lit up. He could see them throbbing through her clothing, growing brighter with each pulse, every rib presenting itself to be counted. Her skull peered out from in back of her face. When she raised her hands to her cheeks, he saw her finger bones stacked on top of one another like the sunstruck windows of a skyscraper. Somehow she managed to support herself, though it must have been agonizing. The boy who was with her said, "Auntie Fen," then turned it into a question, "Auntie Fen?" and tugged at her skirt.

Her knees pivoted and buckled. Ryan caught her just before she fell, holding her up by the arms. Together they waited for the episode to pass. He could not read his watch, so he measured time by the signal-circuit of a traffic light: two reds and a green, and then her pain surmounted some sort of peak and the brightness faded, lingering in a last flush of milky white. A hard sweat had broken out on her face. The boy was saying, "Auntie Fen, Auntie Fen, yo, yo, what's up?" and a car was honking at the end of the aisle, and she tried to lift herself out of Ryan's arms, but in the late-July heat that made the pavement ripple like a reflection in a pool of water, her legs kept keeling out from under her.

He waited until he was sure she had gained her footing before he let go. His work with the church had taken him to a thousand hospitals and nursing homes, so many that he frequently imagined the world was nothing but patients—there were recovering patients, and there were worsening patients, and there were patients whose time had not yet come. He had witnessed the effects of tuberculosis, anthrax, and malaria, of cystic fibrosis and viral pneumonia, Huntington's and multiple sclerosis, lymphoma and dysentery. He had seen cancer after cancer, infection after infection, diseases that filled the body with bales of fluttering light and diseases that brushed lightly over the skin like snowflakes. Never before, though, had he witnessed something like this, a disease that confined itself so tightly to one system and filled it so uniformly, that blazed with such radiance and then vanished so completely. It was as if a firework had detonated in the shape of her skeleton. He could still see the afterimage on his retina. What was wrong with her, he wondered, what was she undergoing, and this time he could not stop himself from asking.

"A little indigestion," she said.

"No, seriously, what just happened to you?"

"A touch of the flu."

Clearly she wasn't going to give him an honest answer. "Do you and your son need some help getting home?"

"Nephew. And I think we'll manage."

She pointed to the one-way street that ran past the cafeteria, where an apartment building was separated from the interstate by a spinney of pine trees. On either side of the walkway, rising from the grass, stood a pair of fluted concrete pillars, their lines meant to carry the eye to heaven, but the cement had fallen loose from them in chunks, exposing veins of black rebar that absorbed the sunlight and directed the eye inward rather than upward.

"That over there," Felenthia said. "That's us."

Ryan watched her cross the road with her nephew, his great big steps and her tiny baby steps, until they reached the apartment building and disappeared behind a screen door. Then he returned to his satchel and his flyers.

That was the afternoon the pastor called him aside to tell him he was being transferred again. "Detroit. August first. Pack your bags, Brother Shifrin." The first of August was only eight days away, and Ryan presumed he would not meet the girl again, but as it happened, he saw her once more before he left town.

He was riding with one of the other missionaries through Wheatley, a small agricultural community a few miles down the highway from their hotel, when they came to a stop sign across from a swimming pool. The sky was thick with tea-colored clouds, the kind that had a yellowing effect on the landscape. The trees and bushes stood motionless to the smallest leaf. Though it was barely noon, the insects were already intoning their night songs. The pool was not crowded, and Ryan was surprised to see Felenthia sitting at the end of the diving board, reading a magazine with her elbows on her knees. She looked wholly at ease, as if she had never suffered so much as a hangnail. The boy treading water beneath her had a glittering infection in his right eye. The other boy, who did a cannonball into the deep end while Ryan sat watching from the passenger seat, wore a fresh puncture mark, a luminous crater high on the shoulder plane of his back. Felenthia swatted at the air with her magazine. She might have been shooing mosquitoes. "Y'all fools quit splashing," she said.

Ryan lost sight of her as his car pulled away. The next day, alone, he swung into the Superstop where she worked and found the gas pumps disconnected. Someone had nailed a sheet of plywood over the door, writing across it in big handpainted letters, CLOSED DUE TO VANDALISM, ROBBERY, AND THE "CROOKS!!" AT PATTERSON INSURANCE. He went over to the window and peered inside. The damage was considerable. Most of the shelves had been overturned. The microwave was missing its door. The cash register was lying busted in a pool of blank lottery tickets. The soda dispenser had been torn from its cords and hoses, staining the wall with plumes of dark brown syrup. The road maps and potato chips, Starlite mints and charcoal briquettes, had all been swept into a reef beneath the shattered glass of the freezers. Suddenly it seemed to Ryan that he had looked out over this same vista a million times before, as if he were a rich man and these broken machines every morning were the city that greeted him as he stood at his penthouse window. He found the feeling hard to shake.

Gradually he would forget nearly everything about Brinkley, Arkansas, just as he had forgotten nearly everything about the dozens of other small towns he had visited over the years, but for the rest of his life, every time he saw a skeleton chandeliering its way down a stand in a biology classroom, he would think of the girl whose bones fluoresced with pain. He never did find out what was wrong with her.

In the unseasonably warm October that followed Ryan's fifty-sixth birthday, he received a letter from the Greater Council of Evangelical Churches thanking him for his fourteen years of service and asking him to give some thought to accepting a post in Ouagadougou, the capital of Burkina Faso, right in the middle of the 10/40 Window. He would be working in the literature ministry, the letter said, consulting with a team of African Christians who were translating the Bible into a local trading language called Dioula. "May God continue to bless you, Brother Shifrin," the last paragraph read, "and may we ask that you give this matter your timely and most prayerful consideration."

Prayerful consideration: that was the phrase that did it. It was one of his sister's pet expressions, and no matter how often he heard it, it always seemed to ring with the sound of her voice.

Dear Lord, we come to You with prayerful consideration.

Well, I've given it some prayerful consideration, and I have to disagree with you there, Ryan.

Look, it failed the first time around, and the second time, too, so let me ask you, Dr. Bragg, with all prayerful consideration, why on earth would I put myself through chemotherapy again?

And so, because Ryan was willing to indulge the idea that there was a path laid out for him and it would be a mistake not to follow it, and because he knew what Judy would have done, he accepted the church's invitation.

On his first day in Ouagadougou, he took a taxi from the airport to the hospitality house. The driver's English was heavily accented, his words popping and rounding in on themselves like water pouring through a concrete pipe. Ryan's brain lagged a few seconds behind in deciphering them, as when he asked what Ryan was doing in Burkina Faso. "Ah fume first of all?"

"Pardon?"

"The film festival, yeah?"

"Ah. No. I'm here on business. With the church."

"The church. Christian, yeah? Not Muslim."

"That's right. Christian, not Muslim."

The driver fell silent as a squadron of polished red and green motorbikes buzzed past him. Soon he pulled to a stop and said something about "the varieties of Heaven." After a moment, Ryan was able to remodel the remark into, "The ride is over, sir." His own misheard version of the words lingered with him, though, and as the months passed, he found himself considering their implications. What was Heaven, he wondered, and what were its varieties? He envisioned a system of countless Heavens, each assembled according to the desires of the person to whom

God graced it. A Heaven of immaculate brushed metal planes. A Heaven of cheeseburgers and big-breasted redheads.

The Burkinabè were developing a new, more colloquial translation of the Bible, modeled after the Contemporary Living Version that had become so popular recently in America. Ryan's colleagues worked with a swift good humor, completing ten to twelve pages a day. There was Souleymane Ouedraogo, a small, courtly man with the gentle speaking cadences and arched hairline of an economics professor; his wife, Assetou, who carried herself like a lamppost, with the rigid back and flexile neck of a woman who was so eager to articulate her thoughts that her body had evolved into nothing more than a structure to prop up her head; and then there was David Barro, barely out of his teens, an amiably bedraggled boy who always had crumbs on his shirt and smelled of the French bakery above which he kept his room. For Souleymane, Ryan imagined a Heaven of ocean waves the texture of long-haired mink. For Assetou, he imagined a Heaven of polite conversations in candlelit restaurants. David Barro, he was sure, would choose the Heaven he had already been given, a Heaven of good looks and youthful well-being and the aroma of bread baking forever in stone ovens.

Ryan was there to assist the three of them with the nuances of conversational English. Often his efforts to clarify some detail of the American vernacular amused them for reasons he did not understand, as when he attempted to explain a verse from the Song of Solomon with the words "making out, you know, heavy petting," and they exchanged stares with one another, struggling to keep their lips twisted shut, then burst into spirited laughter. Little by little he forged a real friendship with them. The Christianity they practiced was colored by the animism that was their cultural heritage, just as his own Christianity, he was sure, was colored by his middle-class Western heritage, a heritage of—

what? Good taste. Christmas gifts. Summer barbeques. But he was curious about their beliefs, and for the first time in his decade and a half of mission work, he did not reproach himself for adopting an anthropologist's stance toward the subtleties of their faith. Often, after they had finished the day's pages, he would join them for a drink, following them around the corner to a posh little bar with casement windows and shea-wood tables. Ryan would quiz them: Did the people of Burkina Faso believe that animals had souls? What about plants, stones, rivers, houses? And if they did have souls, were they capable of suffering? Could the Earth itself suffer? If we wounded it gravely enough, would it burst into light? *No, of course not,* David Barro would answer, chuckling lightly, or, *Yes, of course,* Souleymane would say, shaking his head at Ryan's credulousness, and in return they would ask him various questions about America—how many guns he owned or what his local theme park was named. Every so often, the waiter whose job it was to collect the bottles from the tables would come by and slip their empties into the large front pocket of his apron, striding away with a heavy clinking sound.

For the first time since he was a teenager, Ryan felt the joy and surprise of discovering a whole new set of friends. He looked back fondly on the days when he had to force himself to rehearse their names so he wouldn't forget them. Souleymane. Assetou. David Barro.

The three of them were working on the final chapters of Ezekiel the day the bomb propelled a thousand spurs of metal through their bodies. Ryan was returning from a coffee run when it happened. He stood across the street from the building they all shared, waiting for a gap in the stream of cars and bicycles, and a heavy percussive boom washed over him, and he flinched. At first, he imagined the sound was a lightning strike. The blast was so loud that it temporarily interrupted his hearing—only slowly did the din of horns and engines filter back into the silence. When he lifted his head, he saw a black, almost liquid smoke billowing from the windows of his office. Horrified, he rushed into the street, thinking that he could rescue the others if only he made it to them in time, but a dozen of the city's ubiquitous red and green motorbikes suddenly sped past and forced him to return to the curb.

It wouldn't have made any difference. The building was too hot to enter. By the time the rescue workers extinguished the fire and made their way through the pool of retardant foam, uncovering the table that Souleymane shared with David Barro, their bodies had already fallen dark and stopped moving. Only Assetou remained alive. Ryan watched as they carried her outside on a spinal board, a cataract of light pouring out of the hole where her knee had been. She died a few moments after the sun touched her skin.

What had happened? Slowly, over the next few weeks, the local paper *Le Pays* revealed the story. Unknown agents had apparently loaded a coffee can with thumbtacks, aluminum powder, and liquid nitroglycerine and placed it on a shelf along the front wall of the office. No timer was recovered, no trembler. The investigators' working hypothesis was that the mixture had exploded when someone removed the lid to inspect the can's contents, though it might just as easily have detonated when a shaft of sunlight struck it and raised the temperature, or even when the shelf was jostled by a passing lorry. Much was made of the fact that the office had housed a group of evangelical Christians. A police spokesperson speculated that the bomb had been planted, as similar devices had been, by the small anti-Christian wing of the country's Muslim majority, "ailing and impoverished," the reporter wrote, "visible in increasing numbers, wearing the familiar red and green of Burkina's national colors."

The incident faded quickly from the headlines. The few articles that mentioned Ryan neglected to provide his name, referring to him instead as "the surviving American." And that was how he began to think of himself.

The Surviving American was reluctant to leave his bed in the morning.

The Surviving American lived on a diet of breakfast cereal and millet beer.

The Surviving American spent his nights waking at the slightest sound—a door slamming, an engine coughing—and his days feeling guilty that he had somehow let his friends down by failing to die with them.

The work they had completed was gone, lost in the blaze. The computers and flash drives. The boxes and boxes of notebooks. The ten thousand ink-stained pages where they had put the verses so painstakingly through their variations. And the faces of the dead could be forgotten so quickly. And it was autumn and life was going by. And why should he ever bother to learn a person's name again?

When the church offered to send him to Tunisia, he accepted. He neglected to visit the doctor for his inoculations or to pick up the pills that had been recommended to him. Let what would take him take him, he thought, and six months later, in the city of Sfax, he was walking along a tiled avenue lined with fragrant olive trees when the earth seemed to tilt out of his reach. He reached for an iron post and stumbled to his knees. He was sure he had taken ill, contracted typhoid or malaria or one of the hundred other North African diseases the guidebooks had warned him against. Schistosomiasis. Dengue fever. Then he noticed all the others who had fallen down, a cityful of men and women waiting on all fours as the ground lurched and trembled. All around him the plate-glass windows of the shops and restaurants

burst. The street tiles in their neat rows of yellow and red separated and fell clattering on top of one another. Several of the craft
vendors' carts went rolling and galloping across the sidewalk,
crushing their broad linen umbrellas as they canted over. He
heard buildings cracking along their foundations—it was a sound
he recognized, but how? The roof of a nearby school lifted and
resettled, a first time and then a second, and finally collapsed in
a cloud of white dust that burgeoned into the air and rained down
over the street like chalk, turning to paste in his mouth. There
was a series of crashes, and he turned to see the luxury hotel at
the corner dropping chunks of masonry. One of the chunks
crushed a fruit display. Another snapped a power line, which
went snaking over the rooftops of the cars, throwing off sparks.
Then the entire side wall of the hotel tipped outward in a single
piece and smashed against the pavement like a ceramic plate. He
glimpsed what he thought was a woman clinging to a set of curtains as it toppled. As suddenly as it had started, the earthquake
ceased, its dying tremors dislodging the last few icicles of glass
from the window of a pastry shop. The people around him were
slow to gain their feet. Ryan could hear them cursing in French
and Arabic, could see the light from their broken bones, but aside
from a coruscating blood bruise that had emerged on one of his
knees, he himself was uninjured.

   Two years later, in Indonesia, he was driving through a strip
of shanties along the coast of Sumatra when a block of water
surged over the lowlands, sweeping them flat like an arm clearing a table. The wave took his car, spun it around, and delivered
it upright onto the shoulder of a nearby hill. He held tight to the
steering wheel while the water drained from his floorboards. As
soon as he was certain the ground beneath him was not going to
rise up and carry him away, he pressed the ignition button on his

dashboard, but the motor wouldn't start. He stepped out of the car onto a mat of rattan canes and walked slowly back toward the ocean, picking his way through the wreckage of the country-side: television aerials with drenched flags of clothing wrapped around them, uprooted palms turning their pedestals of earth to the sky. The shanties alongside the road had been reduced to rubble. Through the stones and the sheets of corrugated tin he saw the scraps of a hundred bodies, their lesions and gashes piercing the air with the precise iridescent silver of a mirror catching a headlamp. A few dozen people were limping through the debris, throwing tree branches, baking pans, and strips of plywood off the piles, trying to dig free the buried. Ryan attempted to help them. Some of the lights beneath his hands kept glowing, while others flared out suddenly. Where were they going? To a Heaven of clean white bathrooms with hot and cold running water. A Heaven of knowing, just for a while, how it felt to be rich and healthy.

The next summer, in Costa Rica, he agreed to take a quartet of visiting Spanish missionaries to the final match of the Copa América series, the first major event the stadium had held since its remodeling. Ryan was at the outer ring buying souvenir programs for his guests, listening to the crowd do its stomp-stomp-clap routine, when the midfield stands collapsed. A tide of brown dust went pouring through the entrance bays, tempo-rarily blinding him. The air was filled with moans and screams, electronic feedback, the occasional gunlike reports of wooden buttresses cracking. As soon as Ryan had regained his sight, he shouldered his way past a security guard, under a sign that read SECCIÓN FI A JI2. The walkway ended at a set of twisted handrails extending over a twenty-foot chasm, a man-made canyon of folding chairs and cinder blocks. A woman in a loose black dress had been thrown against the wall while she was leaving. Not since his weeks in Brinkley, Arkansas, had Ryan seen someone whose bones shone so fiercely through her clothing. The stacked blocks of her vertebrae. The strangely shaped elephant's ears of her pelvis. The jumbled gravel piles of her wrists. All around him voices were shouting, "Doctor, doctor." He was surprised to realize his own was doing the same.

It was September of the next year when he finally returned to the United States. He began serving from a small church between a Laundromat and a cashew chicken restaurant in Springfield, Missouri. The Ozarks passed through a beautiful warm autumn, then an icy winter, then a gray and moody spring. The dogwoods blossomed with tiny singed-looking flowers that came down all at once after a single weekend. Ryan was handing out New Testaments from a little knoll on the university's commons one day when a strange light seeped into the sky and the sirens began to wail. He took shelter with several hundred college students in the campus bookstore, crouching in the social sciences aisle and listening to the speakers rustle with white noise. The tornado touched down over them once, for only a few seconds, as fastidiously as a finger pressing an ant into the dirt, and destroyed the building. Ryan covered his head as the textbooks opened their spines and whirled around him, smacking into the walls and floor like birds who had lost control of their wings. All he could hear was the freight-train sound of the wind racing through its circles. Then, in the darkness and silence, he opened his eyes. The two blocks of shelves he was kneeling between had listed into each other, forming a gablelike roof over his head. He crawled into the ruins of the bookstore and rose to his feet. Everywhere there were bodies, radiating from their hands and legs, chests and genitals, faces and stomachs. Their flesh presented a star-map of wounds, glorious and incomprehensible. He felt like a man from some ancient tribal legend who had angered the gods and been doomed to walk the constellations.

Sometimes, late at night, he would find himself reminiscing about the disasters he had lived through, the tornado and the earthquake, the tsunami and the nitroglycerine bomb, and a voice in his head would insist, *The Lord must be looking out for you. Sixty-four years and never a major illness. Sixty-eight years and still going strong. Seventy years and seventy-one and seventy-two and seventy-three . . .* and he would say to himself: *No.* One word: *No.* He did not believe—and who could?—in a God so hawk-eyed and brutal, a God who bestowed a cancer here, a deformity there, for you a septic embolism and for you a compound fracture, selecting one person for grief and another for happiness like a painter experimenting with degrees of light and shadow. And which was the light, he wondered, and which the shadow? If the trials of Job could be a sign of God's favor, then couldn't Ryan's own good fortune be a sign of God's hostility? Maybe the crippled, the bruised, the diseased, the damaged—maybe the reason their wounds shone in this world was because God was lending them His attention from the next, looking on with loving compassion or a cultivated interest in suffering. Compassion. A cultivated interest in suffering. Compassion. A cultivated interest in suffering. Those were the possibilities that played across Ryan's mind as he lay in bed watching the darkness conduct its usual late-night scintillations. He listened to the legs of an insect ticking across the floor of his bedroom. Say that God's attention was a product of His sympathy: well, then our pain came first, and it brought His gaze, and from His gaze arose the luminosity of our suffering: $y + z = a$. Say, on the other hand, that God's attention was a product of His esteem for certain forms of afflicted beauty:

then our pain came first, and it brought with it the luminosity of our suffering, which summoned His gaze: $y + a = z$. One was the cause and the other the effect, one a and the other z, though either way, our pain came first, our pain was inescapable, our pain was always y. What frightened Ryan—horrified him—was not the possibility that God did not love us but that He did love us and His love was merely decorative. Aesthetic rather than unconditional. That He loved us because we suffered, and our suffering was pleasing to His eyes. The Illumination had overturned all the old categories of thought. For a while Ryan had believed, along with the crystal healers and the televangelists, that the light that had come to their injuries would herald a new age of reconciliation and earthly brotherhood. You would think that taking the pain of every human being and making it so starkly visible—every drunken headache and frayed cuticle, every punctured lung and bowel pocked with cancer—would inspire waves of fellow feeling all over the world, or at least ripples of pity, and for a while maybe it had, but now there were children who had come of age knowing nothing else, running to their mothers to have a Band-Aid put on their flickers, asking, *Why is the sky blue?* and, *Why does the sun hurt?*, and still they grew into their destructiveness, and still they learned whose hurt to assuage and whose to disregard, and still there were soldiers enough for all the armies of the world. And every war left behind the shrapnel scars and shattered limbs of a hundred thousand ruined bodies. And every earthquake and every hurricane produced a holocaust of light. And when his sister died she had looked at him with the panic of someone who had no idea what was coming next. And when his friends in Burkina Faso died their wounds seemed to flood the sky. And the gun shops and munitions factories were as plentiful as blades of grass. And the emergency rooms were as full as they had ever been. And there were towns in the great open middle of the country where the cemeteries outnumbered the churches. And in the hockey stands and the boxing arenas, a cheer went up with every split lip, every burst capillary. And in the video games the schoolkids played, the aliens erupted in geysers of blood and golden tinsel. And in the tent cities and domestic violence shelters, the poor and the beaten huddled over their sores and bruises, cradling them like fussy children. And Ryan felt that he had spent his life in a darkened room, groping for meaning or at least consolation. And so, it seemed to him, had everyone else. And their bodies were aging and one day they would fail altogether. And every heart would be soaked in brightness. And every brain would burn out like an ember. And there was God, high on His throne, attending to the whole terrible procession of sorrows and traumas, corrosions and illnesses, with a cool, cerebral dispassion. He took His notes. He never uttered a syllable. He had the whole world, all the little children, you and me, brother, in His hands. And it seemed to Ryan that He viewed their bodies as a doctor would—so many sorry aging structures of blood and tissue, each displaying its own particular debility. Their wounds were majestic to Him, their tumors and lacerations. And perhaps it had always been that way. Perhaps the light He had brought to their injuries, or allowed the world to bring, was simply a new kind of ornamentation. The jewelry with which He decorated His lovers. The oil with which He anointed His sons. *The Earth was crammed with Heaven, and every common bruise afire with God, but only he who saw took off his shoes.* And if that was the case, Ryan thought, if it was our suffering that made us beautiful to God, and if that was why He allowed it to continue, then how dare He, how dare He, and why, why, why, why, why? He loved us, or so He said, but what did His love mean? What was it good for? It didn't change anything, it didn't improve anything, it only lingered in the distance, fluttering like a bird around the margins of their wretchedness. It was a sad little robin of a word, His "love." It fled at the first sign of cold weather. Its bones were hollow and filled with air. Anyone could see how feeble it was, how insubstantial. How wrong. And here was the question that kept Ryan awake at night: Was it possible for God to sin? Or were God and sin the opposite poles of a binary system? Was sin whatever God was not—the cold to God's warmth, the darkness to God's light? Or was it stationary, absolute, and was God as capable of venturing into it as anyone else? Because it seemed to Ryan that if God could sin, and if their suffering was as needless as it appeared, and if He had permitted or even abetted it, then His love had soured into hatred, and He should take to His knees and repent. Never mind the foundations of the earth. Never mind the morning stars singing together. Never mind the sea shut up with doors. He had formed His children, endowed them with the breath of life, and set them free in a world of poison and fire. Of endless diseases and natural disasters. Floods and landslides. Volcanic eruptions. A world of spinal meningitis. Of cerebral palsy. Of neurochemical imbalances that made the weakest among people hate having to exist. Of genetic disorders that blanketed their skin in ulcers. Could He see them in their pain? Was He awake at all behind the lit windows of Heaven? For this was the hope that Ryan found himself nursing—that God had merely gone to sleep for a while and was not paying attention, that the glass of Heaven was dark, and the curtains were drawn, and the suffering of humankind was like the sunlight that gradually suffused the sky in the morning. And maybe, Ryan thought, that was all there was to it. Maybe the hour was still too early. Maybe they hadn't yet suffered enough to rouse Him from His bed. A little more pain, a little more light, a few more blows and afflictions, and God would stretch His limbs and waken to the grand celestial daybreak. And the Earth would experience its restoration. And everything would be changed. The older Ryan became, the more the notion preoccupied him. He lay beneath his sheets watching the dim plane of the ceiling. Inside it he could see the same hallucination he had seen ever since he was a child forcing his eyes to make sense of the darkness, a thousand lambent spots that leaped and circled around one another like the static on an ancient television. And he knew that if he stared at them long enough they would come together as they always had, in a single overlapping field of Catherine wheels and carousels.

In the fourth decade of the Illumination, shortly after Ryan's eighty-first birthday, he was selecting an orange from a display at the supermarket when a whistle rang in his ears, beginning with a greaselike sizzle, then rising slowly and leveling off. Suddenly the floor was cool against his cheek. Dozens of oranges were rolling around him like billiard balls. He did not remember lying down, but he must have. The woman hovering over him said, "Are you all right? Took a little spill there, didn't you, sir?" and though he could see the arthritis shining in her fingers like a string of pearls, she gripped his hand to help him stand up.

Maybe that was when it started, or maybe it was a few days earlier, when he lost track of himself while taking his afternoon walk and regained his thoughts wandering through the lobby of an office building several blocks away, but soon Ryan realized that something had happened to his mind. It became difficult for him to distinguish the past from the present. He could no longer be sure he knew where he was. One minute he might be an old man waiting in line at the bank to make a cash withdrawal, and the next he would be nine years old and in Miss Fitzgerald's music class, sitting crisscross applesauce between Jeffrey Campbell and Jessica Easto, angry that the instrument box had been nearly empty by the time it reached him, which meant that he had gotten stuck—again!—with the rhythm sticks instead of the hand drums. He might be jimmying a spoon under the lid of a jar and look up to see the sun shining on a snowcapped Russian mountain, or clouds breaking over the Gulf of Mexico, or the moon wavering in the bug-stitched mirror of the lake where his college girlfriend kept her cabin. He could never tell. Or perhaps he would be watching the palm trees streak past his windshield, flinching at their trunks as the wave spun his car in circle after circle, then find himself attending an air-conditioned Midwestern church service where someone he could not recollect having met, a pastor with the pliant, swaying voice of a yoga instructor, was offering a sermon in celebration of his retirement from the mission. That was where he seemed to be right now: the church.

"We are here today not only to worship the Lord," the pastor said, "but to pay tribute to a man who has dedicated his life to His service, Brother Ryan Shifrin," and that was *him*, Ryan thought, *he* was Brother Ryan Shifrin. And his sister was Sister Judy Shifrin, and his father was Father Donald Shifrin, and his mother was Mother Sarah Beth Shifrin, and his dog was Scamper Shifrin—Scamp for short—and there she came bounding across the lawn with her tongue lolling over her lips, the tag on her collar jingling like a sleigh bell.

"Scamp! Scamper! Here, girl!"

Either she did not hear him, or Ryan merely imagined he had called out, because she disappeared beneath the pulpit, and when she reemerged, she was not his dog but Mr. Castillo's, Max—no, Trinket—barking and lunging at the pastor's vestments. And then there was no dog in the church at all. The stained-glass window was casting its tinted shapes onto the carpet. The communion rail was riddled with plum-size holes. The banner on the pulpit read, I LOVE THE HOUSE WHERE YOU LIVE, O LORD, THE PLACE WHERE YOUR GLORY DWELLS, and for the first time in years, Ryan thought of the beaten journal of love notes the boy with the bruised backside had given him a few days ago.

I love driving to the bluff and drinking cheap red wine out of paper cups with you.

I love how beautifully you sing when you think no one is listening.

I love it when the computer freezes up or we get stuck in a traffic jam and you lean back and pull out your old "Ahhh! This is the life!" routine.

When had he lost it, he wondered, where had he left it behind?

"Now, some of you may not know this," the pastor was saying, "but Brother Shifrin has been working for the church in one capacity or another for more than forty years. Kids, that's longer than some of your parents have been alive. You may not believe it"—he patted his chest—"but that's longer than old Pastor Wallace himself has been alive."

Ryan was sitting at the outside corner of the left front pew, directly beneath the giant black box speaker on its crossed metal stilts. The altar was lined with Easter lilies. He couldn't wait to start high school next fall, and his hip was aching with a soft lucidity, and his hands were stained with liver spots and petechial hemorrhages, but that did not keep him from catching the Frisbee his scoutmaster was throwing through the crisp November air, nor from knocking on a hundred doors each afternoon with his satchel and his leaflets, though he confessed he found it hard these days to tie his shoelaces and operate his telephone, and he had been away from home now for such a long time.

It seemed to him that he had grown old not in the usual way, day by day, but in a series of sudden jerks. His sister died, and ten years fell on his shoulders. The flames burst from the building in

Ouagadougou, and down came another twenty. The street tiles cracked, the stadium collapsed, the shanties were flattened, and the years fell over him like rain.

Why had he never married or fathered children?

He wanted a Heaven of starting over, a Heaven of trying again.

The pastor was speaking gently into the microphone. "And when you listen to the testimonials I've received, I am sure you will say to yourself, as I have, Truly, this is a man whose work has been blessed by the Lord. For what better life can we imagine than a life of Christian service, a life of waiting upon the Creator and His beloved children? Before I read the first of these letters to you, though, I'd like to ask that you all please rise and join me in a song that exemplifies the spirit with which Brother Shifrin has dedicated himself to the church, number two hundred fifteen in our hymnal, 'Teach Me Lord to Wait.' "

As the organ resounded and the benches creaked, Ryan thought of his sister: how she had loved to sing, and how young she had been when she relinquished her life, and how assiduously he had taken it up and lived it.

What do you think, Judy? What do you make of that? Did I keep it warm enough for you?

Now the worshippers were on their feet, performing a hymn he knew by heart, their voices flowing just alongside the melody, as if tracing the banks of a stream. And if a bomb were to land on them as they sang so humbly and sincerely, the splendor of their bodies would bathe the town in silver. And if every bomb flew from its arsenal, every body displayed its pain, the globe would catch fire in a Hiroshima of light. And maybe, from somewhere far away, God would notice it and return, and the cinders would receive Him like a hillside washed in the sun.

Nina Poggione

"You quarrel with your sickness," Thomas said calmly. "Everyone has a sickness. It should be cared for but not cured."

"What?" Pearl said dully. She wished that he would pour more wine. Thomas' way of talking made her dizzy.

"I said, each of us has a sickness. It is not something that should be cured. To eradicate the sickness would be to eradicate the self."

—Joy Williams

She was in Seattle, at the bookstore across from the university, with the high windows and the wooden chairs and the microphone that lent a floating electric quality to her voice, and *The Age of Girls and Boys* kept creaking as she flexed its spine, and her mouth was shedding a raw white light that sharpened to a knifepoint every time her lips came together, and she could see that she had wrested the audience's attention, their genuine attention, though whether they were listening to her or watching the light show was anyone's guess, and there in the second row, sitting with his tousled hair and his loose-necked posture, was the man who had approached her the night before, at the event in Bellingham, to sign a galley proof of *Off-Campus Apartments*, her sad sunken ship of a first novel. She could hear him reacting to the story she was reading, making half-voiced subliminal noises of agreement or fascination, chuckling when she mentioned the widow's inexplicable accent, and nodding vigorously, *gymnastically*, as if choosing sides in a debate, at "the world, the good and beautiful world, where people got married and had children and slowly grew old together." Was he experiencing his feelings or merely demonstrating them? She couldn't decide. Afterward, he made sure to claim the last spot in line, mothing away to investigate the new releases, when a woman with a tote bag fell into place behind him, then drifting back over to the procession. She had already autographed twenty or thirty books by the time he reached her.

He took a copy of *Girls and Boys* from the stack and said, "Hi there again. I was at that thing you did last night. Remember? The guy who said you were his favorite writer?"

She tried her best to smile without using her mouth—to *express* a smile—but even that was difficult. The ulcer on her lower lip was stinging, stinging terribly. She felt as if someone had taken the flesh, right there where her incisors met, and run it through a sewing machine: *zt–zt–zt–zt–zt.*

Before she could steel herself to answer, he hurried on: "Anyway, what I neglected to tell you yesterday is that I absolutely love this collection. Love. It. Especially 'Small Bitter Seeds.' That one's my favorite. I read it in the *Pushcart,* and afterward I ordered all your books. *Everything.*"

To talk meant to suffer, as it had for much of the last four years, and she had become practiced at finding the most efficient path through a conversation. Usually she could touch all the major landmarks so glancingly and yet so deftly that the average person failed to notice she was even taking a shortcut. "Thank you. I knew you looked familiar. That was actually the title story until my editor told me no one would buy a book called *Small Bitter Seeds.* Now how would you like me to sign this?"

"Oh, this one's for my father. Write, 'To Jon Catau.' That's *J-o*-no *h-n,* and then Ka-too: *C-a-t-a-u.*"

After she finished the inscription and shut the book, she found him staring over her shoulder. The windows crowning the poetry shelves were filtering the light so that the trees outside, the lampposts, the buildings, all seemed to swim in blue Easter egg dye, but that wasn't what had caught his attention. He was examining his reflection in the glass, and specifically the incandescent bruise on his arm. Gaze too long at your wounds, she had discovered, and your eyes would fill with phantom colors, like a sunbather drowsing on a beach towel.

One of the booksellers was repeating her name. "Ms. Poggione? Excuse me. Ms. Poggione?"

"Mm-hmm?"

"We were hoping you would sign some stock before you leave. And also we have this guest album with a page for all our authors. Would you mind writing something in it for us? Nothing fancy— just a few words will do."

He slid the books across the table one by one, like a line cook prepping burgers, marking each title page with the jacket flap so that all she had to do was take a copy from his hand, cross through her name, and replace it with her signature. In the guest album she wrote, "Thanks for hosting me on this, the final leg of the great spring *Age of Girls and Boys* tour." She added a doodle of a girl boosting a boy over her head like a circus strongman. The man with the bruise on his arm had withdrawn to the sanctuary of the employee recommendations shelf, but when she began gathering up her purse and jacket, he came loping back over to the table. With a sudden sweeping feeling of magnification she intuited that he was going to ask her to dinner, and in fact he did, forcing himself to meet her eye, then saying something that began, "I hope you don't mind," and ended, "a great little seafood place, the best in Seattle." He was certainly sweet enough—a sweet, brave kid, and starstruck, by *her,* of all people—but the truth was that it hurt too much to talk, and she just wanted to return to her room and lie in bed with a mouthful of hydrogen peroxide foaming up over her gums.

"That's very nice, but I'm afraid I'm not feeling well."

"Oh. All right. I understand completely." Meekly he asked, "So at least can I give you a ride back to your hotel?" Maybe it was the way his voice seemed to slip through the center of itself and form a knot, so like Wallace's when he thought he had embarrassed himself, but she realized all at once that she could not disappoint him again. She resigned herself to another ten minutes of conversation and nodded fine, okay.

"Great! I'm parked out back."

He led her down the staircase and across the ground floor, past circular racks stuffed with purple and gold sweatshirts, shelves stuffed with pennants and soda cozies, and out into the evening, which was not blue at all but a soft, waning pink. The floorboards of his car were littered with textbooks and old CD cases, the carpets gritty with road salt. As he drove her across the bay, he spun an excitable little monologue, telling her about the inlet they were passing, where his friends Coop and Mia kept their catamaran, and the neighborhood off to the right, where his favorite coffee shop was located, and not far away, near the arboretum, was the unpainted furniture store where he had worked after high school for eighteen months, while he "decompressed," he said, "and figured the whole thing out," and there up ahead you could see the car wash with the elephant sign, a smiling neon behemoth hosing itself down with its trunk, which was his very favorite car wash—easily, no contest.

It took an effort of will to interrupt him. "You live in a wide world of favorites, don't you?"

"That's what Coop says. I guess I do."

"So how did you hurt your arm?"

He searched the sagging cloth of the ceiling for an answer. "You know, I honestly can't remember. Bumped into a doorway. Got punched."

He slid into the turning lane at a red light and leveled his gaze at her. "But *that*," he said, and he tugged his lip down to display the tissue, a healthy rose color, unlit by trauma or disease, "must hurt like all hell."

Impulsively she grazed the ragged fringe of her sore with her tongue. It flashed the way a shard of glass does when it's struck by the sun. "Mm-hmm. Like all hell."

"Yeah, I can totally tell. You know, I really respect you. My football coach—don't worry, I'm not one of those football guys. I quit when I was in eighth grade. But what my coach used to say is that you've got to play through the pain. And that's what *you* do. It must be hard to get up in front of an audience and talk when your mouth is like it is."

And that was her situation exactly. There were entire weeks when she did everything she could to avoid speaking to other people: letting her voice mail take her phone calls, using the self-service lane at the grocery store, waiting for the UPS truck to drive away before she collected her packages. The problem began shortly after the Illumination, when she punctured her soft palate with a tortilla chip. With fascination and disgust, she watched over the next few days as the mark sank into her skin and filled with a luminous fluid. It took nearly two weeks for it to heal, by which time she had generated another by jabbing her gums while brushing her teeth. After that the wounds came in clusters, appearing whenever she bit the inside of her mouth or ate something too salty or spicy, but just as often for no reason whatsoever, or at least none she could determine. At first she thought the problem was only temporary, but four years had passed since then, and she had not gotten any better. Four years of withdrawing from her friends, her son, her parents, of declining to go on dates because she couldn't bear to pretend she was all right. Four years of pinprick-size cavities on her lips and her gums, her cheeks and the roof of her mouth, on the tender border of her tongue, tiny inflamed holes that expanded slowly and clotted at their edges, then whitened, distended, and lost all form. Some of the sores grew as large as nickels, flooding her face with light even when her lips were clamped shut. No sooner did one vanish than another would appear. Often, when things were at their worst—when she came into morning thinking she might have healed while she slept and gave the spot where one of her ulcers had been an experimental tap and felt so ill with pain that her hands tightened and the wells beneath her eyes grew damp—she would find herself repeating, *Why me, why do I have to be sick all the time, what possible purpose could it serve? And why* this *sickness, why* this *pain, why not some other? Take my eyes so that I cannot see. Take my legs so that I cannot run. Anything, anything, but my mouth so that I cannot speak, my mouth so that I cannot eat, my mouth so that I cannot kiss, my mouth so that I cannot smile. Make me better. Make me better. Make me better. Make me better. Or at least make me better tomorrow than I am today, make me better next week than I've been this one.* This was the voice in her head, a veritable Niagara of words, pouring over one another in their own immense cloud of turbulence and spindrift, but trailing alongside it was her other voice, her speaking voice, the one her ulcers had forced her to adopt, which employed as little motion as possible, so that she wound up rejecting even the shortest words in favor of easier ones, saying *mm-hmm* for *yes* and *mm-mmm* for *no,* and obliged her to take great care with every sentence she uttered so that avoiding her lesions would not distort her pronunciation. She was afraid that the voice she used in public would change the voice she used in the privacy of her thoughts, that fluid, unfearing voice with which she had once written her books. Presuming, of course, that it had not already. Your mind was not free of your body. That was the lesson.

"Well, this is it, Ms. Poggione," the boy said, and she realized they had reached the hotel.

"Thanks. What's your name now?"

"John Catau."

"I thought that was your father's name."

"It is. I'm a junior, or unofficially I am. My dad is Jon Catau: *J-o*-no *h-n*. I'm John Catau: *J-o*-with an *h-n*."

"Well, John-with-an-*h*, you can call me Nina."

"Nina." He took her wrist, rubbing his thumb along the pulse point as if he were calming an injured animal, and she understood what she should have all along: that he was hitting on her. His touch was warmer and more muscular than she had supposed it would be. "Are you sure I can't buy you a drink?" he said.

She risked stretching her mouth to smile at him. "Some other time." And she opened the door and went into the hotel.

Upstairs, standing at her bathroom mirror, she drew her lower lip cautiously away from her teeth. The flesh sent out a spike of pain, shimmering as she exposed it to the open air. She had ruptured some fragile seal over the sore, and blood came brimming from the threadlike crack, spilling into the pocket of her gums. Though the edges of the canker had softened, she knew from experience that it would get worse before it got better.

She sat on the ledge of the tub and made her ritual evening phone call. Wallace didn't answer, so she left him a message. Each time her lips came together or her teeth bit into a letter, she had that terrible sewing-needle sensation. She tried to conceal her discomfort, but the effort gave her voice an oddly convulsive sedative quality, as if her limbs were twitching while she slept:

"Hey, honey. I know you ha*v*e *p*lay rehearsal tonight, *b*ut I'*m* wi*p*ed out, and I'*m* going to slee*p*, so I'*m* calling early. Your *m*o*mm*a lo*v*es you. I ho*p*e you had a *p*er*f*ect day. Don't *b*urn the house down. Re*m*e*mb*er, the Stegalls are right next door i*f* you can't reach *m*e and there's an e*m*ergency."

She hung up. For the thousandth time, she reflected that she should write a story that used no *b*'s, *f*'s, *m*'s, *p*'s, or *v*'s, one she could deliver without aggravating her mouth. "A Story to Combat the Pain," she would call it.

But what if it wasn't her lips that were ulcerated?

She would have to write a second story to avoid her hard palate, one without any *c*'s, *d*'s, *g*'s, *h*'s—oh so many letters.

And a third that would let the tip of her tongue lie still, a story that was all vowels and labials, unspooling with a long underwater sound.

So then: "*Three* Stories to Combat the Pain."

She washed her face and brushed her teeth, all but the bottom incisors, then changed into her pajamas and slipped into bed. Four more days of readings, she thought. Four more airplanes to four more cities. She wondered how Wallace was doing without her. Had he remembered to lock the door? Was he eating the food she had Tupperwared? He was the kind of boy who would nibble at a hot dog, offering half of it to a stray animal, and consider himself fed for the day—but he was fourteen, and old enough now, they had decided, to stay home alone while she was on tour.

Fourteen! In another year, unless she recovered as mysteriously as she had fallen ill, she would have been this strange sick creature for fully one-third of his life.

She yawned, and her mouth flickered at the boundary of her vision, as if a distant ship were sending out signals in Morse code.

Once there was a country where no one addressed the dead except in writing. Whenever people felt the urge to speak to someone they had outlived, they would take a pen and set their thoughts down on paper: *You should have seen the sun coloring the puddles this morning,* or *Things were so much easier when you were alive, so much happier,* or *I wanted to tell you I got all A's on my report card, plus a C in algebra.* Then they would place the message atop the others they had written, in a basket or a folder, until the summer arrived and they could be delivered.

In this country it rained for most of the year. The landscape was lush with the kinds of trees and ivies that flourish in wet weather, their leaves the closest green to black. The creeks and pools swam with armies of tiny brown frogs. Usually, though, in the first or second week of June, the clouds would thin from the air little by little, in hundreds of parallel threads, as if someone were sweeping the sky clean with a broom, and the drought would set in. This did not happen every summer, but most. Between the glassy river to the west of the country and the fold of hills to the east, the grass withered and vanished, the puddles dried up, and the earth separated into countless oddly shaped plates. Deep rifts formed in the dirt. It was through these rifts that people slipped the letters they had written. The dead were buried underground, and tradition held that they were waiting there to collect each sheet of paper, from the most heartfelt expression of grief to the most trivial piece of gossip:

You won't believe it, but Ellie is finally leaving that boyfriend of hers.

What I want to know is whether you think I should take the teaching job.

The crazy thing is, when the phone rang last night, I was absolutely sure it was you.

Do you remember that time you dropped your earring in the pond and it surprised that fish?

I just don't know what I'm doing these days.

So it was that people surrendered the notes they had saved with a feeling of relief and accomplishment, letting them fall through the cracks one by one, then returned home, satisfied that they had been received.

This was the way it had always been, for who knows how long, with the dead turning their hands to the surface of the earth, and no orphans praying out loud to their parents, and no widows chitchatting with the ghosts of their husbands, and all the wish-it-weres and might-have-beens of the living oriented around a simple stack of paper and a cupful of pens. Then something very strange happened.

In Portland the bookstore was a labyrinth of aisles and staircases, with shelves that stretched to the rafters and let out the sugary smell of old paper, columns that shone with textured gold paint, and the floor was a worn industrial concrete that resembled a pond abounding with gray-green silt, and as she walked through the stacks she could see the vague form of her reflection passing underneath her, vanishing and reemerging in the grit and gloss of the stone, and on the store's top level, where she gave her reading, the art books stood directly behind the audience in a long panorama of faces, so that Ms. Erin Colvin from Hillsdale and Mr. Jim Fristoe from the Pearl District seemed to sit alongside Andy Warhol and Mona Lisa and one of Modigliani's radiant, blank-eyed women, and when it came time for Nina to take questions and someone asked her how she developed her titles, she gave her usual answer, comparing the title to a target toward which she shot the arrow of a story and confessing that she had never been able to write so much as the first sentence until she had taken careful aim. In the case of the story she had just presented, she said, a fairy tale of sorts, she had tried "A Fable Beginning with a Glimpse of Blue Sky," "A Fable Ending in a Thunderclap and a Rain Shower," and "A Fable Occurring Between Two Thunderstorms" before she hit upon "A Fable from the Living to the Dead," after which followed a dozen variations on that one idea—"A Fable *to* the Dead," "A Fable *for* the Dead," "A Fable *for* the Living *from* the Dead," "A Fable *from* the Dead *to* the Living"—until at last she settled upon "A Fable for the Living."

A Fable.

A fable.

A *fab*le.

Her ulcer had begun pussing out, which meant that it was healing, but meant, too, that if she kept her lips closed for even half a second, the discharge would glue them together and pulling them apart would transfix her jaw with light. It was shameful, her pain, appalling. She hated to exhibit it, hated the attention it brought her. And yet she couldn't stop thinking about it, couldn't stop trying to justify or understand it. Most of the people who gathered to collect her signature were too young and fit to display more than a few minor sports injuries and shaving rashes, along with the occasional gleaming cincture of a hangover headache, but there were others in line, too, the sick and the insulted, *her* people. The teenage girl confined to a wheelchair by cancer or arthritis, hip dysplasia or osteonecrosis, her pelvis a shining cameo of bones. The old man whose heart was failing, pulsing the way a star pulses. The woman nursing a glowing thyroid, surreptitiously pressing a hand to her neck. The doctor in her hospital scrubs, who seemed so healthy as she stood facing Nina but turned to hobble away with her spine iridescing through her shirt like a string of frightful pearls. Nina looked at them, and something softened inside her. She wondered if her face showed what she was thinking: *Yes. That's it. I understand. You don't have to tell me.*

Capping off the procession was a college student who wanted Nina to "sign this note" certifying that he had "gone to this reading." As soon as she scratched her name on the page, he whisked it away from her, zipping it into his backpack as if it were some wild creature trying to buck its way out of his grasp.

Now it was only Nina and one of the booksellers. She fell silent as she autographed the remaining stock, fifteen copies of her new collection and twice that many of her most recent novel, *Twin Souls,* a sort of parable in the guise of a love story, about a world in which there were two of everybody and it was forbidden to interact with your other self—the first book of hers that had sold well enough, miracle of miracles, to earn out its advance. Her signature slowly changed beneath her fingers, rearranging itself, *purifying* itself, plunge by plunge and bend by bend until it was no longer a set of letters at all but a curious abstract design. It was like the pattern she had once watched a moth draw with its wings in the condensation on her bathroom mirror. She remembered switching off the lights and opening the window so that it would fly away and then, when it did, calling Wallace in to see the strange hieroglyph of sweeps and flickers it had left behind.

"I bet it was trying to communicate with you," he mused. "Maybe it was my dad, reincarnated as a moth, and the only way he knew how to get in touch with us was to write something with his wings." He looked more carefully at the mark. "Except he's illiterate."

Wallace, her wonderful, brilliant Wallace, was the product of a fling she had allowed herself one night when she was drunk and twenty-two with a man whose name and face had abandoned her the moment he put on his clothing. Nearly five years passed before she found his business card behind her dresser and in a flash remembered who he was—his fingernails with their clean white crescents, a banker's nails, and the way he bathed her thighs with kisses, stopping just short of her pubic mound as though he had encountered a brick wall. How, she wondered, would she ever work up the courage to tell the man what their one sodden hour of sex had engendered? The question, as it turned out, was academic, since a Web search informed her that not long after Wallace was born his father had been killed in a speedboat accident, "age 28, survived by his wife and childhood sweetheart, Tammy." Wallace knew little more than that his father had died a long time ago and the two of them had never married.

When the last book was signed and the "Thank you so much, Ms. Poggione" came, Nina said good-bye with a handshake and collected her possessions. It wasn't until she was on her way to the staircase that she noticed him standing at the first-editions shelf, John-with-an-*h* Catau, running his fingers over the covers as if he were fascinated, absolutely fascinated, by the various Gail Godwins and Curtis Sittenfelds in their clear plastic sleeves.

She stopped short. "What on earth are you doing here?"

"Why, of all the places to run into each other," he joked. Clearly he had been rehearsing what to say, but he made it only midway through the sentence before his voice tightened in a plexus of timidity and self-doubt, the same slipknot effect she had noticed the day before. "I'm sorry," he continued. "Is this too much? This is too much, isn't it? It's not a long drive from Seattle to Portland. Two and a half hours. It was just that you said 'some other time,' so I thought maybe . . . well . . . *tonight.*"

For some reason she could not work up any anger toward him, or even any distrust. He was so obviously harmless—and not harmless in the thin-veneer way of countless serial killer movies, but truly harmless. He wore the fixed expression of a child caught filling the saltshaker with sugar. If only she weren't so exhausted.

"I'm sick." She said it once for herself and a second time for him. "I'm sick, John. And your attention is flattering, and if things were different, I would be happy to get a drink with you somewhere, but every minute I'm not holed away in my hotel room, *alone,* is hard for me. Do you understand?"

He grinned. "You remembered my name."

"Bye, John."

"Look, how about some coffee? There's a coffee shop right downstairs. And then you can go back to your hotel and get some sleep and maybe tomorrow you'll feel better than you do today."

Make me better tomorrow than I am today. Make me better next week than I've been this one.

She was the type of person who never read her horoscope, never saved the slips from her fortune cookies, and yet there were times when she was all too willing to be guided by coincidence and intimation, those fleeting signals that flagged the air like torches and suggested the universe had lit a trail for her. Which was why, she supposed, she agreed to have a cup of coffee—one cup—with him. She ordered a small vanilla latte, iced, so that she could conduct it to the corner of her lip with a straw. Did she want something to eat? A scone?

"God no."

She missed the days of dining out with her friends and lovers, indulging her appetite for lobster or curry, pad Thai or seasoned French fries, before she knew how much would be taken from her, and how quickly. Occasionally, in the stillness of a taxi or an airplane, she would catalog the pleasures she had lost. Cigarettes. Chewing gum. Strong mint toothpaste. Any food with hard edges or sharp corners that could pierce or abrade the inside of her mouth: potato chips, croutons, crunchy peanut butter. Any food that was more than infinitesimally, *protozoically*, spicy or tangy or salty or acidic: pesto or Worcestershire sauce, wasabi or anchovies, tomato juice or movie-theater popcorn. Certain pamphlets and magazines whose paper carried a caustic wafting chemical scent she could taste as she turned the pages. Perfume. Incense. Library books. Long hours of easy conversation. The ability to lick an envelope without worrying that the glue had irritated her mouth. The knowledge that if she heard a song she liked, she could sing along to it in all her dreadful jubilant tune-lessness. The faith that if she bit her tongue, she would soon feel better rather than worse. The coltish rising feeling of sex or mas-turbation, and the way, as it gripped her, she no longer stood between herself and her senses. The problem was that the more aroused she grew, the dryer her mouth became, so that she could never reach culmination without experiencing that awful germi-nating sensation she felt before an ulcer erupted, like a weed spreading just under her skin. She no longer knew when she was being sensible, when overcautious. She was tired, very tired, and she hurt. Writing about it did not make it better.

She and John Catau took an empty table in the center of the shop and sat across from each other sipping their drinks. While he spoke, she covered her mouth with her palm, trying to usher the coffee past her lips without visibly wincing. He was offering another one of his meandering narratives, about a rock concert where the crowd was "so raucous" that it spilled out onto the sidewalk and he had traded jackets with the guitarist. Every so often she would punctuate the story with an *mm-hmm* or a *right*, thinking *Make me better, Take me home,* while he nodded and stroked the stubble on his chin. He must have been talking for nearly fifteen minutes when he made a remark that caused him to laugh, a quiet little two-beat arrangement, as if he were exhaling once through each nostril. "You know, like in 'Sunset Studies,' " he continued. "Remember, that bit you wrote about the door hinges flapping loose from the house like butterflies?"

"Where would you have seen 'Sunset Studies'?"

"*The Lifted Brow* began archiving its old issues online."

"Hmm." A group of teenagers in crowlike black clothing had stationed themselves by the graphic novels, their faces irradiated with patches of cruel red acne. "This place"—she gestured at the stiltlike columns, the vista of windows—"it reminds me of a bead shop I used to visit in college. Not that I had any interest in beads. I went because it reminded me of this art gallery where my friends and I spent all our time in high school. Freestanding counters everywhere. Polished white pine floors. It made me feel like I was reliving my past."

"Mm-hmm. Very esque-ish."

"What?"

"Esque-ish. It's a word me and Coop came up with. First *esque* and then *ish.* Something that reminds you of something that reminds you of something."

"That's good. I like that."

"Yeah? You think it will catch on?"

"John, how old are you?"

"I'm twenty-three. And a half."

She made the mistake of smiling. One of her teeth snagged

her lip, and there it was, that unsparing light, a spasm of pain that spread across her mouth as if a metal barb had punched through the skin, tugging it outward so that a living pink tent rose up from the tissue.

"Jesus H.," said John Catau. "I absolutely did not realize. I'm so sorry."

She waited until she was sure she could speak. "It's okay. I a*pp*—I a*pp*—I thank you for your concern."

"Will you show it to me? Your ulcer?"

"No. *No. John. God.* It's not pretty. You don't want to see it."

But the look he gave her was full of such humble curiosity, with his eyes lingering on her mouth and his hair dangling over his creased forehead, that she placed her fingers on either side of the sore and slowly everted her lip for him. He inhaled sharply. In the space of that breath, between one second and the next, he understood. She didn't have to tell him, didn't have to explain or apologize. She didn't have to combat the impression that she was undergoing some kind of joke ailment, like a hangnail or an ingrown hair, the kind of thing that could be remedied with tweezers or a topical cream. *A canker sore, yes. I had one of those myself a few years back*, people liked to say. *Grin and bear it, that's my motto*, and they would clap her shoulder and wait for her to chuckle along with them at the human body and all its darling haplessness. And now here was this boy, this ridiculous boy, and he seemed to know everything about her. *Make me better.* His fingertips and the base of his palm were resting lightly on the table, creating a shadowy little hidden cove, and she found herself resisting the impulse to slide her hand into it.

"I'm so sorry," he said a second time. "That's terrible. Terrible. You really don't want to be here at all, do you?" And then, before she could answer, he added, "You know, I read that there are more nerve endings on the lips and the tongue than anywhere else in the body. Were you aware of that? Genitals included. Which means that your mouth is the most sensitive place you've got when it comes to things like hot and cold and pleasure and pain."

"Mm-hmm. I know."

"Okay. I'm going to drive you back to your hotel now."

"No. Please. It's not far. I can walk."

"Right," he said, "I understand," and she believed he did somehow. "Nina? How long before you're better, do you think?"

"I wish I knew. Not tomorrow. Two days, I hope."

"Two days." He made it sound like a fact he was memorizing for a quiz. "Listen, this bruise on my arm, on my biceps?" He notched the contusion with his thumbnail. "I got it from punching myself after your Bellingham reading. I kept saying, 'Catau, you're going to ask this woman to dinner.' I was mad at myself for chickening out. That's all. I was just embarrassed to tell you before."

And then his hand was on top of hers, and he was saying goodbye, and she felt that old carnal tightening in her knees, that flush of heat in her chest, and suddenly, in her imagination, she was sinking into bed with him and his caresses were covering her body in babyskin. How long had it been since she was well enough to unbutton someone's shirt and dot his stomach with kisses? And did she *have* to be well enough? Maybe she *was* sick and despondent, broken into a thousand pieces by an illness that would not go away, but so what? Couldn't she pretend she was whole for just one night? How much of yourself could you manufacture out of the fragments and the spare parts?

In her hotel room, she cried and then set her clothing out for the next day, turned her blanket down, and called Wallace. For half an hour, she lay in bed debriding her mouth with hydrogen peroxide, letting the watery chlorine taste spread down her tongue and into her throat as she wondered what had happened.

She switched on the TV. A sitcom was starting, the image sharp and true on the plasma screen. She tried to pay attention to the story rather than the play of shapes and colors, but it was nothing special, a show like every other, where all the people were assembled from light, and their problems made them lovable, and their smallest gestures set off waves of swirling photons.

There was a woman, not quite old but not quite young, whose fiancé had died unexpectedly. It was barely a month into their engagement and the two of them were attending a chamber music concert when he began coughing into his sleeve and excused himself from his seat. Because they had quarreled earlier over the cost of the wedding, she did not worry about him when he failed to return. Instead, with exasperation, she thought, What could possibly be keeping him?, little realizing that what was keeping him was death.

When she went to the foyer to look for him, she found a ring of ushers clustered around his body as if he were a spill for which no one wanted to accept responsibility. She would never forget the sight of his tongue pressed to his teeth, struggling to form some word he had just missed his chance of saying.

More than a year had gone by since then, a terrible year of ill health, sleeplessness, and rainy days that layered themselves over her like blankets. Who was she? Who had she become? Her skin was paler than it used to be, her hair grayer. Recently she had noticed creases lingering around her eyes in the morning, and also across her forehead, as if she had spent the night squinting into a harsh light. The lines did not go away when she rubbed them, vanishing only gradually as the hours wore on, and she could foresee a time when the mask of age that grief had placed over her face would simply be her face. She missed her fiancé terribly. Sometimes it seemed to her that he was only a beautiful story she had told herself, so quickly had she fallen in love with him and so quickly had he left her. It was hard to believe that that man who refused to button his collar, whose kisses began so shyly and ended so fervidly, who never once looked at her as if she were foolish or tiresome or even ordinary, was the same man she had found splayed across the theater's staircase like an animal pinned to a board.

Frequently she had the feeling that he was standing just behind her, his breath tickling her ear like it used to when he came prowling over to seize her waist while she was cooking. All the same she did not speak to him.

Instead, like everyone, she accumulated letters that would never be answered. *I don't understand how this can be my life,* she wrote, and *What am I going to do?* and occasionally, late at night, when she could not sleep, something longer such as *Do you know what it feels like? Shall I describe it for you? It feels like the two of us got on a boat together, and the deck tossed me into the water, and you went sailing away without me. Thrown overboard—that's how it feels. So I want you to tell me, because I really need to know, why did I spend my whole life waiting to fall in love with just the right person if you were just going to leave and it would all be for nothing?*

That first summer, immediately after he died, she had barely been able to pick up a pen, but by the time the earth split open a year later, she had amassed three heavy baskets of letters. One afternoon, she went to the parched field where the fair sat in the autumn and the soccer team practiced in the spring and dropped them into the deepest opening she could find. The ground swallowed them as neatly as a pay phone accepting coins, except for the last page, which continued to show through the dirt until gravity gave it a tug and it slipped out of sight. That was where her heart was, she thought, cradled underground with the roots and the bones.

As she stood in the dust listening to the insects buzz, she dashed off one last note and let it go: *Are you even out there?*

The next morning, she received her answer.

The streets seemed to quiver and spark in the rain, and water cascaded from the roofs of the old Victorians, and the gray ash of the sky made the inside of the bookstore appear lustrous and unfamiliar, saturated with color, like a movie theater where the film has snapped and the seats have been engulfed in light, and in the bathroom, where Nina went to disinfect her mouth with Listerine, the walls were covered with photos of third-tier pop stars in unflattering poses, bizarre headlines clipped from tabloid newspapers, and when she stepped back into the store, she saw that the Newbery displays had been taken down and replaced with chairs and a microphone, and to the seven people who had braved the San Francisco weather to hear her read, she presented "A Fable for the Living," coaxing each syllable carefully past her open sore, which was even worse than it had been in Portland. Every time someone entered the building, she could hear the storm drumming and resonating on Haight Street. Then the door swung shut, and the noise softened to a rustle, and once again they were all sealed together in their bright and cozy den. She kept waiting for John Catau to come slouching out from behind the survival guides, wearing a sly look of guilty satisfaction, as if by following her across three states he had allowed her to defeat him in some subtle contest of expectations, but it soon became obvious that he was not there. She was not prepared to feel so disappointed.

Though the audience was small, the weather must have put them at their ease, because they posed an uncommon number of questions: "Do you go into an office every day? A coffee shop? Or do you write from home?"

"I have a spare room with a desk and a computer. That's where I do most of my work. Except the revisions—those I finish by hand, usually at the kitchen table."

"Are there any words you feel you overuse?"

"*Strange, great, little*—I heard an interview with an editor who was asked about her pet peeves, and she named those three words, I suppose because of the way they adjust a phrase's rhythm without actually changing its meaning. And *soul* probably. *Terrible.* And also *lambent,* but I love that one."

"Do you read your work out loud when you're writing?"

"No. Never. The truth is I'm embarrassed by the sound my voice makes in an empty room, that grand pronouncement effect. And there's something else"—*and it hurts, it hurts*—"which is that, in my experience, and this might sound completely absurd, but stories have a certain power the first time they're read out loud, don't they? An energy, or an honesty. The way the words cut through the air. And it seems a shame to squander that power when there's no one else around to hear it."

"This isn't a question. I just want to say that I enjoy listening to you read, the care you take with your pronunciation. Have you ever considered reading your own audiobooks?"

"Thanks, and no, but nobody ever suggested I should until now."

"If *Twin Souls* were made into a movie, who would you cast as Mary Ruth?"

"I get people wondering that all the time, but I never know how to answer. Why, did you have someone in mind?"

In a theatrical, almost *moony*, tone of voice, the girl who had asked the question said, "I think Julia *Krukowski* would be *perfect*," which made the friend sitting next to her stifle a smile. Nina nodded as if at the essential rightness of the idea, though she had never heard of Julie Krikowski. She suspected the name might be invented—if not, in fact, the girl's own. More and more, though, she found that she was required to take the stardom of certain people on faith. The world presented an endless sequence of celebrities replacing celebrities replacing celebrities, like cheap wooden nesting dolls, each bearing a tinier and less persuasive likeness than the one that had come before. It exhausted her.

"My son says it would make a good anime film. So are there any more—" She felt an itch in her sinuses and turned her head. A sneeze tore at her lips with a startling photographic flash. She gasped and closed her eyes, waiting for the pangs of light to subside, for the blood to stop beating in her jaw. *Make me better.* Maybe if she never ate or drank or spoke or laughed or smiled or kissed anyone ever again—maybe then she would be all right. "Are there any more questions?"

The audience took pity on her. She thanked everyone for coming, signed a few books, and phoned for a taxi. Before she left, the manager gave her one of the trading cards he had printed to publicize the event, number 1,972 in the series, with her photo on the front and a description of the book on the back: "In *The Age of Girls and Boys*, Nina Poggione has crafted an elegant collection of love stories and fantasies, unique, lyrical, and haunting.

Whether in the award-winning 'Small Bitter Seeds,' with its gifted physician struggling to retain his practice after losing his voice to cancer, or in the daring title story, in which the children of a world sinking into infertility attempt to transcend the circumstances of their lives, she evokes the souls of her characters with compassion and an exquisite clarity."

She relied on the cabdriver to find her hotel, a narrow brick and stone structure, latticed with balconies, that she recognized from her *Twin Souls* tour the instant she saw the waxed wooden floor that stretched across the lobby in a sunburst of multiple browns. She had gone directly from the airport to the bookstore, so she had to check in at the front desk before she could ride the elevator to the third floor, unlock her room, and open her nightstand. It held a phone book and a Gideon's Bible, but was otherwise empty. Two years before, in the same hotel—though not, surely, the same suite—she was searching for a stationery pad in her bedside drawer when she discovered a journal someone had left behind. The cloth had been razed from the cover, revealing a kidney-shaped patch of gray board, and a buckle ran through the first thirty pages or so, as if they had been dipped in water. It was filled with handwritten love notes, she discovered, page after page of them, *I love this*es and *I love that*s stacked tight as bricks against one another. *I love the "bloop" sound you make whenever you drop something. I love remembering the evening we sat on the roof at your parents' and watched the sunset reflecting off the windows of that old church. I love your silver chimneysweep charm, the one you wear around your neck for good luck.* That night, she lay in bed and read the whole thing. Slowly a pair of personalities emerged from the sentences, taking on mass and texture. The man's name was Jason, the woman's Patricia, and at first Nina felt like a spy, eavesdropping as he turned the most quotidian details of their life into endearments, but after a while she might have been their closest friend, sitting between them as he cupped his hand to Nina's ear and whispered all the beautiful things he wished her to relay to his wife. Maybe the words weren't meant for Nina, but they were wonderful all the same, if not *I love you* then at least *Somebody loves somebody.*

The next morning, before she left, she asked the concierge if there was a Jason Williford registered at the hotel. He tapped on his keyboard. "No, I'm sorry, ma'am."

"A Patricia?"

"No. No Patricia Williford either. Perhaps they've already departed?"

"Maybe so. Could you find out for me?"

"No Jason or Patricia Williford for the last . . . six months, at least. I'm sorry."

So she kept the journal, taking it home with her, and one day, when she was running a fever from the cluster of sores under her tongue, five or six of them scattered along the midline, and the shining vitric crater of an ulcer on her hard palate, she took a Stanley knife and excised a page from the book. Immediately, she felt ashamed. What was she thinking? Why had she done it? Rather than tape the page back in place, though, she folded it in quarters so that she could carry it in her pocketbook.

And now, as she did every so often, she took it out and read it:

I love watching you sit at your desk, the sun striking you through the philodendron leaves. I love that game where you draw a picture on my back with your finger and I try to guess what it is. I love those blue jeans with the sunflowers on the pockets, the ones that hug the curves of your waist. I love your gray coat with the circles like cloud-covered suns. I love the joke you told at Eli and Abbey's wedding reception. I love how easily you cry when you're happy. I love your question marks that look like backwards s's, your periods that look like bird's beaks. I love the way you stand at the mirror in the morn-

ing picking the ChapStick from your lips. I love how you laugh with your mouth open wide, and how you snort sometimes, and how embarrassed it makes you when you do. I love to think of you as that bored little girl designing adventures for herself, riding your sleeping bag down the staircase, or taking a running leap along the hallway and trying to flip the light switch in midair, or walking from your bedroom to the far side of the kitchen without stepping in the sunlight, or else you would die. I love how your eyes grow wet whenever you talk about your grandfather. I love that first moment, at night, when you trace the curve of my ear with your fingernail. I love planning vacations with you. I love how good you are to me when I'm not feeling well. I love the inexplicable accent, from nowhere anyone has ever visited or even heard of, that you use when you're trying to sound Italian. I love the bull story. I love helping you shave that tricky spot behind your knees. I love the way your hair fritzes out in all directions when you work up a sweat. I love your many doomed attempts to give up caffeine. I love that perfect little cluster of moles on your wrist. I love the yellow tights you wear when you're feeling—how you say?—sparky. I love every—

There the page ended.

She had not yet shut her curtains, and when a bright light swept across the window, she saw a million raindrops speckling the glass, a column of white beads tilting through them with a minute quiver as the drops along the border vacillated and were swallowed into the center.

Her phone buzzed. She read her home number on the display. It was Wallace, calling to ask if he could have some friends over for Cities in Dust, the role-playing game he moderated. "Do you mind? Tomorrow's Friday, so there's no school afterward. We'll order a pizza, and everyone'll probably spend the night. It'll be me and Conrad and Nathan and a few others."

"Are any of these 'few others' girls? You know you can't have Camarie spend the night if I'm not around."

"But Camarie is our Forged One!"

"Forged One or no, I'm not comfortable with it. Tell me, has Camarie asked her parents what *they* think about your great coed, unsupervised role-playing extravaganza?"

He changed tacks. "Camarie is only twelve, you know, Mom. I wouldn't *do* anything with her. It would break the Creep Equation." This was the lesson his algebra teacher had used the first day of eighth grade to demonstrate the practical value of higher math: you took your age, divided it by two, and added seven, "and that's your dating boundary," Wallace had explained to her, hunched over a cherry Danish at the kitchen table. "Any younger than that, and it's creepy. I'm fourteen, which means I can only date someone my own age, since fourteen divided by two is seven, plus seven is fourteen."

She had overheard enough heedless mid-game snack-break conversations to know how he and his friends really interpreted the equation. *And that's your fucking boundary. Which means I can only fuck someone my own age.* She also knew that, like most eighth-graders—or at least the science fiction kids, the British comedy kids—they were all talk, all roostering, their lasciviousness just another role-playing game, a way of trying on their manhood and simultaneously mocking it.

She cleared her throat. "Be that as it may."

She managed to lay a stress on the last word without making her discomfort audible. Or so she thought. But after four years, Wallace could derive her condition from her voice with some authority. "Your lip?" he asked.

"Mm-hmm. It's at that hurts-to-talk stage."

"Would you like to talk about it?"

"Ha ha."

"All right, listen, no Camarie. But everybody else is g——eah? Hey, there's another call coming in. I'm gonna take it, Mom, okay? See you Sunday."

"Sunday. Be good."

She returned her phone to her purse, then lay back and gazed at the window, waiting for another car to breast the hill, its head-lights taking just the right angle to send a field of stars Big Bang-ing over the glass.

$37 \div 2 = 18$, or thereabouts, and $18 + 7 = 25$, so a certain overzealous someone who had punctuated her dreams last night by kissing her neck, disquietingly, like a lover, was too creepy for her by one year.

And a half.

A bit of tissue had come loose from between her molars. She tried to dislodge it with her tongue, and a prickle of light appeared where she had scraped the papillae. *Damn. Damn damn damn.* It was yet another tiny injury, almost too small to notice, and yet she worried that, like so many others, it would rupture and lose all shape, growing more and more indistinct as the pain took hold. She brought her travel kit to the bathroom, prepared a capful of hydrogen peroxide, and tipped it into her mouth. She had to be so careful with herself. And here was the question: Was it worth what it cost?

Her house was built like all the others, with its roof projecting over the front door to keep it from opening directly into the rain, and it was her pleasure upon waking in the morning to step out onto the porch and take stock of the day. This particular morn-ing arrived hot and bright, with the sky that oddly whitened blue it became when there was no moisture in the air. She was surprised to find a fissure interrupting her lawn. She kept the grass carefully trimmed and watered, and she was sure she would have seen the rift if it had been there the day before. It ran as straight as a line on a map. She traced it with her eyes, following it across her neighbor's yard and a few others before it vanished into the woods at the end of the block, and then back again until it deadended at her front steps.

But that was not the strange part. No, the strange part was the sheet of paper that was protruding from it. She picked it up and unfolded it.

Of course I am, it read.

The handwriting was familiar to her, with its walking-stick *r* and its *o*'s that didn't quite close at the top. But it took her a moment to figure out where she recognized it from.

She spent the next few hours twisting her engagement ring around and around her knuckle. A potato chip bag was dipping and spinning in the middle of the road, and she watched it ride the breeze until a boy rode by and flattened it beneath his bicycle.

Finally, on a blank sheet of paper, she wrote, *If you are who I believe you are, tell me something only you would know about me.*

She was unaccountably nervous. She knelt on the porch, closing her eyes as she slipped the note into the fissure. Something deep within the ground seemed to wrest it from her fingers like a fish plucking a cricket from a hook.

For the rest of the day, every time she went outside, she expected to see a flash of white paper waiting for her in the grass. But it was not until the next morning that she found one: *I love your gray coat with the circles like cloud-covered suns.*

She stared closely at the breach in her lawn. If she followed it on foot, she calculated, she would eventually reach the scorched field where she had gone to deposit her letters.

On a fresh sheet of paper, she replied, *Everyone we know has seen me in that coat. It doesn't prove a thing.*

Early that afternoon, an answer arrived: *I love how you laugh with your mouth wide open, and how you snort sometimes, and how embarrassed it makes you when you do.*

She wrote, *Well, yes, that's definitely me.*

I love the joke you told at Zach and Christina's wedding reception.

She wrote, *If this is a trick . . . this had better not be a trick. Is it?*

I love how easily you cry when you're happy.

So the correspondence went on, hour after hour and day after day, pushing across the distance of the soil. All his letters were love letters, delivered while she was sleeping or mopping the kitchen, weeding the garden or out buying milk. When she held them up to the sunlight, the faded marks of earlier messages emerged through the stationery: *Bailey had two kittens last week, and I named the first one Bowtie, and the second one Mike! I hope you're better now, I truly do, because I am, I tell you, I am. I think there's something terribly wrong with me.* They came in a variety of hands and were often hard to decipher. She presumed he had salvaged the pages from under the ground, a few dozen among the many hundreds of thousands that had rained down over the generations of the dead.

I love the way you stand at the mirror in the morning picking the lip balm from your lips.

I love the inexplicable accent, from nowhere anyone has ever visited, you use when you're trying to sound French.

I love that first moment, at night, when you trace the curve of my ear with your fingernail.

Soon the situation no longer seemed strange to her. It was as if the two of them were kneeling on opposite sides of the bedroom door, sliding notes to each other along the floor. Then it was as if the door had vanished, vanished entirely, and they were simply sitting in the bedroom together. When she had crossed the threshold she could not say, only that she had. He was her fiancé—she did not doubt it—but what had brought him back to her?

It was one of those peaceful mid-April evenings with a coral sky the uniform hue of a paint sample, and from the hills of Los Angeles came the *shick-shack* of insects, and from the highways came the gusting sound of traffic, and because of a broken stoplight at Sunset and Laurel Canyon, she was fifteen minutes late to the bookstore, so one of the cashiers escorted her directly to the reading annex, a dimly lit room lined with shelf after shelf of remainders, where twenty or thirty people sat in poses of quiet thought or conversation, their shoulders touching as they swiveled around in their chairs, and he was not there, or at least she did not see him, and *Once there was a country where no one addressed the dead except in writing*, and *Who was she? Who had she become?* and *She sensed that every word had demanded some mysterious payment from him, a fee that could only be understood by those who had already been laid to rest*, and by the time she finished presenting the story, reaching the *ever* and the *after*, her eyes had adjusted to the darkness and she knew for certain—he had given up on her. It was just as well. The ulcer on her lip was still stinging, but a seal had begun to form over it, a clear bandage of skin with the texture of overlapping threads. She was recovering in spite of herself. She gave her mouth a quick investigation with her tongue. Deep in the pocket of her gums was the firm polyp of a sore, like an unpopped kernel of popcorn, that had developed without ever quite breaking the skin. On one of her cheeks was a minuscule dimpled lesion, and on her tongue itself was the same small scuff she had noticed the night before. None of them had become painful yet, though. If, after the reading, she spoke as little as possible, there was the slim possibility they would die away without getting any worse, and the ulcer on her lip would heal, and she would be graced with a few days of well-being before the next outbreak began.

She would bake a pizza—or better yet: a lasagna—and eat until she was stuffed.

She would have a long conversation with Wallace about his father.

She would find someone to fuck and she would fuck him.

A woman in the front row asked, "So that part where the dead begin to glow—is that supposed to be because they're in pain? Because they don't *seem* to be in pain. Are they?"

Well, there was physical pain, Nina answered, and there was emotional pain. This particular story offered little evidence of the former, maybe, but abundant evidence of the latter. Ever since she was a child, she answered. English Lit, she answered, with a minor in biology. No, she answered, not yet. She was afraid that as soon as she decided to incorporate it into her stories, the phenomenon would end as mysteriously as it had begun, and everything she had written would be cemented to a particular time and place. Now, she supposed. Now and here. (What else could she mean?) Constantly, she answered. At least two or three books a week. In fact, it was reading that was truly at the center of her life—experiencing stories, not making them. She was sure most other writers would say the same. No, she answered. Usually, she answered. Once or twice, she answered. Certainly she had changed since then, in innumerable ways. With her first book she had seen the world as a narrative, seen human lives as narratives. Now, instead, she saw them as stories. She wasn't sure what had happened. Maybe she had experienced too much sickness. Maybe her sickness had made her less intelligent. Maybe her sickness had made her more sentimental. Maybe her sickness had returned her to the simple receptiveness of her childhood, when fitting people together seemed more important than taking them apart. No, it wasn't that, she answered. She was just as interested in characters as she had ever been. But somehow she'd come to believe that characters were made up of their ideas and perceptions rather than their actions. A mistake, perhaps. She couldn't argue with that. Yes, exactly, she answered. The traveling, she answered. The fact that she could go to work in a T-shirt and shorts, she answered, along with the privilege of participating in other people's dreams, and most of all the thrill she got, the feeling of wondrous correctness, when a handful of words she had been organizing and reorganizing suddenly fastened themselves together, forming a chain that seemed to tug at the page from some distant, less provisional place, as if through an accidental pattern of sounds, rhythms, and insinuations she had linked herself to the beginning of the world, a time when words were inseparable from what they named and you could not mention a thing without establishing it in front of your eyes. It was the same feeling, she was convinced, that painters experienced through color, dancers through movement, photographers through light. The same feeling that mathematicians experienced through equations and actors experienced through emotion.

The sun had fallen behind the audience. In the deepening shade of the room, it was easy to see their wounds and contagions: the wrenched backs and sciatic hips, the legs cramped with heat lightning, a glittering pathology of sprains, rashes, and carcinomas. Nina sat at the table by the lectern and signed the books she was handed—a half-dozen *Girls and Boys* and twice that many *Twin Souls*, plus a mint-edition copy of her ancient small-press poetry chapbook, *Why the House Loves the Fire*, preserved in an acetate sleeve for the store's first-editions case.

She had spent too much time talking and had worn the seal off her ulcer. She could feel it shining through her lips. *You've been stung by a bee or a wasp before, haven't you?* she answered. *You know how at first it's only a faint irritation, and you can almost disregard it, but then the venom spreads and suddenly, in the smallest division of a second, the injury blossoms open and becomes alarmingly, almost* hyperphysically, *bright? Well, it was like that blossoming-open moment, continually renewing itself, for days and days. Yes,* she answered, *she had seen a doctor about it. The problem was that nobody knew what caused them. Rumors,* she answered. *Rumors and folk remedies. Flaxseed oil. L-lysine. Hydrogen peroxide. Warm saltwater. For a while she had tried burning them closed with a sulfuric acid compound that left a cap of white crust over the top, but every time she used it her mouth filled with the sickening taste of aluminum foil, and often the sores would keep expanding underneath the cauterant and absorb it anyway. All the time,* she answered. *Because words on paper didn't hurt. No,* she answered. *No. They had made a ruin of everything she cared about. She didn't want adulation anymore. She didn't want love. She only wanted to carve a small path of painlessness and blunted feeling through her life until she came out the other side.*

Back at the hotel, before she phoned Wallace, she stood at the mirror practicing her diction. "Hello. Hello. *M*ake *m*e *b*etter. *M*ake *m*e *b*etter. This is your *m*other. *M*other. Mother." She would wait for him to ask her how she was doing, and "I'm better," she would say. Which was true, or very nearly. She would be better soon. She was sure of it. The trick was to speak deliberately enough to rid her consonants of that lunging electric quality that gave her condition away, but not so deliberately that it sounded unnatural or calculated. Even the slightest measure of strain in her voice, and Wallace would pick up on it. He was like a hero in a classic detective novel: Father Brown, Hercule Poirot. She worried sometimes that she had passed her syndrome along to him, that one day in his mid-thirties he would wake to discover that his immune system had broken apart inside him like a crossette, bursting open in an eruption of pus and cankers, and everything he loved had become difficult. She hoped the thought would never occur to him. She didn't want him to dread growing up.

She called her home number. Someone answered on the first ring, speaking with the heavy gravel of a smoker or a barroom blues singer. She thought she heard him ask, "Who am I, and how can I help you?" but in the initial air pocket of the connection, she might have been mistaken.

"I'm sorry?"

There was a whispered flurry of *dudes*, and then the man said, "This is the wrong number. Say good-bye. Hang up," and the line went silent.

She stared at the phone. After a few seconds, the LCD became dim from inactivity, and her face peered back at her with the blank puzzlement of a prisoner in a cage. She pressed redial. Her home number marched across the screen, appearing digit by digit beneath the phone icon transmitting its telepathy waves.

This time Wallace answered. "Hello?"

"*Wallace. What* is going on?"

"Hey, Mom. Nothing. Just me and the campaigners are taking a break. What's up?"

"Who was that man who answered our phone?"

"Man?"

"Wallace, I *just* called you, and a man *just* picked up."

She could always tell when he was lying by the seesawing quality of his voice, as if some hidden athletic force were propelling his sentences up and then catching them as they fell back down. "I don't know. You must have dialed the wrong number or something."

"I pressed redial." In the background the same deep voice that had spoken to her earlier said something like *wonder who* or *hundred and two* before the others hushed him. "*Him. That* man."

Wallace paused. "Okay. Listen," he said. "Don't freak out. There's this guy we met. He sells books from a blanket over by that Chinese place. Mom, I'm telling you, he had a first-edition Cities in Dust manual, still in the wooden box, with both the Twelve Nations supplement *and* the original Gazetteer. We're negotiating the price down, that's all."

"Out! Get him out of our house!"

"Give us just a . . . second . . . more," Wallace told her, "and we'll be—"

She heard someone say, "All right, man. You can have that one and one other. But that's it."

"—almost—"

"Kendall Wallace Poggione!"

"Finished," Wallace concluded.

"Now!"

"Okay, okay, we're done. Jesus! Problem solved. He's leaving."

The front door opened and closed, its damaged hinge clacking against the frame. With a cavernous sigh her son declared, "You know, Mom, just because *your* life frightens you doesn't mean *my* life has to frighten me."

The next day, a message came while she was sitting on her front steps. She glanced away for a moment, and there it was, nestled in the thick fringe of grass around the fissure, like a mushroom springing up after a thunderstorm. *I love you*, it read, *and I want you to join me. I want us to be together again, my jewel, my apple. Whatever the cost, I want it, I want it. And I don't want to wait until you die, because God knows how long that will be.*

It was his longest letter yet. She sensed that every word had demanded some mysterious payment from him, a fee that could be understood only by those who had already been laid to rest. What was he asking? That she end her life? That she suspend it? Or something else altogether, something she could hardly imagine?

For the next few days he left no love notes in her yard, no entreaties, only a single question that appeared late one night on the back of a chewing gum wrapper: *Hello?*

He was giving her time to think. He was waiting for her belowground—she knew it, she knew it. Every day the crack by her porch grew a little larger. At first it was only a chink in the dirt, no wider than the slot where she dropped her mail at the post office, but gradually it stretched open until it was as big as an ice chest, and then a steamer trunk, and then a gulf into which she could easily have fit her entire body. She wondered what it would be like if she accepted his invitation. She began to dream that she was living beneath the field on the far side of the woods, moving through a long procession of rooms and hallways where the dead milled around like guests at a trade convention. Throughout the day, at various angles, the sun pierced the hills and the pastures, sending bright silver needles through the ceiling of the earth, so that it was never completely dark, and at night, when the land was soaked in shadows, the people around her glowed with a strange heat. She watched them flare and shimmer through their skin, their bones going off like bombs, every limb a magnificent firework of carbon, phosphorus, and calcium. It seemed that the surface of the world had two sides: on one were the bereaved spouses, the outcast teenagers, the old men and women who had no one left to reminisce with, and on the other were the lovers and friends and parents they had outlived— all of them, whether above or below, aching for those who were gone; all of them, whether above or below, pressing their fingers to the soil. Her eyes flickered in her face, and her teeth shone in her mouth, and when she woke, before the dream had lost its color, she felt that she was recalling some earlier existence, like a house she had lived in as a child, familiar down to its last curved faucet and last chipped floorboard.

The truth was that the thread connecting her to the world was as thin as could be. A sunrise here or there, the feel of suede against her skin, the aroma of strong coffee in the morning, and a few moments of forgetful well-being—that was it, that was all she had, and she knew that it could snap at any moment. She had always believed that one day someone would come along and love her and she would understand how to live. Maybe the idea was juvenile, but she had carried it with her all her life, like an ember smoldering in a pouch of green leaves. It was only the past awful year that had forced her to give it up. And now here it was again, the hope that she had finally found him, the man who would wrench her into the world, the good and beautiful world, where people got married and had children and slowly grew old together.

One afternoon, as she was standing at the kitchen counter eating a turkey-and-diced-olive sandwich, she realized that she had made up her mind. She swept the bread crumbs into her palm and brushed them gently, caressingly, into the sink, as if she were stroking a cat. Then she went outside and knelt at the edge of the crevice. Her neighbor was grilling a steak in his backyard. A forsythia bush rustled in the wind.

There she was, and then there she wasn't, and two large, pale ants were exploring the impression her knees had left in the grass.

It was the last the world would see of her, or at least the last the sun would, the last the sky.

I am here to tell you what happened next.

In Phoenix the streets ran flat and straight, and the jacaranda blossoms made strange ghosts in the slipstreams of the cars, and even at seven, after the sun had set, when the hotel's valet motioned one of the taxis over for her, the city was clothed with a lustrous violet sky that seemed to have the full force of the day shining inside it, and her driver asked her why she was in town, and, "No kidding. Have you ever read those Stainless Steel Rat books?" and, "Tempe Square, d'ya say?" and she kept flattening her tongue against the sleek patch where her sore had been, reassuring herself that it scarcely hurt anymore, though her tongue itself was already perforated where she had rasped it against her teeth, and it felt as if she were balancing a seed, a small bitter seed, on the tip, and she knew it would be only a day or two before the tiny pock spilled out of itself and ulcerated, but for tonight at least she was better, she was better, and the bookstore smelled of bread and coffee from the bakery next door, and there was something about the way the microphone dislocated her speech, taking her Annie Lennox contralto and the slightly too-long hiss she gave her *s*'s and making them gigantic, directionless, that she was still unpracticed enough to find amusing, as if she were nothing but a voice, a big spectral voice, and she could lose herself in it, forgetting all the people who sat before her with their tics and abscesses, their blisters and swollen glands, the intestinal disorders that floated in their abdomens like foxfire, the conjunctivitis infections that made their eyes gleam and shimmer, gathered in their chairs between the podium and the horror shelves, and when she reached the end of the story, someone raised his hand and asked, "What's wrong with your people?" and then, "Don't mistake what I'm saying. I liked that. I really did. But you write these stories about characters who have great sectors of what one would ordinarily regard as the common human experience entirely unavailable to them. I mean, they don't seem to realize it, but they do. I'm just trying to understand why," and the only answer she could think to give was that she had spent the last four years doing exactly the same, trying to understand why, and then there arrived the usual questions about her favorite books and her writing schedule and her teaching philosophy and her cover designs, and after she was finished responding to them, when she had thanked the audience for attending and signed the bookstore's stock, one of the managers gave her a T-shirt with the words FICTIONAL CHARACTER printed on the front, and the bandage on the inside of his arm held a single brilliant point of silver that reminded her of the picture on an old cathode ray tube, collapsing to a starlike remnant of itself as the power was switched off, and the arches along the back of the

store were crowned with paintings of mountains and houses, and
the gold pillars were washed in light and shadow, and she was
getting ready to leave when there he came, *him*, striding past the
magazine racks, giving her his funny, bashful, enthusiastic smile,
and he said, "Two days, you told me. Well, it's been two days. It
took me almost that long to drive here. I was wondering if—"
and she interrupted him by gripping his wrist and stroking it
with her thumb, slowly lifting her hand free until her fingers were
barely skimming the risen tips of the hairs, and she asked him if
he would mind too much, too terribly much—"John. John-with-
an-*h* Catau"—if he would mind driving her back to her hotel,
and she wondered if she had lost her senses, but she felt only the
slightest nettling of pressure on her lip, and all she had was this
one night, and he only had to look at her to see her.

Soon after the woman went to join her fiancé, as the final swel-
tering days of summer came to a close, an unusual event took
place. Late one night, while everyone was sleeping, something
shifted beneath the brown pastures and the dry creek beds, and
a hundred thousand fissures spread across the landscape, leading
to a hundred thousand front doors. Shortly after the sun rose, in
one house after another, the lights went on, and people showered
and got dressed, and then they stepped outside to go to work.
Earlier that week, a mass of clouds had been seen at the horizon,
which meant that it was almost time for the rains to begin again,
but this particular day had dawned hard and clear. The heat rang
out like a coin. The grass twitched and straightened in the morning air. And the lawns—they were split down the center, and from
every rift projected a sheet of paper:

I love that perfect little cluster of freckles on your wrist.

I love the way your hair curls when you work up a sweat.

I love how good you were to me when I got sick.

I love watching you sit at your desk, the sun shining on you through the philodendron leaves.

I love your many doomed attempts to give up caffeine.

Once there was a country where it rained for most of the year, and everyone resided underground, and no one was quite sure who was dead and who was living. But it did not matter because they were happy. And they were ever. And they were after.

Morse Putnam Strawbridge

It is enough that the arrows fit exactly in the wounds they have made.

—Franz Kafka

At first he was sure he had died. When the one with the shaved head gave him another blow to the midriff and his stomach erupted with four long shears of light, he believed he was watching his soul flee from his body. He had never been certain he had a soul, but there it went, like a flock of birds flooding through an open gate. Out it poured from the gash on his arm. Out it poured from the puncture on his thigh. Out it poured from that frog's neck of tissue between his thumb and his forefinger, where the one with the ski jacket had nicked him with a paring knife and forced him to splay his hand open until the skin split to the muscle. So much light. What else could it have been?

Then he noticed that the one who had caught him below the knee with the tire iron was glowing from his front tooth. And the one with the shaved head was examining the scuff marks on his knuckles, foiled with drops of blood. And the smaller one, the talker, who had started things off by pushing him against the wall and saying, "Where are they, huh? Where did you hide them, buddy?" was swiping at a glinting bruise on his arm, eyeing it with aggravation and curiosity, like a cat batting at a laser pointer.

So either all of them had died or none of them had.

He decided they were still alive. Abnormal but alive. Luminescent but alive. The cars were still gunning their engines at one another. New Fun Ree was still steaming the air with its smell of noodles and battered chicken. And his wounds were still pulsing and burning. The only difference was that he could see the nerves working now, growing brighter with each burst of pain.

The one whose tooth was shining said, "What the hell is up with you guys? Have you seen yourselves?" and the others said, "Have *you* seen *your*self?" and, "Look in a mirror, Stephen Hawking," and, " 'Oh, my tooth, my tooth. Christ, fellas, I've gotta get to a dentist. This thing is about goddamn killing me.' " They traded a laugh at the impersonation. From the mouth of the alley he listened to the four of them argue: What was happening? How long would it last? Who else was it affecting? Every so often they paused to smack him or use the knife, but without any real brutality now, as if they were hurting him just to see the light blossom open beneath their fists, the glittering silver stream the blade left in his skin. His head was clear despite the pain. He was no longer angry or frightened. He watched with interest as his body was chafed and torn, thinking, *Look what's here inside me. Who ever would have guessed?*

Finally the one with the hoops in his ear said, "Um, listen, guys, which was it? Did Vannatta say the twelve hundred block or the twenty-one hundred?"

"Look for the Chinese place with the red awning is all I remember."

"It was twelve hundred, right, wasn't it?"

"No, twenty-one, I thought."

"Shit, did somebody keep the note?"

The one with the insect bites spattering his neck took a square of yellow paper from his jacket and unfolded it. "Twenty-one hundred," he read.

The conversation seemed to drop down a well. Somewhere

overhead an exhaust fan was whirring. On the street a basketball slapped the pavement.

"Well," the smaller one said. "I don't think the King of the City here's our man."

Which was exactly what he had tried to tell them when they marshaled him into the alley: he wasn't their man, he didn't have the bricks, he wasn't even sure what the bricks were. But as usual, somewhere between the thought and the statement, his words had hit a blind curve and been wrenched out of shape, so that what he said was not at all what he had intended to say: "No, no, I'm him. Bricks, uh-huh, bricks."

"All right," the smaller one decided. "Here's the agenda. You, you, and you—go find the other Chinese restaurant. Red awning. Twenty-one hundred block. Track down the dude who's got our stuff. Me, I'll stay here and clean up *this* mess." The three of them tramped past the dumpster, the one with the ski jacket rubbing his neck with the bent end of a tire iron, his insect bites pricking the air like a firework.

As soon as the others were out of sight, the smaller one made a study of the damage they had done to him, his eyes pausing at each radiant wound like a kid playing with his first magnifying glass. When he had finished, he gave a long drawn-out whistle and said, "Hey, I'm sorry, man. We really worked you over, didn't we? Look, let me help you get home. Where do you live? Somewhere around here?"

"Around here." He gestured farther down the alley, to the alcove where he kept his shopping cart, with his books and his blanket all bundled up inside.

"Jee-zus. All right, then. Let me get you to the ER."

It took the smaller one a while to persuade him to leave his shopping cart where it was, concealed between a dumpster and a plat of cardboard. He helped him totter to the sidewalk, supporting him as he limped on his busted kneecap, which thrilled with light every time his foot struck the ground. By the time they reached the curb, the glare was unremitting. The smaller one looked up and down the street and complained, "Those dumb assholes took the car, can you believe it?" He hailed a taxi. At the hospital, he removed a horseshoe of hundreds from his jacket, thumbed off five, six, seven bills, and reached across the seat with them. "Good luck, man," he said. "No hard feelings, I hope." He tucked the money into his pocket, then opened the door and urged him outside.

He stumbled into the entrance bay, where several tired-looking doctors sat watching people arrive, pointing, nodding, shaking their heads, as if at a street performance they were too exhausted to appreciate. No one seemed to know what was going on. The halides were altering the whites and yellows of everyone's clothing, lending them a flat blue baseball-park color, but the strained tendons and broken bones of the incoming patients were still plainly visible, even to him. There was the one in the tank top, the young mother, two big shimmering battery bruises on her back. The one with the star cluster of hives on his face. The elderly one with a dog bite showing through her stockings, as round and dazzling as a crown tipped with diamonds. But in all that shining parade of injuries, none was so spectacular as his own. As the taxi sped away, the doctors saw him stumbling along the handicap ramp and sprang up from their benches, calling for a stretcher. A radio was playing at the front desk. He heard a newscaster intoning, "From all over the world this evening we are receiving similar reports—of the ailing and the wounded, shedding light from their bodies," which meant it wasn't just them, it wasn't just here, it was everyone and it was everywhere.

Quickly he was wheeled down the hallway. In the waiting

area, he saw a man he knew from the camps, the one with the old photo of himself heat-pressed onto his T-shirt, a young peroxide-blond lifeguard with a girlfriend on his arm and a stripe of zinc on his nose. And there at the water fountain was another, the one with the braided gray beard and the Scottish terrier. And later he would hear that a third, the one who sold hairbrushes from the sidewalk in front of Fantastic China, had been hospitalized and died that same night with six broken ribs and a cerebral hemorrhage.

Two of the doctors lifted him onto a bed, and the room flooded with technicians and orderlies, anesthesiologists and nurses. The one whose eyes were two different colors asked him his name. If ever there was a question whose answer he had rehearsed, it was this, but he must have been in more pain than he realized, because his tongue let him down again. "More. More Put. More." He felt something brushing his fingers and looked down to find himself holding a notepad and pen. His left hand, his dominant one, the hand that was torn at the webbing, kept filling with a silver mercury he eventually recognized as his blood, so he used his right, spelling his name out one slow letter at a time: Morse Putnam Strawbridge.

"Well, Mr. Strawbridge, hang in there, and we'll get you put back together."

He watched as his clothes were shorn from his body, felt a pinch on his arm, and much later, when he woke up, a pair of women were standing over him, the high clouds of their faces hovering against the blue ceiling. The one with the hint of a headache glowing on her brow said, "It's good to see you again, Mr. Putnam. Are you ready for your morning exercises? We're going to start with the heel slides today. Last night we made it to ten. We're going to shoot for fifteen this time, okay?"

He tried to swallow, and everything shuddered slightly. The

one with the headache was Diane, and the one gazing out the window, watching the buckeye pluck at the wind with its leaves, was Cici. Cici, who believed she was so much better than Diane, so much prettier, so much more sophisticated. Cici, who earned twice the pay for half the work, the lazy sponge. Diane lifted Morse's blanket aside, exposing the fearsome light show of his joints and muscles. Her temples were pounding. She didn't want to touch him. There was dirt and then there was *dirt*, she thought, God's good soil and the grime that sank into a person's flesh and never went away, no matter how thoroughly you scrubbed his filthy body. Heaven forbid her Billy end up like that one day. It's your job, Diane. You don't have to like it. Just brazen up and do it. One hand on the ankle, and the other on the hip. That's the way.

He left the hospital with seven scars decorating his body. To his fingers they felt like segments of fishing wire, taut little lines threaded just below his skin, except for the cut the doctors had made to his peritoneum, which had swollen with infection while he was in recovery and now rose rippling from his stomach like a fat red hairless caterpillar. He was still in pain, still recuperating. An aurora flickered through his gut every time he stretched or coughed, sneezed or bent over. Someone had stolen his shopping cart and blanket from the alley, dumping his books into the alcove behind New Fun Ree, and he sorted through them, throwing out the ones that were rat-gnawed or waterlogged, glued shut by grease or mildew. He bought another blanket from Goodwill, stole another shopping cart from Costco, and four years after the Illumination, that day when something struck a switch in his injuries, he was still sitting cross-legged by the subway entrance, selling books to pedestrians.

"One for two or cash money. One for two or cash money."

He was only nine years old the summer he learned that he could speak more easily when he had practiced what he was going to say. His parents had enrolled him in a workshop at the children's theater. His teachers tried to lure him into their acting-is-believing games, but he was terrified, and nothing worked, until the hairy one, whose clothes gave off the musky smell of tennis balls in a freshly opened canister, took a gamble and cast him as Owl in *The House at Pooh Corner*. Morse studied the script until he had his part memorized, and taking the stage on the last day of camp, he discovered he could deliver his lines with grace and authority, as if he truly were perched on his floor that had once been a wall, telling a story to Pooh and Piglet on the blusterous morning his tree blew down. He spent the next few years believing he would become a movie or TV star when he grew up. Then one of his high school teachers explained that in proper Stanislavskian acting you should live in the moment, as if you were pioneering your words the second you spoke them, and that was it, it was all over, whatever eloquence he had imagined he possessed went bursting into the sky like dandelion snow. He could live in the moment or he could speak in it. He could not do both.

"One for two or cash money. One for two or cash money."

That was his first method—memorization. His second was replication—sorting through the expressions he heard, weighing this piece and that, until he found the right words to mimic a real conversation. He was like a cashier returning a handful of change. In his imagination, each time he spoke, a drawer slid open and a silver bell *ka-chinged*.

How are you doing today? "How are you?" *I'm fine, and yourself?* "I'm fine, I'm fine."

Or: *Our records indicate that your full name is Morse Putnam*

Strawbridge—is that correct? "Correct. Morse Putnam Strawbridge."

Or: *Hello, and welcome to KFC. Would you like to try our new two-piece white-meat value meal?* "New two-piece white-meat value meal."

Though the technique could be surprisingly effective, he used it sparingly, since people tended to become angry when they realized what he was doing. Usually he relied on the dozen or so stock phrases he had already learned by heart.

"One for two or cash money."

"What have you got here, books?"

"Books. One for two or cash money."

"Let's see. I think I'll take the Poggione. How much is it?"

"Price inside the cover. Cash money."

"Here you go then."

Here you go then, he would think. *You go here then. Then here you go.* And he would accept two or three dollars from their hands, scrunching the bills together and stuffing them in his pocket. Then it was, "God bless you, brother," or, "God bless you, sister," and on to the next prospect. The one with the army surplus backpack and the wire-rimmed glasses. The young one, the schoolkid, rehearsing a mustache on his upper lip. The one with the in-town shoes and the out-of-town boyfriend, hoping to impress him with her daring and generosity by buying a book from the scruffy guy with the dirt browning his face. Never the one shifting her child protectively to her outside arm. Never the one discussing the stock market on his cell phone. The Readers and the Good Samaritans—that was who he wanted. He could identify the Good Samaritans from half a block away, zeroing in on him in a fury of benevolence, their fingers sharp and rigid, but the Readers were harder to spot. They could be young or old, sickly or robust, attractive or disagreeable. They inspected the books on his blanket as if they were meeting his eyes. Sometimes they would reach for one with a tiny bated coo of recognition, and he would think they were going to buy it, but no, they had already read it, and they only wanted to know if he had liked it as much as they did. They cherished certain books and disdained others with a zeal that seemed totally genuine yet totally arbitrary. Frequently they wore too much clothing. They rarely haggled. The one feature they seemed to share in common was a tightness at the nape of the neck, as if someone had fixed a stiff metal lozenge where their spine emerged from their shoulders. Though Morse himself was not a Reader, he had been studying them for years, alert for that compressed diamond of tension and the light it cast over their collars.

Sometimes, on the gray-soaked days of February and March, when the sun seemed to dissolve into the clouds like an antacid tablet, he would peer down the street and see nothing but a gleaming field of injuries, as if the traumas and diseases from which people suffered had become so powerful, so hardy, that they no longer needed their bodies to survive. From the doors of shops and art galleries came strange floating candles of heart pain and arthritis. Stray muscle cramps spilled across the sidewalk like sparks scattering from a bonfire. Neural diseases fluttered in the air like leaves falling through a shaft of light. A great fanning network of leukemia rose out of a taxi and drifted incandescently into an office building, and he watched as it vanished into the bricks, a shining angel of cancer. On sunny days, like today, the light was still visible, but Morse had to look more closely to make it out. It was people—they were the problem. Their bodies got in the way. A team of Mormon missionaries walked by in their shirts and ties. It was only after examining them carefully that he noticed that the heavy one, the one with the lumbering gait, had a crescent of athlete's foot glowing from the heel of his shoe. The Chinese family who operated New Fun Ree wheeled their baby into the restaurant, her colic the same silvery white as her jumper. A young couple emerged from the subway, stroking each other's hands. They turned toward the street, and their outlines blurred like plucked wires. The one with the poison ivy rash was named Adam. Just that morning he had stepped into the shower and found an awful prickling Nike swoosh of blisters crimsoning his calf. "I'll be damned," he said, poking his head past the curtain. "Hey, honey? Did you take me hiking or something this weekend and forget to tell me about it?" In the mirror, Helen had cocked an eyebrow, spitting her toothpaste out. "I don't think so. Did you go away and miss me when I wasn't looking?" She was always doing this—amazing him by drawing up some half-forgotten endearment of his, a flirty little line she had greeted with a muffled *thank you* months before, and offering it back to him like a petit four on a tray. She *did* love him. She *did*. He steered her past the street bum with his milk crate and his blanket. Goddamn poison ivy. Goddamn nature. If he grazed his calf with his shoe while he was walking—accidentally, let's say— would that count as scratching? Do it, Adam. Go ahead. No one will mind. "Don't you dare, mister," the one in the turtleneck, Helen, warned him. "If that stuff spreads, it will be your own fault." She took a sip of the coffee she had bought from the subway vendor, the Exotic Autumn blend. *You'll love it,* he had said. *Best of the season,* he had said. But it had an ultrasweet botanical taste she couldn't stand, like the dried cloves her mother always punched into the hams she prepared at Easter. Yuck. Why bother? She tossed the cup in a trash can. An alley cat leaped out from behind the pizza boxes and newspapers and sprang between her legs, bawling at her with its teeth bared, a shrill iamb of hatred. She backed away. Sometimes it seemed to her that she had no place in the world. There was no pity, no consolation. Everything she did ignited these wild billows of spite and resentment. She couldn't even throw a cup of coffee away without causing trouble for herself. She used to be so at home in her life, so happy, and now there was Adam, only Adam, and he was too lovestruck to see her properly. How could she explain that the woman whose sweat he liked to lick off his fingers, the woman he wanted to marry, wasn't Helen at all but the ruins of Helen, the shipwreck of Helen?

Morse lost his grasp on them as they crossed the street. Ever since he was a child he had experienced these occasional episodes of deep understanding. Now and then, unpredictably, things would shiver as if from the cold, and he would know what someone nearby was thinking and feeling. It was happening more often all the time. One day, he was afraid, his life would be nothing but other people's minds. Across the street, for instance, were a pair of glaziers unloading a sheet glass window from a truck flashing its hazards. The one supporting the lower end was named Ezra. A scrim of clouds breezed across the sky, filtering the sunlight, and there in the glass suddenly, as he tilted the pane, he saw his reflection, his dreadlocks spilling out of their elastic band like snakes from a can of novelty peanut brittle. Behind him the world was a claylike city color, the gray and brown of weathered sidewalks and high-rises stitched with fire escapes. It was so strange, so strange. He was backing up when the heel of his boot struck the curb. His reflection lurched away from him. He barely managed to steady the glass in time. Have a nice trip, Ezra. See you next fall. To his partner he said, "Take it a little slower there, why don't you, yeah?" Every word was like a blade in his sore throat. The pain showed through his Adam's apple, a dazzling string of broken beads. He hated himself when he got this way, hated his voice, hated his body. It was the city that did it to him. The crowds, the noise, the pollution. Two years, and he still wasn't used to it. There were days when he could not close his eyes without seeing his Moms and Pops, his four younger sisters, his old bedroom, the luminescent stars on his ceiling, the above-ground pool in his backyard, the beautiful green and yellow of the trees sashaying in the breeze along the coast. He wished he could hear them rustling the way they did on those sunlit summer afternoons when he and his friends stood shaking them for nuts. I don't like this place. I don't want to be here.

And then he was gone.

Morse heard a train grinding metal, that unmistakable city sound, and from out of the subway came an enormous spreading tide of pedestrians. Bike messengers pedaled along the curb and swerved across the median, their wheels tilting back and forth. Cars followed one another into empty parking spaces like bowling balls *tock*ing into a ball corral. A bus stopped at the corner to discharge its passengers. In scarcely a second they broke apart, disappearing down side streets and alleys, into clothing stores, restaurants, and apartment buildings. To all of those who crossed in front of his blanket Morse repeated his sales pitch.

"One for two or cash money. One for two or cash money."

Their skin was raw from the wind, their eyes glowing with fatigue or fever, allergies or conjunctivitis, and almost always they passed him by. Occasionally, though, one would stop and look at his merchandise.

"What does that mean, one for two?"

"One of my books, two of yours. Or cash money."

"What if I don't have any books with me?"

"Then cash money."

"How about for the Basilakos? The hardcover there? What would that set me back?"

"Price inside the cover."

It happened the same way every day, eight to ten hours of work for a few dollars in sales. No one ever came to him with books to trade, except for a handful of his regulars. The one with the clip-cloppy high heels and the endless collection of alternate history novels. The one who shopped for his bedridden grandmother, picking out the kind of mysteries that had the name of the author embossed across half the cover. The one who sorted through Morse's entire stock every Monday and Thursday, deftly and selectively, as if culling the almonds from a jar of mixed nuts. And the smaller one, the talker, who had left Morse staggering across the hospital parking lot the day the Illumination began, his body whitewashed with lacerations.

"How goes it, MP?" That was what he called him, MP—short, he said, for Morse Putnam, Missing Person, Mister Popularity. "Keeping busy?"

"Yeah, yeah, keeping busy."

"Selling a few books?"

"Selling a few."

"And how are you feeling today? Feeling good?"

"Mm-hmm. Feeling good."

This was their ritual, although sometimes it was "Are you feeling groovy today?" and Morse would say, "Feeling groovy," or "Are you feeling lucky today?" and Morse would say, "Feeling lucky," which made the one with the gold watch and the vein in his forehead chuckle and tell him, "You're okay, my friend. Nothing wrong with the old Morse-man, is there? Anyway, two of yours for one of mine, right? That's the bargain?"

"*One for two.* One for two or cash money."

"Yeah, I know, I know. I'm just twisting your balls a little. Here you go," and he would hand Morse a pair of hardcovers he had just purchased from Barnes & Noble, the printing sheen still on the jackets. Sometimes, if the smaller one was in the middle of a job, he would leave immediately, but often he would stay and chat with Morse for a while, telling him about the college girl, a real looker, he had goated around with at his cousin's wedding, or the flatbed truck that had woken him grinding its engine that morning, or the trouble he was having with one of the smackheads over on Spring Street. His first few visits to Morse had been guilt visits, pity visits, his way of showing faith to a living thing he had hurt and tried to help, like a man stopping off at the pound to look in on a stray dog he had clipped with his car. Let's take a peek at the poor battered son of a bitch. Let's see if we can't donate a few bucks to the cause. Soon, though, somehow, he had developed a real affection for Morse. He began confiding in him, telling him dirty jokes, asking after his health. On torrid summer days, when Morse's old wounds lit up, the smaller one would make a wincing noise of drawn breath and shake his head in apology. He seemed genuinely sorry to have injured him—and in spite of himself, Morse responded to his contrition.

"All right, then, take it easy, MP," he would say after he had plucked some yellowing old best seller from Morse's blanket. "Don't let the bastards grind you down," and once he had left, Morse would turn the books he had given him spine-side-up and riffle through the pages, watching the shower of fives and tens that fell ticker-taping to the ground.

In the winter you could never stay comfortable. It began with your hands, which grew chapped from the cold and turned a frayed, weather-bitten red. You could breathe on them, you could wedge them under your arms, but it made no difference. They would not stop aching. Your blood showed its pain in them with every pump, phosphorescing through your skin like those deep-water krill that glowed in the wake of a ship. Your eyes dried out, and your stomach gripped you. You experienced a piercing sensation in your eardrums. There was a specific dental pain, brought on by the way you clenched your teeth against the chill, that you could see throbbing through your gums in the morning, bouncing up at you when you cupped your palms to your mouth. As for your feet, you could not feel them at all. Sometimes, walking, you were amazed to see them stumping away beneath you. It was as if they belonged to another being who had fallen mysteriously under your command. You wore layer after layer of clothing, wrapping everything you owned around yourself—jackets on top of sweaters, jeans on top of flannels—and as the sun rose, your sweat wicked gradually into the fabric. Because you had nowhere to do your laundry, colonies of fungus formed around you. You did not notice the smell usually, but now and again, caught in the warm burst of air from a subway grate, an awful fetor would billow up around you. There was the outdoor life, and there was the indoor life, and you had far too much of the one and far too little of the other. The outdoors offered speed, commotion, and freedom of movement. The indoors offered comfort, security, and its own kind of freedom, freedom from the jabs, nicks, and toothmarks of the cold and the rain. Occasionally, when the smaller one had been unexpectedly generous with you, you would check into a cheap hotel for the night, taking advantage of the warmth, but such nights were rare, and from time to time, in your desperation, you were willing to settle for something less—if not the indoors, then at least the illusion of it.

So it was that Morse made up his mind one day to pay a visit to the camps. He went to the bus station and stowed his shopping cart in one of the large roll-in storage lockers across the lobby from the ticket counter, then caught the northbound train from the platform across the street. He got off at the third stop after the river, hiking past strip malls and used-car dealerships until he reached the warehouse with the painting of the American flag on its side, where he slipped through the rent mesh of a chain-link fence and cut through the tree line to the freeway. The culvert was dry, so he followed it under the road, then scaled the bluff that looked down over the traffic. Sometimes, during rush hour, he would sit on the bare mass of marble at the top and watch the cars and trucks streaming by. Every so often a squirrel or a possum would dart out of the woods and vanish into the chaos of wheels, reappearing as a flash of golden light that popped open and scattered across the concrete.

The camps were a quarter-mile into the trees. Morse walked through tussocks of yellow grass and over the slanting roofs of half-buried stones, then past a rickety wire coop where a line of chickens sat meditating eggs. Suddenly a clearing opened up, and there it all stood: the lawn chairs and the clotheslines, the circles of charred dirt, the clumps of nylon tents that seemed to bloat out of the ground like sheeny orange mushrooms. A stop sign had been nailed to the trunk of a white oak and along the bottom someone had spray-painted the word TIBET. Toward the back of the clearing was a pile of trash, filled with all the waste pieces and bits of metal the camp's countless fires had not succeeded in consuming—beer cans with their labels whitened away, clothes hangers straightened into antennas, the spoonlike keel bones of chickens. And to the west, beneath the arms of an ancient chestnut, was a canvas tarp with a soft glow leaking from inside.

Something drew Morse toward the light. He found a dozen men sitting hunched on crates and logs around a gas lantern. Their bodies seemed to whisk around inside themselves. Tucker was the one with the eczema scales on his face and the respiratory ache in his chest, the cramps in his stomach and the chilblains on his feet, and God only knew what terrible baroque infection casting its glow from the beds of his fingernails. His body had become a horror novel: *The Fall of the House of Tucker.* He couldn't remember the last time he truly felt like himself, the last time he sensed that old strength of spirit pulsing inside him. When he was thirteen or fourteen, probably, around the time he met Jeff Moody and that crowd and his parents tossed him out for huffing paint and breaking into storage units. Those were the days. All that ravaged holiness. Things had never been better. Show me a person who rambles on and on about his childhood and I'll show you a person whose life has disappointed him. Tucker watched a praying mantis take a few stiltlike steps across the ceiling of the tarp. Praying, preying, praying, preying. Praying, he decided. It seemed to be moving in slow motion. He put his knuckles to his eyes and rubbed them. The hissing sound surprised him. Then he looked up and realized it was just the lantern, venting propane into its chamber. The one letting the matchstick bob between his teeth had turned up the burner. His name was Aaron, and he'd be damned if he went back to the shelters, where they tried to steal your backpack while you were sleeping, except you weren't sleeping at all, were you? No, no, you were pulling the old fluttery eyelash trick, and when you bounded up from the mattress to bust some skulls, they nailed you from your weak side with a twelve-inch Maglite. So what if the volunteers gave you a hot meal and let you use the showers? So what? The place was full of crooks, perverts, and evangelicals—f-a-c-t *fact*. Him, he would rather be safe and freezing on a pallet of oak leaves, lying where he could stare out of his own sleeping bag, and not at the walls or rafters but the sky, watching the birds light up the trees with their own little infections and heart attacks. He held his hands out toward the Coleman lantern. His fingertips seemed to waver in the fumes. What was with everyone? A silence had fallen over the group, a heavy quilt of exhaustion. Screw that shit. Time to liven things up with his favorite joke. "Hey, fellas," he said, and he nodded across the circle. "Why does David here smell so bad?" David. That was the one whose hair was receding in a perfect arc, like the gently spreading ripple on the surface of a pond after a goldfish lips at a mayfly. Her real name, though, was Kristi, and she had known it ever since she was a little boy, gazing at herself in the mirror as she tucked her penis between her legs. That wonderful tightening of the skin. That glorious nectarine smoothness. She should have paid for the operation fifteen years ago with her student loan money, just like she had threatened she would. Whose body was it, after all? I mean, really, Mom—whose? A bent green insect dropped onto the lantern, casting its giant shadow onto the tarp. In a million years Kristi could never explain why it startled her into beating Aaron to the punch line, but it did. "So that blind people can hate me, too," she said. Everyone laughed. The joke never changed. Oh what a riot. What a fucking, fucking riot. How dismal it was to wake up every morning as the same gamy, balding mammoth of a man she had been when she went to sleep. Oh to wake up one morning as what she truly was—a gamy, balding mammoth of a *woman.* Hah! Now *that* really *was* funny. Good one, Kristi.

Morse picked up an orange crate and edged his way into the circle. Reluctantly the others made room for him. He had just settled down when the one with the smudge of oil on her glasses asked, "Say, man, you got a cigarette?"

"A cigarette?" Morse made a show of checking his pockets. "No cigarette."

"*Pfft.* What makes you think you're welcome here without any cigarettes? I don't even *know* you. Does anyone else here know this joker?"

"I don't know him."

"Never seen him before."

"Yeah, that's what I figured. You got a light, at least?"

"No, no, got no light."

"Then here's a question: what exactly are you good for?"

"Good. Good. Good. Good." Morse took a breath. "Good question."

Accidentally he had delivered a wisecrack. That, it seemed, was all it took—he had established his credentials. He was the squirrelly guy, the comedian, quiet but sort of funny if you gave him half a chance, and nobody would object if he sat with them around the lantern, watching as they held their fingers to the heat or drank from a bottle of liquor, smoked a joint or played high-card-low-card. The one suffering from the trembling disease that caused a hard light to glare from his body invited Morse to join the game, but he declined with a shake of his head. The one who had been chewing on the matchstick touched it to the burner, watching it ignite with a fizz of sulfur. The one with the dragon-fly tattoo squeezed the knee of the one whose long black hair fell almost to her waist, and she closed her eyes and passed him a slow, stretching, easy-baked smile. Morse had the impulse to squeeze her other knee, that fat little beanbag he saw marking its shape in her skirt, but he knew better than to try it. All the good-will he had earned would evaporate in an instant if he did. The sun was nearly gone. It was only a few seconds before the last moment of left light came angling over the field and disappeared.

An hour or so later, shortly after the one with the broken veins on his cheeks snuffed out the lantern, Morse dragged a sheet of cardboard to the border of the clearing and lay down. For warmth he brought his legs together and pulled his arms inside his clothing. As usual, he found himself tracing his scars with his fingers. His wounds had healed long ago, forming raised white lines that remained stiff and pale no matter how flushed he became. He was fascinated by them, by their singular alien braille. They still hurt when he prodded them, not unbearably, not even unpleasantly, but enough. Enough so that he noticed. Enough so that his awareness yielded itself over to them and whatever else he had been thinking about gradually gave way and drifted out of his mind. He had learned to love them, those firm embossments of stitched skin. They gave him the same feeling of comfort he imagined devout Catholics must experience fingering the beads of a rosary.

Nearby an owl filled the night with its blooming sound, a strange low death call that grew softer and softer until Morse woke to the sight of the morning graying the trees. His heart sank. Once again, it was a question of inside versus outside, a question of proportions. The hotel rooms he rented were 90 percent inside; all they lacked was another living person—a wife, say; a child—to round them off to 100. The alcove behind New Fun Ree, by contrast, was 90 percent *outside;* sure, now and then, as he crouched behind the barrier of his shopping cart, a dreamlike inside seemed to form itself around him, wrapping him in an illusion of protection and tranquillity, but it was only that—an illusion—and he never quite forgot it. The camps were something else altogether. They were just as outside as the alcove, but because he was surrounded by other people, with their odors and their voices and footsteps, the illusion was even stronger, even worse. And when that beautiful inside fantasy of his finally thinned away and broke in the sunlight, he felt completely exposed and forsaken.

It happened the same way every time. Why could he never remember?

——

On Friday afternoons, when the weather was clear, he liked to go book hunting. He would push his shopping cart from one block to the next, rattling over every seam in the sidewalk, every steel vent, until he had returned to the subway entrance. To walk the whole circuit of thrift stores and libraries took him two hours and forty-five minutes. His cart's left front wheel had become detached, and when he forgot to apply his weight to the handle, the empty holding bracket scraped the pavement and left a streak of orange rust. He was always nervous some police officer would cite him for vandalism and arrest him, so he shuffled along with his head down, glancing up only when he saw a light so bright he was sure someone must be dying, though invariably it was only the sun rebounding off a windshield or a manhole cover. Or almost invariably. One day, shortly after the Illumination, when Morse had just returned to his books, he was offering his usual pitch to the pedestrians when a few yards away, beneath the lamp-post in front of the subway entrance, the one plugging quarters into the parking meter put his hand to his head and collapsed. The one walking her dachshund rushed to his side to perform CPR, and the one in the business suit phoned 911, but already the rules were second nature to Morse: light equaled pain, and as the glow from the man's body sharpened to a million pinpoints that bleached together and then faded to a shadow, he knew that death had taken him, in his polished shoes and Burberry coat, away.

By now everyone along Morse's route knew him so well that his question—"Any books for me today?"—was merely a formality.

"Well, someone donated a few Harlequins I can give you," they said.

Or, "I left a couple for you back by the restrooms."

Or, "Sorry, brother. Try us again next week."

Or, "Here you go. They're in pretty ratty shape, but you're more than welcome to 'em."

Welcome to 'em, he thought. *Well come two um. Welc'm to'm.*

One mid-April evening, he had just completed his itinerary when he passed a pile of furniture resting at the base of someone's stoop, the remnants, he guessed, of an estate sale or an eviction. The lamps, chairs, mirrors, and such had already been picked over, but he found a stack of old books sitting in a cardboard box and loaded them into his cart. When he reached the subway entrance, he fanned them out next to the rest of his merchandise. At the bottom of the stack was a flat wooden coffer that hardly resembled a book at all, but he included it anyway, using it to shore down the corner of the blanket.

A school bus backfired, striping the air with a plume of black exhaust. The sidewalks were bustling with people. The one taking the tiniest, most judicious steps as she walked out of New Fun Ree winced at the blast. She felt as if she were crossing a high wire hundreds of feet above the ground. Her name was Zoe, and for her it had been a long life of falling ill whenever the seasons changed, regarding her body as it slowly broke down and defeated her. Its agonies and odors. Its sad animal deterioration. They always followed the same pattern, her sicknesses: first the raw burred patch of a sore throat spread slowly across the roof of her mouth, and then she felt a tack in her left ear when she swallowed, and then her neck grew stiff, and her eyes burned, and finally her joints ached and her nose ran and every inch of her incandesced inside the bright aura of a fever. But that wasn't right, was it? The pain was old, as old as she was, but the light was new. It was easy to forget it had not always been there. It was so soft, so intimate, like the colors in a Giroux print. Or that was how she saw it, at least. Some of her colleagues in the Art Department described it rather differently: like the marshy blotches of a Jaeger painting; like the sun-streaked elliptica of an Ozu film. She would not have been surprised if every person in the world observed her own distinct version of the phenomenon, eight billion unique, privileged variations. Another car honked. She tried to keep going. How would she ever cross the street to her apartment? Feed a cold, starve a fever, they said, but she really needed to get something solid in her stomach.

Because the sky was bright and the air was warm, Morse worked later than usual that night. The traffic was fitful, moving forward in clots and gaps, and the moon was already rising over the buildings when three boys dashed across the street, cheating the signal. They leaped onto the curb a few steps in front of a pickup truck and headed toward New Fun Ree, the colors of their clothes shuddering around them. The one whose shoelaces were whipping at the pavement was named Wallace. He had three pizzas from Pie R. Squared in his hands: a cheese, a pepperoni, and for Camarie, the vegetarian, a black olive and pineapple, which was pretty damn disgusting, if you asked him. He was thinking about the campaign he was running—how if the group followed the Eastern path, they would encounter the last of the elder folk, and if they followed the Western path, they would find the seal of Raxhura, but if they strayed toward the Smoke Mountains, the fire genasai would consume them in flames—when he spotted it, a pale wooden box the size of a laptop computer, sitting at the margin of that old book guy's blanket. Holy shit, was that what he thought it was? He said, "Hey, hold up, guys," and Ben P. and Conrad turned around. Wallace handed the pizzas over to them, then bent down to give the wooden box a closer look. His palms were sweating something ridiculous. His heart was racing like he didn't know what kind of crazy engine. Everything was exactly right: the scorched brown lettering, the blurred illustration of the Phoenix, the "Arise, Oh Generations of the Dead" slogan with the famous "Generations of the Dad" misprint. No doubt about it—what they had here was a first-edition Cities in Dust manual. And not only that, but the brads on the corners of the box were still in place, which meant that odds were the set was intact, with both the Twelve Nations supplement and the original Gazetteer. Unbe-fucking-mazing. Buy it, Wallace. Buy it. Borrow the money. Do whatever it takes.

"How much is that book right there?" he asked, keeping his voice nonchalant.

"One for two or cash money."

"Mm-hmm. What exactly does that mean?"

And after Morse had explained it to him, the one with the loose shoelaces said, "Dude, my mom's got a whole wallful of books at home. Come with us. You can take your pick." So Morse followed the boys to an apartment building on the 1400 block, then onto an antique elevator with an operator's stool in the corner. The walls were so narrow the four of them were barely able to fit inside. He had to leave his shopping cart in the lobby. The one with the crickety voice led them into the front room of his apartment, which, just as he had promised, contained seven full-length rows of recessed shelving, jammed with several thousand books.

Morse took his time looking over the selection. In the next room, gathered around a coffee table strewn with dice, papers, and metal figurines, was a cluster of seven young teenagers. The one with the green silk fillet braided into her hair, the only girl in the bunch, was sitting on a futon with her knees folded to her chest, clutching a throw pillow like a mother protecting her baby.

Camarie was her name, and no matter what she tried, she kept falling in love. With Wallace and that ribbed blue sweater of his— its smoky sort of pencil-shavings smell. With Mr. McKim, her math teacher, and the dry-erase marker bruises on his knuckles. With the *News at Nine* anchor—the weekend guy—and the way he pressed his lips together and made a little *mm* sound, as if he were scratching a hard-to-reach itch, whenever he had to report something tragic. With Ben P. and that lock of hair he couldn't keep out of his eyes. With Ben F. and his strong brown tennis-player's arms. With Wallace again and how he laughed louder than anyone else at his own jokes. With Nathan and the hundred different ways he had of saying "dude." With Conrad and how he bit the loose threads from the cuffs of his shirt, bringing his per-fect white teeth together like nail clippers. With her brother's friend Hal and his beard that looked as soft as Jesus'. With Wal-lace one more time and that night she rolled a ninety-nine for agility and he said, "Kick-ass," and then winked at her. Boys!

Morse had already chosen the first of his books, a thick volume of Impressionist paintings he knew would sell right away, when the phone on the table rang. Without thinking, he picked it up. The one who lived there flung his hands about as if flailing at a mosquito. "Shit, man. That's gonna be my mom. Why did you answer? Give me the phone. No, quick, find out who it is, and say, 'How can I help you?' "

The words plunged at Morse like bats, filling the room with their clacks and their squeaks, and he barely had time to fight his way through them before he spoke. "Who am I, and how can I help you?"

"I'm sorry?" the voice in his ear said.

The one folding the slice of pepperoni pizza said, "Tell her, 'This is the wrong number,' dude."

The red-haired one dove in with, "Dude, say good-bye. Hang up."

Morse repeated the phrases as best he could, then returned the phone to its cradle.

A second later, it rang again. This time the one who lived there answered: "Hey, Mom. Yeah, just me and the campaigners are taking a break." The blandishing tones of his voice became more bruised, more salted. "You must have dialed the wrong number or something. Okay, listen, don't freak out. There's this guy we met and—"

Morse scoured the shelves for the second of his two books. *Impressionist Masterpieces in Full Color* was the kind of oversize hardcover whose thick, coated paper was cool to the touch and gave off a smart perfume of expensive ink. The binding was so heavy he had to support the book on his hip. He wanted his other choice to be smaller, lighter. He was sure he would know it when he saw it. Dimly, as he scanned the bookcase closest to the front door, he heard the noise of an argument, or half an argument, the raised voice of the one letting the dice clitter in his hand, but it was of no significance to him.

The one whose retainer was drawing a silver line across his teeth groaned. "All right, man. Hurry it on up. You can have that one and one other, but that's it."

On impulse Morse selected a worn volume with a frayed silk bookmark dangling over its spine from the corner of the top shelf.

"Fine. Fantastic. You have your two books. Now go. Go. You have to go now."

Morse heard the one on the phone saying, "Okay, okay, we're done. He's leaving. Problem solved," as he placed the wooden box with the brown lettering on the sideboard and took his exit. In the hallway he made the call button glow beneath his index finger. In the elevator he sat like a king on the stool's satin cushion. From the lobby he retrieved his silver chariot. And then he was gone, back outside, among the night smells and the speeding cars and the bars with their gray windows and the diners with their bright ones.

Because it was late and the alley behind New Fun Ree was unilluminated, Morse wasn't able to page through the second book until the next day. It turned out to be a diary, handwritten in blue ink, each page lined from top to bottom with thousands of small slanting letters.

I love how dark your hair gets after you wash it. I love waiting for you in the airport at the bottom of the escalator. I love the way you run your hands under the hot water a hundred times a day when it gets cold outside. I love how you "dot all your t's and cross all your i's." I love my birthday present—thank you so much. I love hearing you rise to someone's defense, and twice in one night, too: Woody Allen and Neville Chamberlain. I love watching you upend a whole bottle of water after you've exercised: that little bobber working in your throat, and the gasp you make after you finish swallowing, and the way you slam the bottle back down on the counter. I love how cute you are when we're watching basketball together and you pretend to care who's winning. I love your idea for a hard rock supergroup made up of the members of Europe, Asia, and America—Pangaea. I love your cleansing rituals (but I love your dirtying rituals even more). I love your morning breath.

That was all it was, line after line of love notes, none of them longer than a sentence. They appeared to be from the father of the one with the loose shoelaces and the crickety voice, addressed to his mother.

I love the e-mails you send me in the middle of the day.
I love trying to coax you to pick out a restaurant.

I love the way you groan whenever adult human beings start talking about comic books.

The cover was scuffed, the pages were buckled with moisture, and Morse was uncommonly disappointed. No one would ever buy such a thing. He presumed the one who had allowed him to take it would come looking for it within a day or two. He decided to save it for him.

The next week, when the smaller one, the talker, came by to swap his books and slide Morse a few extra dollars, he made a show of considering his choices. "No, not the Lawrence," he said. "And not the Ramirez. And definitely not the Railey. A man's got to have *some* scruples. How about that one?" and he reached for the diary of miniature love letters.

Morse surprised himself with the force of his objection. "No! Not that one."

"MP!" The smaller one shook his head. "I'm ashamed of you. A businessman never gets attached to his own merchandise. That's the first rule of success: sure, fine, love the product, whatever—but love the *sale* more. I thought I taught you that."

"Sure, fine, whatever." Morse slipped the book into his coat. "Not that one."

The smaller one's hand cuffed Morse's shoulder. "Hey, I'm just screwing with you. Hell, give me the Railey. It doesn't make any difference to me."

That afternoon, when it began to sprinkle, Morse rolled a sheet of Visqueen over his books. The diary seemed to broadcast its message straight through the plastic, *I love you, I love you, I love you, I love you,* pulsing like a beacon. All around him people were braking their cars or ducking into buildings, zipping their jackets or opening their umbrellas. He fixed his mind on the pretty one standing under the awning of the jewelry store and thought, *I love your green dress and your loneliness and your matching green shoes.* He turned to the one who was limping into the subway station and thought, *I love how you have a foot cramp and you keep saying "Stop it, stop it, stop it" to yourself.* He watched the one carrying the grape cluster of plastic bags and thought, *I love it that you're walking down the sidewalk and now you've turned the corner and I can't see you anymore because you're gone.* He had expected it to be effortless, expected his love to ease right out of him, as gently and clearly as notes from a piano, but soon enough he realized it was impossible. It couldn't be done, or at least he couldn't do it. He did not love anyone, he only understood them, and who in this world would choose understanding over love?

It was a different rain, nearly eight months later, and Morse was watching the water create beads on his poncho, when the smaller one brought him two new books. The first was called *Mister Parsons,* the second *Mansfield Park,* and he said, "Two MPs for my main MP. Don't let them get wet now. I think you'll like these."

"One for two or—"

"Yeah, yeah, I know, one for two or cash money. Give me that hardback number right there. The big red fella. It'll match my sofa."

Morse weaseled the book out from under the Visqueen and handed it to the smaller one, and the smaller one slipped it into his coat, gave a little *cha-cha* with his tongue, and pretended to fire his finger at Morse. Then he walked away whistling. Morse would never understand people who exulted in bad weather.

It was barely noon, but it seemed as if the sun had already gone down. The sky was a solid brick of gray, so dark that Morse lost sight of the smaller one long before he made his turn onto Tenth

Street. The rain that dotted his poncho formed tiny solid-looking drops that merged by threes and fours into trembling half-domes, then broke free of their shapes and streamed away. The effect was mesmerizing, soporific. It was an effort for him to look anywhere else, though eventually he did. On the corner, beneath the black canopy of a newsstand, he saw an abscessed tooth blazing like a newborn star. The stacked blocks of a degenerative disk disorder came leaning out of a taxi. Behind the window of the drugstore were a pair of inflamed sinuses, by the counter a shimmering configuration of herpes blisters, on the bench a lambent haze of pneumonia. And across the street Morse saw a great branching delta of septicemia slide through the rear doors of an ambulance and disappear in a glory of light.

The subway shrieked and released its passengers. Up they trudged from under the street, hunching and shivering. The one shaking the water from his hands was named Charles Dennison, the Attuned and the Obedient, Beloved of the Lord and His Angels, and issuing its proclamations in his mind was the Divine Vibratory Expression named Hahaiah. Hahaiah had given Charles a single holy task: to provide fresh experiences to Eternity. The responsibility was profound. *Fish the magazine out of that trash can. Whack the sports car with it. See the license plate: DADSTOY. Yes, that one. No, not the window, the door! Hit the DOOR! Now bite your hand, there where the palm thickens at the base of the thumb.* Charles set his mouth to his palm. *HARDER.* His teeth drew light from his skin. *Good.* In Eternity everything had already taken place—that was the problem. Nothing happened there that was not happening again. Only here, in the Physical and Contingent World, could one generate fresh experiences for the Lord and His Elect, which was why it was incumbent upon Charles to do exactly what Hahaiah bade him. *Stop that woman, the one in the fur jacket.* Charles took the woman by the sleeve. *Say, "Truly, my lady, it is a Marvelous and a Blessed Day."* "Truly, my lady, it is a Blessed and a Marvelous and Day." *A MARVELOUS and a BLESSED.* "A Marvelous and a Blessed." The woman wrenched herself away from Charles and continued through the door of the hotel. He saw her standing in the lobby with a look of vexation and disordered pride, trying to tease the oil from her jacket with her fingers while the doorman folded her umbrella. This was what the world was: the one and only place where things could still happen for the first time.

It was late afternoon before the rain finally drove Morse to his alcove and he had the chance to give the books the smaller one had traded him a shake. From *Mister Parsons* fell a thousand dollars in hundreds. Another thousand fluttered from the pages of *Mansfield Park*. The bills were authentic, newly printed, with that sweet, antiseptic smell that reminded him of window spray.

Never before had the smaller one given him so much cash money. Not for the first time Morse wondered where it all came from.

He was having one of his indoor moods, so he took his cart to the lockers at the bus station, then checked into a hotel, the old Beaux Arts building across from the modern art museum. He put his clothing in a drawstring bag to be laundered, showered until the water no longer ran gray, then settled down in a bathrobe and slippers to ply his way through the TV stations. He had brought only a single book with him, the diary of *I love you*'s with the torn binding and the foxed pages, which the one with the loose shoelaces had never retrieved. Every now and then, when Morse had nothing better to do, he liked to open it and read a few lines at random. *I love your avocado and Swiss sandwiches. I love the way your neck arches like a cat's whenever you hear a car slowing down on the street outside our window. I love the story of the Sticky Bandit—aka Mr. Splat. I love your fascination with crop circles, but as landscape art, not UFO indentations or messages from the Circlemakers of the Beyond. I love swipping your triggle gitch.* He was fascinated yet vexed by the book. Between each sentence, it seemed, there was a gap, a chasm, a whitening away of meaning. He did not understand how something so sweet, so earnest and candid, could also be so wayward and enigmatic. He kept expecting to return to the book and discover that it had pondered all his questions while he was gone and then fortified itself with the answers.

For two nights, Morse stayed in his hotel room eating grilled steak and cheese agnolotti, seared scallops and grilled duck breast, and drinking sparkling water and tempranillo and white burgundy. The cake he ordered was too rich, and the raspberry sorbet gave him an ice cream headache, the kind that smoldered across his temples for thirty seconds and then flared out, but he barely noticed it. It felt good to eat and drink, to stand at the window looking out over the city, to sleep in a soft bed, to wake without quite realizing he had. It felt good to be alive. Wounded but alive. Shining but alive.

By the time he returned to his milk crate and his six squares of sidewalk, the weather had turned cold and serene, ice-still. Everyone was puffy with extra clothing—coats, jerseys, sweat suits, long johns, wool socks, and ribbed hats. He could see the cars breathing from their tailpipes like looming metal monsters. A station wagon rabbited forward to beat the light, then braked to a stop behind a delivery van. The family inside leaned into the momentum. Their bodies seemed to quiver, their minds seemed to dance, and Morse waited for them to reveal themselves to him. The one sitting Indian-style in the cargo area was named Evie. The *chump seat*—that was what Tom and Amy called it. Or sometimes the *chimp seat*. Which meant that Evie was the chump.

Or sometimes the chimp. But she didn't care. She liked riding back there with the groceries and the jumper cables. It was like camping out in her own private fort, a fort that was also a space-ship, a spaceship that was also a go-cart, a go-cart that bumped down the track at sixty miles an hour while she pretended to steer with her hands and also sometimes even her feet. "Are you okay back there in the caboose, Evie-girl?" her mom called out, and Evie said, "I'm fine," and most of the time her mom asked, "Whatcha doing?" next, but fortunately she didn't this time, because what Evie was doing was peeling the scab from her knee. It was nearly the size of a silver dollar, or maybe a piece of gum after it's been flattened on the driveway, and just like the gum it was crisp on the top side but gummy on the bottom, and just like the silver dollar it sparkled in the light. It hurt a little as she lifted it free, trailing a few strings of something wet and sticky. Total and complete grossness.

All that day, Morse kept up a patter of *one for two*s and *cash money*s, but it made no difference. No one was willing to stop in such a chill. He busied himself rearranging his books. His lips froze together each time he licked them, separating with a slight click. Whenever he moved, gusts of detergent wafted from the folds and gathers of his clothing.

I love your Elvis impression—the worst Elvis impression I've ever heard, or ever will hear, in my entire life. I love your thing for lips and hands—and the fact that, thank God, my own lips and hands received a passing grade. I love the little meditative puffing noises you make when you're exercising. I love watching you dive into a swimming pool, the way your body wavers underneath the water, the way your legs frog open and closed, the way you breach the surface with your eyes shut good and hard.

He had just set the diary aside when a shadow stretched across his blanket. The smaller one was standing there, his body all doubled in on itself. His arms were crossed, his knees locked tight, and his left eye wore a lustrous white bruise. A two-day growth of bristles covered his face. It was the first time since the Illumination that Morse could remember seeing him without a pair of books in his hands. The first time, for that matter, his voice sounded so thin and frightened, though he tried his best to manufacture some of his old swagger. "MP! Maximum Penalty! Listen, those books I gave you on Tuesday? The money? That was a mistake." He scuffed the pavement with his shoe. "And, well, I need it back, just this once."

"The money." Morse shook his head and shrugged. "The money."

"Jesus Christ, you stupid dimwit, what's that supposed to mean? What, are you telling me that you spent it already? Great! Perfect! What the hell have you been feeding yourself, gold-dusted truffles?" The smaller one stalked away, then turned back around. "Thanks for your help. MP. Buddy. Friend of mine. It's good to know I can count on you in my time of need." He flinched at the sound of a car door slamming, then stiffened his neck, like a brawler recovering from a punch, and descended into the subway station.

Several months passed before Morse saw him again. By then the trees were leafing out, and the last hard saddles of gray snow were melting from the recesses of the alleys. Warm breezes kept pushing at the ground, as if an invisible highway were running just overhead. From the ledges and the power lines came startling polyphonies of birdsong. All over the city people had taken to the streets to enjoy the first breath of spring. Morse watched the one with the bad case of acne—his neck, cheeks, and forehead a glimmering and resplendent red—pop a wheelie on his racing bike. The one whose bare legs were goose-pimpling in the breeze crossed the street. The one holding the paper bag and the soda bottle hummed along to his own private music. He stopped short as he was passing Morse's blanket. "Tell me, is that Tevis you've got there, the original Gold Medal paperback?"

Morse opened the book he had indicated and displayed the copyright page.

"It is, isn't it? I'll be damned. How much?"

"One for two or cash money."

"One for two what?"

"Books."

A car pulled up to the curb, its parking lock clicking and chirping.

"I don't have any books with me. Hmm. Hey, look, this is going to sound ridiculous, but what about a bowl of chili?" He extended his paper bag. "Can I trade you a bowl of chili instead? It's good. Good chili is worth two books easy, right?"

"No chili. One for two or cash money."

"Yeah, but I just spent my last five dollars. How's this, look—a bowl of chili, a bottle of 7Up, *unopened,* and"—his hand fished a few coins from his pocket—"a quarter, a dime, and one-two-three-four-five-six-seven-eight . . . twelve pennies?"

And because Morse was thirsty, he nodded.

The one with the soda bottle gave a firecracker-like clap. "It was a pleasure doing business with you," he said once the exchange was made, and strutted away.

Morse decided to eat his lunch in his alcove. He picked up his milk crate, parceled his blanket around his books, and lifted the bundle into his shopping cart. In the alley behind New Fun Ree, on the blind side of a dumpster, he found the smaller one crouching like an injured dog. His eye had long since healed over, but a hundred other injuries illuminated his body. The fingers of his right hand, wrapped in a T-shirt, yielded a flat and powerful light.

His bruised ribs and galled right cheek printed the air with their sigils. His face shone from beneath the skin, slung over his skull like a scarf over a lamp. He said, "I think I'm in some trouble here, MP," and once again Morse watched as the film of the world came loose on its spindle. His name was Lee, Lee Hartz, and oh Jesus, oh Jesus, how was he going to protect himself? Vannatta would find him and finish what the others had started. He would rip him open, flay him apart, proceeding digit by digit, layer by layer, until there was so much blood that whoever found him would have to shield his eyes from the light. *The currency of punishment*—that was what Vannatta called it. As in, "We're going to give our friends on Ninth Street an important lesson in the currency of punishment." A blow for every hundred, he meant. A broken bone for every thousand. A human life for every million. Lee had seen it happen to countless thieves and swindlers, watched their fragile bodies spraying outward from themselves like the glass from a hurled bottle, shattered and gleaming on the pavement. Where could he hide? Where? Vannatta knew the city down to its pores, its nerve endings, its last filthy alley and its last wind-etched bridge bearing. He could find Lee wherever he went. He could snap his fingers and kill a man. He never rested, never slept. Oh my sweet Lord above.

Lee used his good hand, his left one, to grip Morse's arm. "I need someplace to hide. I need to flat fucking vanish. Can you hide me, buddy? Can you do that?"

"Someplace to hide." And it came to Morse like a crack of thunder. "I can do that."

He led the smaller one out of the alley and around the corner, then past a modest streetside park where the benches were peppered with men and women whiling away their lunch hours. The one with the ulcer flaring from her lip was named Nina. The foul thing shone like a penlight, with much too bright a brightness, though she wasn't talking, wasn't chewing, wasn't even moving. Why? she wanted to know. What was wrong with her? For nearly five years, *five years,* it had been one ulcer after another, a plague of shining sunken wounds. She was hungry, but she could not eat. She was lonely, but she could not speak. And she no longer believed it would stop. Oh, there had been a lover once, and he kept e-mailing to ask her when he could visit, and maybe someday she would say *yes* to him, maybe someday she would say *now,* but every time she dared, she felt that briary sensation on her lips and tongue, and she knew that it would soon be getting worse. She had never found love, or if she had, she had rejected it, and she was nearly certain she would die young—or at least younger than she otherwise would have—because no one had ever come along and saved her. She leaned back, distending her arms behind the bench. Overhead a pair of gray squirrels were sparring around the trunk of a beech tree. She watched as they dashed in and out of sight, their tense little brushes flickering a half step behind them. If only she could have been one of them, she thought—could have been anyone, or anything, else for a while, a bird, a kite, a cloud. What sense did it make that such a thing wasn't possible? It would take so little. Who had created this world, anyway? All her life she had avoided bar fights, contact sports, political protests—anywhere there was the slightest chance she might get hurt. She had been so careful, so excruciatingly careful. Not once had she ever been punched in the mouth, and yet that was how she felt now, all the time: as if she had just been punched in the mouth. But it's not my *fault.* I didn't *do* anything.

The train platform was only a few blocks away. Morse guided the smaller one through the turnstile and onto the northbound express. On the other side of the river, in the gas station by the used car lot, he borrowed forty dollars to buy a carton of cigarettes and packed them into the smaller one's jacket. The smaller one's stomach shone and guttered through his shirt, its lancinations casting their light over Morse's hands. As he closed his zipper, he felt like a doctor stitching an incision. The two of them shuffled past the pumps and the repair bays, the pawn shop and the nail salon, the warehouse with the giant American flag painted on its side. Then it was through the chain-link fence, under the freeway, up the bluff, and into the trees. The last thing the smaller one said as Morse banked him away in an empty tent was "What we did to you that day—I had no clue, man, you gotta believe me."

It was nine days later, and Morse had stopped hearing footfalls in the alley at night, stopped feeling the wind on his neck, stopped, in short, expecting trouble to find him, when it did. He was sitting on his milk crate by New Fun Ree, reading one of the diary's late pages by the light of the sun, the pigeons strutting past his blanket like mindless little kings.

I love feeling your hands reach behind me to adjust my collar when I'm wearing a shirt and tie. I love the way, when we haven't seen each other for a while, you'll run to me with one of your patented spring-loaded hugs, your arms outstretched and then BAM! I love the hard time you have with fractions. I love the soft blue veins on your wrist. I love the beautiful pink cushions of your lips. I love hearing you sing old R&B songs when you don't know I'm listening, love your bright little meadowlark of a voice. I love it when we finish having sex, and we don't have anything to do, and I can just lie there twitching inside you for a while. I love the way you'll put a few spoonfuls of palak paneer on your plate, eat it, then put another few spoonfuls on your plate, eat it, and so on. I would love to have a baby with you.

He had just turned the page when the book was plucked from his hand, taken almost delicately, as if someone were twisting a blueberry from a vine. He looked up, and there they were, the one with the shaved head and the one with the paring knife and the big red beefy one with the metal hoops in his ear. He recognized them right away, though he had not seen them since the day they put him in the hospital.

The big one, who had loosened his necktie and rolled up his shirtsleeves, fanned through the pages of the diary. "What's this we got here?"

Morse tried to ask him a question. "Doing some? Some some?"

"I'm gonna do me some reading."

"Doing some reading?"

"That's just what I said now, isn't it?"

He handed the book to the one whose missing tooth, a bicuspid, gave a jack-o'-lantern quality to his face, and the one with the missing tooth cocked his wrist and flung it into the street. The cover jackknifed over on itself with a ruinous crack before a truck sent it skidding into the gutter. Several of the pages fluttered loose. Morse watched them follow one another across the asphalt, spilling words the way a car wreck spills oil.

"Now, I understand you've been seen with a friend of ours. Man by the name of Lee Hartz. What we want to know is where he's hiding out these days."

"Hiding out?"

"I think you take my meaning."

Morse shook his head.

And then it was, "Looks like our man here doesn't know anything," and, "That's a shame really. A real shame," and they seized him by the arms and marched him around the corner. The people on the sidewalk stood hard to one side or else shied away into the entries of shops and restaurants. At the dark end of the alley, beneath the fire escape, the one with the smile said, "All right. Lee Hartz. Name ring any bells for you yet?" and the one with the tire iron said, "I don't think he understands the question," and the one whose neck muscles stood out like wood vines said, "I guess we'll have to find some other way to ask him."

They came at him with their fists and their boots and their knives. The light left his body in a flood of silver. Perhaps this time it really was his soul.

He sank against a cellar window, shielding his face with his hands until it was over. He was not sure how long the three of them took, only that a moment came when someone belted him on the ear and one last kick made its mark on his hip. Then there was just the quiet of their breathing, their lungs laboring as if they had finished a race. The one with the necktie said, "Rest up now, buddy," or maybe it was the one with the shaved head. He couldn't tell their voices apart anymore. "We'll be seeing you soon."

Morse listened as the traffic absorbed the sound of their footsteps. Slowly, slowly, he uncovered his eyes. The alley was so narrow he had become invisible to most of the people on the street. He watched them passing in the distance as if through a sheet of water, the strange reeds of their bodies blurring this way and then the other. The one sliding a letter into the mailbox, his frayed leather satchel looped over his shoulder, was named Masaki. At the lab he and his team were working with silica fiber and an attosecond laser on an experiment in quantum optics. Their thesis—and the Hval equations had already borne this out—was that there was no such thing as photonic degradation, that light was effectively immortal, or at least as immortal as the universe itself. If he was right, their research would cement the principle

as fact. Masaki imagined himself standing before a hushed audi-
torium. "Distinguished colleagues," he would say, "members of
the press," and he would gesture toward the spotlight illuminating him on the dais. "This light you see, and the light of the
candles on your tables"—it would be an awards banquet, he
decided—"and even we ourselves, all of us here, our own images,
are, in a word, imperishable. This is what my team's experiments
have demonstrated." They were so close, so close. He could
hardly wait to publish their results. A quarter was resting by the
toe of his shoe, and he stooped over, collected it into his palm,
and stood back up. A wave of passengers poured from the subway
tunnel. Another wave surged across the asphalt. And all of them,
the whole great press of men and women, children and teenagers,
jostling and coughing and checking their text messages—they
believed their lives were like falling silver coins, flashing for
merely an instant before they returned to the darkness. They
were wrong, but it was what they believed. Masaki's heart was
moved by their weakness and their splendor. He heard a commotion and glanced down the alley. Take that gentleman lying
against the brick wall in a heap of wet clothing, crying out so
gravely and unintelligibly. Yes, his moans were awful, and yes, his
wounds burned out of him like a fire, but his pain would cease,
and his body would heal, and the light would last forever.

Acknowledgments

I owe thanks to my editor, Edward Kastenmeier, and to everyone at Pantheon and Knopf who has supported this book, including Tim O'Connell, Rita Madrigal, and Josefine Kals; to Alex Bowler and everyone at Jonathan Cape; to my agent, Jennifer Carlson, and her colleagues at Dunow, Carlson & Lerner; and to Heather Swan, for her early encouragement and her help with the title.

THE BRIEF HISTORY OF THE DEAD

The City is inhabited by those who have departed Earth but are still remembered by the living. They will reside in this afterlife until they are completely forgotten. But the City is shrinking, and the residents clearing out. Some of the holdouts, like Luka Sims, who produces the City's only newspaper, are wondering exactly what is going on. Others, like Coleman Kinzler, believe it is the beginning of the end. Meanwhile, Laura Byrd is trapped in an Antarctic research station, her supplies are running low, her radio finds only static, and the power is failing. With little choice, Laura sets out across the ice to look for help, but time is running out. Kevin Brockmeier alternates these two storylines to create a lyrical and haunting tale about love, loss, and the power of memory.

Fiction/Literature

THINGS THAT FALL FROM THE SKY

Weaving together loss and anxiety with fantastic elements and literary sleight-of-hand, Kevin Brockmeier's richly imagined *Things That Fall from the Sky* views the nagging realities of the world through a hopeful lens. In the deftly told "These Hands," a man named Lewis recounts his time babysitting a young girl and his inconsolable sense of loss after she is wrenched away. In "Apples," a boy comes to terms with the complex world of adults, his first pangs of love, and the bizarre death of his Bible coach. "The Jesus Stories" examines a people trying to accelerate the Second Coming by telling the story of Christ in every possible way. And in the O. Henry Award–winning "The Ceiling," a man's marriage begins to disintegrate after the sky starts slowly descending. Achingly beautiful and deceptively simple, *Things That Fall from the Sky* defies gravity as one of the most original story collections seen in recent years.

Fiction/Short Stories

THE TRUTH ABOUT CELIA

While playing alone in her backyard one afternoon, seven-year-old Celia suddenly disappears while her father, Christopher, is inside giving a tour of their historic house and her mother, Janet, is at an orchestra rehearsal. Utterly shattered, Christopher, a writer of fantasy and science fiction, withdraws from everyone around him, especially his wife, losing himself in his writing by conjuring up worlds where Celia still exists—as a child, as a teenager, as a young single mother—and revealing in his stories not only his own point of view but also those of Janet, the policeman in charge of the case, and the townspeople affected by the tragedy, ultimately culminating in a portrait of a small town changed forever. *The Truth About Celia* is a profound meditation on grief and loss and how we carry on in its aftermath.

Fiction/Literature

THE VIEW FROM THE SEVENTH LAYER

In this collection of fiction, Kevin Brockmeier shows us a fantastical world that is intimately familiar but somehow distant and beautiful. From the touching title story, in which a young, antisocial woman imagines her escape into the sky with an apparition only she can see, to the haunting story of a pastor tempted by something less than divine, Brockmeier moves effortlessly from the extraordinary to the everyday, while challenging us to see the world anew. Stunning, elegant, profound, and playful, *The View from the Seventh Layer* cements Kevin Brockmeier's place as one of the most creative and compassionate writers of his generation.

Fiction/Short Stories